# FINAL CUT

## A Corie McKenna Mystery

# Acknowledgments

Thanks to my fabulous writing group–Amy, Bob, Charlie, Dean, Laura, Leann, and Millie. Your friendship and invaluable help with my work are greatly appreciated. Special thanks to Susie and Isabella for sharing their home with us every week. Thanks to the Fort Bend writers–Bill, Michelle, Rebecca, Roger, and Stacey–for their input. Any mistakes or misstatements made in the novel are mine. For their encouragement and advice, I also thank Bill Manchee and my agent, Mike Farris. Special appreciation to my husband, Benton, for putting up with my countless hours at the computer.

To Benton, for always being there.

# FINAL CUT

A Corie McKenna Mystery

Volume 2

by Kay Finch

Top Publications, Ltd.
Dallas, Texas

Final Cut

A Corie McKenna Mystery
Volume 2

A Top Publications Paperback

First Edition

Top Publications, Ltd.
12221 Merit Drive, Suite 950
Dallas, Texas 75251

ISBN#:978-1-929976-68-3

Library of Congress Control Number 2010921363

*I'm tired of this cat and mouse,*
*I know you're sittin' in that house.*
*Come out and take it like a man,*
*You'll soon know what she has planned.*

# CHAPTER 1

I hid behind the trunk of a live oak, senses on high alert. Jack Litchfield had eluded service of the divorce citation in my pocket for a week. The moment he walked out of that house, he was mine. I peered around the tree. Sun split the morning haze and glinted off the bay window. The blinds opened.

Finally, some activity. I tensed, waiting. When my cell phone vibrated, I nearly came out of my skin. Checking the caller ID, I groaned. Not her. Not now. I glanced at the house. Still quiet, so I answered the call and tried to put a smile in my voice.

"Corie McKenna."

"Have you served him yet?"

No hello, no good morning. The plan hadn't changed since our chat last night, or the eight calls before that. I was doing a humongous favor for my friend Wade by dealing directly with his divorce client, Nora Litchfield, until after the papers were served. He owed me.

"I'm waiting outside the house now," I said. "This isn't a good time." Not to mention, I'd rather carry on a conversation with the mockingbird squawking in the tree above me.

"Are you sure he's in there?" she said. "I can't imagine Jack house-sitting for anyone."

God, this woman irked me. I had tracked her husband down when she couldn't give me one single clue to where he'd been living since they separated.

"He's in there," I said. "If he's planning to jog today,

it's a done deal."

"I told you – he jogs every day."

"Then today's the day. I'll chase him all the way downtown if I have to."

"Dear," Nora said, "one look at you in jogging shorts, and my husband will be chasing *you*. Trust me."

Oh, goodie. "In that case, consider the job done."

"It's about time."

I clenched my teeth. As owner of Houston's swanky spa, Serenity in the City, Nora was a potential source of referrals for Wade's divorce practice. Not good to make waves, even if I suspected her big mouth had tipped Jack about the papers coming and sent him into hiding. I checked the house again. The front door was opening.

"Gotta go," I told Nora.

"Wait. What about the subpoenas?"

"I'm serving them today," I said, lowering my voice. "We've been over this." A tortoiseshell cat slipped out the door and picked its way across the dew-tipped grass. The door shut. I slumped against the tree.

Nora was still blabbing. "There's a change. Carmen called in sick, so she's not at the spa. The address–"

"I *have* her address. No problem." I'd just as soon never set foot in Serenity Spa, if for no other reason than it was one of my mother's hot spots.

"Call me the second you're finished."

"Right." I powered the phone off. Nora would have to cool her jets until I was ready to talk to *her*.

I hummed a song appropriate to the occasion–*goin' through the big D and don't mean Dallas*–until finally the door opened again and Jack Litchfield poked his head out. He looked around before stepping onto the porch. He was dressed in all white, a stark contrast to his leathery skin. A man who, according to Nora, spent ninety percent of his time playing while she worked.

Jack inched his way to the sidewalk and surveyed the area like he feared a S.W.A.T. team waited to swoop down. I'd have to play out Nora's jogging suggestion rather than approach the man directly. I wasn't taking any chance he'd dart back inside when he spotted me. After a minute he returned to the shade of the porch to stretch. The cat lurked behind the shrubbery near Jack and watched me.

The mere thought of jogging made me sweat. Only mid-May and already the humidity was off the charts. I swept damp bangs off my forehead, waiting for the right moment to come out of hiding. When Jack dropped into a runner's stretch, I emerged from behind the tree and jogged casually down the sidewalk.

He glanced up as I passed the house, and I flashed my best come-hither smile. From the corner of my eye, I could tell he'd frozen in mid-stretch to stare. I kept going and, true to his reputation, he caught up with me at the first corner.

"Well, hello there," he said.

"Hi. Nice day, isn't it?"

"More gorgeous than usual." His gaze traveled the length of my body. "How 'bout we keep each other company?"

I gave him a suit-yourself shrug.

I'd heard that Jack thought he was God's gift, but I couldn't figure out why. He was paunchy with bird legs, and he wore his salt-and-pepper hair like something from the Bee Gees era, curling over his collar.

When we'd gone a good distance from the house, I paused to catch my breath. Litchfield stopped on cue.

"You all right, darlin'?"

"I, I think so." My ragged breathing was no act. I'm not a jogger, but he probably thought I was panting for him. "Just out of shape."

"Your shape looks great to me." He eyed my sweat-drenched tank top, trying to x-ray through my sports bra. "You need a breather. Why don't we find us a place to sit down, get to know each other better?"

I struggled to keep a straight face and poured on the Southern charm as I edged closer to the man. "Good idea. You're so kind, Mister–"

"Call me Jack." He offered his hand. "Jack Litchfield."

Pulling the wrinkled citation with its thick packet of attachments from my pocket, I slapped it into his palm.

"Good to meet you, Jack. You've been served." I couldn't suppress a satisfied grin.

He dropped the papers as if they'd scorched him. They plopped on the sidewalk.

His eyes narrowed. "Damn you. What's this about?"

"Read carefully," I said. "There's a hearing next week."

"I'm not reading shit," he said, his voice a low growl. "Keep your stinkin' papers."

"Too late. You've been officially served with a TRO and a notice to appear in court." Weasels like Jack always think they need to hold the papers. Not true. I could have thrown them at his feet, but I like the official feel of placing a citation directly into a person's hand.

"I didn't accept a damn thing." He stomped on the papers and ground his foot back and forth like he was crushing out a cigarette butt. "Here's what I think of your papers. You tell her that. Tell that little slut to drop it."

I had a few of my own descriptive titles for Nora. "Little slut" wasn't one of them.

"I think you should calm down," I said, backing away.

He went to grab my arm, but I dodged him and took off running for my truck.

"You tell her what I said," he yelled. "She's not getting a red cent."

I glanced back. At least he wasn't following me. He had, however, picked up the papers and was busy ripping them to shreds. Pieces fluttered to the sidewalk. I reached the truck and jumped in, shaking my head.

What was it about being served that turned men like Jack into blathering idiots? He and Nora had been separated for months with no attempts at reconciliation. Surely he knew a divorce was blipping on his radar screen. Like it or not, she'd end up with fifty percent or more of their community estate–which is probably what bugged him most. That or the fact that I'd hoodwinked him.

Driving down San Felipe toward the Loop, I decided Jack would settle down in a day or so, hopefully before the hearing. At least I was out of it now. Or I would be soon–after the two witness subpoenas were served. Nora felt sure Jack's secretary, Phyllis Keene, and his former mistress, Carmen Messina, could put an interesting twist on next week's testimony. Especially interesting, I thought, since Carmen was employed by Nora.

At a red light, I grabbed the subpoenas off the passenger seat. A Post-it note bearing Carmen's home address was stuck to her subpoena, along with her required witness fee, a ten-dollar bill that flapped in the breeze from my A-C vent. Nora thought Jack's affair with Carmen began shortly after she came to work at Serenity in the City, and though Jack had long since moved on to younger women, he and Carmen remained pals.

The woman lived on South Braeswood, an easy trip when traveling against rush-hour traffic. If she was truly sick, she might head out later to a doctor's appointment. If she was playing hooky, no telling what she'd planned. Better to get out there early. I stopped at a Rice Epicurean Market and ran inside to pick up some fresh flowers, my sure-fire method of ensuring a single woman would open her door to me. Then I hit the 610 Loop and headed south.

Fifteen minutes later, I approached Carmen's front door, wearing my neon yellow "Corinne's Flowers" T-shirt and carrying a bouquet of pink roses in a glass vase. The door had sidelights, so Carmen could easily identify me as a floral delivery person. This usually worked—except for that one time the jealous husband didn't realize I was on his side and came after me with a shotgun.

I rang the doorbell and glanced around to make sure I was alone. The sun ducked behind a cloud. Across the street, a bicycler zipped down the path around Braes Bayou. Behind him, a female runner pushed a baby stroller. The houses in the area seemed expensive for a single woman. Made me wonder how much money a hairdresser made these days.

I turned back to the door and peered through the sidelights. C'mon Carmen. Be home. I wanted this over and done with. Nora's pushy attitude was bugging the heck out of me. Plus, these roses might not last for a second visit. I waited, then stabbed the doorbell again, drummed my fingers on the vase, reached into my pocket to assure myself Carmen's subpoena was in place.

Still, no answer.

I left the porch, then crossed the sidewalk to the driveway where I'd parked. Carmen's garage door didn't have windows, so I couldn't snoop to see if her car was inside. Maybe I'd get lucky and find her sitting on the patio, enjoying her morning coffee. Worth a try.

I walked up the drive, tipping the flowers forward to

keep them out of my face. Water sloshed onto my shoe. The neighborhood seemed eerily quiet. No dogs barking. No traffic noise. Even the birds were silent.

Carmen's back yard was divided from the driveway by the standard six-foot cedar fence. I rapped on the gate and called, "Hello? Anybody home?"

Nothing. As I put my face up to the fence to look between the slats, rose thorns grazed my cheek. *Ouch.* I set the vase down and tried again. I could see a patio table and some potted plants. As I moved down the fence, looking through wider openings, I saw that Carmen had a pool.

Somebody was swimming. Floating, actually, with face down and arms outstretched. Long dark hair splayed out from the person's head like seaweed.

"Ms. Messina?" I yelled, trying the gate. It didn't open. Frustrated, I jiggled the latch. "Hello? I have a delivery."

I moved down a couple feet and peered through another crack. Jeez. The woman was skinny dipping. No wonder she was ignoring me.

A door slammed behind me, followed by a booming, "Hey, what are you doin' over there?"

I spun around. An elderly man in a blue plaid shirt crossed the neighboring driveway, mopping his bald head with a handkerchief.

"You're on private property, missy," he said. "What's your business here?"

"I'm delivering these roses to Carmen Messina." I pointed at the vase.

"Roses?" He frowned. "From who?"

"That's not any of your business," I said. "Who are you?"

"George Doyle." His eyes narrowed. "You'd better not be another one of those gosh darn satellite dish people. Bunch of scammers."

"Sir, I'm delivering, not selling," I said.

"You still got no business poking your nose around. You got flowers to deliver, I'll sign for 'em. Carmen's at work."

"No, she isn't."

"I live here, missy, and I'm telling you she's gone to work."

"Not today," I said. "She called in sick. And I believe she's in the pool as we speak."

"In the pool? No way. Carmen doesn't swim."

I stared at him for a second. The woman in the pool hadn't actually looked like she was swimming.

He went to the fence and put an eye up to a crack, then twisted toward me. Panic flooded his face.

Oh, damn.

*Did she go out on a whim,*
*And meet up with disaster?*
*Should I be blaming him?*
*Wish that I could ask her.*

# CHAPTER 2

I vaulted the fence like a Marine in training camp, then took a long running dive into the cold water. Two strokes brought me to the dark-haired woman. She didn't react when I lifted her head. With a quick glance I noted the pale face, swollen lips, hands and feet wrinkled as prunes, like she'd been in here forever.

*Don't think. Move.*

Treading water, I wrapped an arm beneath her nude breasts, holding on to her icy skin. I knew the drill from my teenage lifeguard days, but waterlogged shoes slowed me down.

George Doyle had managed to unlatch the gate, and he danced back and forth alongside the pool, watching us. When I got closer, I could hear him chanting, "Carmen, Carmen. Oh Lord, Carmen."

"Call nine-one-one," I yelled.

He kept up the dance, until I hollered again. "George. Call nine-one-one. Go. Hurry."

My words must have finally registered, because he took off through the gate, toward his house. Normal reaction, I guessed, though surely Carmen had a phone that would have been closer.

I reached the shallow end, climbed the cement steps, and pulled Carmen out onto the pebbled poolside surface. Gasping for breath, I knelt next to her and felt for a pulse. Couldn't find one. Oh, God.

My mind raced, trying to remember the correct procedure for CPR. Was it two breaths? Three? Damn. I couldn't remember. I decided on two, but her chest didn't rise, so I repositioned her head and tried again. I gave her two more breaths, then began chest compressions, alternating compressions with breaths, fifteen to two.

Where was that man? The way my shoulders were shaking, I didn't know how long I could keep this up without a partner. Blood pounded in my temples, and I was beginning to lose my equilibrium when Carmen's back door opened. A twentyish kid with spiky black hair loped out, saw me, and did a double take.

"What's going on? Aunt Carmen?" His gaze flitted between me and Carmen.

I kept up the compressions, huffing to catch my breath. In my heart, I knew it was too late, but that wasn't my decision to make. I had to continue CPR until the professionals arrived.

The kid looked down at Carmen, grimacing. "Shit, where are her clothes?"

That was the least of our problems, but before I could respond George came through the gate, putting himself between Carmen and the kid. He started to unbutton his shirt, then grabbed the lapels and ripped the buttons open, taking the shirt off and covering Carmen. He scowled at the kid, then turned to me.

"Help's on the way," he said. "Carmen's okay, right? She's gonna be okay?"

The kid said, "Man, she's dead."

"No, she can't be." George looked at me. "She's not dead, is she?"

Seeing the elderly man's ashen complexion, I was afraid of having another victim on my hands. "We'll see," I said, counting compressions. Nine, ten, eleven. "Either one of you know CPR? I could use a hand."

George shook his head. "I don't, I never–"

"Give it up," the kid said. "She's dead."

The old man's face screwed up as he gazed down on Carmen's lifeless body. "Do something," he said, his eyes begging me.

"I'm trying," I said. "But I'm afraid it's too late."

George's expression turned hard. Without warning, he lunged at the kid. "What did you do to her, you rotten little–"

The kid stepped aside, and George rammed into a chaise lounge. He spun, arms swinging at the kid.

"Stop it," I yelled. "What's wrong with you?"

"That no-good punk had something to do with this," George said.

"Did not," the kid said.

"Little creep," George yelled. "Carmen should have turned you away from the start."

"Stupid bastard," the kid shouted back. "Get out of here."

"STOP!" I yelled. "Think about Carmen." I checked for a pulse again. Still nothing. I resumed CPR anyway. Sirens sounded, growing closer.

George and the kid were glaring at each other when the ambulance crew stormed the back yard. Minutes later, police officers and a squad of firemen arrived. Rescue workers crowded around Carmen, making their last-ditch attempts to save her though I felt sure nothing short of a miracle would bring the woman back now.

I retreated to the patio, noticing for the first time a striped beach towel draped over a chair back. I sat down, shivering, and began to pull the terrycloth around me. Wait–was I contaminating evidence? No. Drowning accidents happened. Carmen had made a bad choice in staying home today. Maybe she'd gotten a cramp or something. But there was no crime here.

I used the towel to push sopping ringlets of hair back from my face and neck. The tragic scene before me seemed even more depressing now that clouds had rolled in to hide the sun. My eyes burned from the chlorine, or maybe from tears that threatened to spill out. I'd wasted all that time at the front door. If I hadn't dawdled, maybe I could have saved her.

A police officer honed in on the fact that the kid was next of kin and led him off to a corner. Before they were out of earshot, I heard the nephew identify himself as Trey Salinas.

George Doyle slouched on a bench by the back door in his white undershirt, elbows on knees and holding his head in his hands. I got up and approached him. With all the ruckus of two-way radios and people talking over each other, he didn't hear me coming. When I sat beside him and put a hand on his shoulder, he jumped.

"Are you all right?"

He turned to stare at me with red-rimmed eyes. "What do you think?"

"I'm sorry. I tried my best to save her."

George nodded, his lips quivering. "I was right next door the whole time. I should have checked on her." He spotted Trey Salinas and stared daggers into the kid's back. "I swear he's behind this."

"Why would you say that?"

"You'd know why if you saw how he pushed his way in here uninvited." George's complexion reddened as he spoke. "Tried to take over the place from day one."

"Day one? What do you mean?"

He frowned at me like he resented my questioning. "Carmen's lived here for near to three years. She never mentioned no nephew. All of a sudden, kid shows up, moves in."

"He lives here?" I asked.

George nodded. "Mooches off her and treats her like dirt."

So the kid didn't respect his elders, I thought. That would irritate an old-timer like George.

"I understand how you feel." I patted George's arm. "He's young and immature. But sometimes an accident like this turns people–"

"Accident?" George straightened. "This was no accident, missy."

"Maybe Carmen wanted to cool off," I said. "Maybe she slipped and fell."

"I said she didn't swim." George had raised his voice.

"It's awfully muggy." I said. "Who wouldn't be tempted to take a dip with this great pool in their backyard?"

The old man jumped up, indignant. "Carmen did not swim," he said. "She never swam. And she did *not* come outside willingly like, like that."

I doubted Carmen would have advertised to the neighbors that she liked to swim in the nude or that she made a habit of doing so with a young nephew living in the same house. I would have said so to George, except for the fact that his shouts had drawn the attention of the officer with Trey, who now plodded our way, wearing the hang-dog expression of a man who'd witnessed far too many tragic scenes.

"I'm Officer Belton," he said when he reached us. "I hear you two found the body." He poised his pen over a notebook page.

"Who told you that?" George said. "Was it that–"

"Yes, officer," I interrupted. "We found the body."

Belton eyed George, then asked for our names and wrote them in his notebook. He beckoned another officer to come over and they separated us. Belton took me inside.

Blue-cushioned chairs surrounded a white-tiled breakfast table just inside the door. Belton pulled out a chair and sat down, motioning for me to do the same. I checked out the kitchen as I arranged the dry side of my towel over a chair before sitting. The room looked unused, sparkling like something out of a Mr. Clean commercial.

"What time did you get here, Ms. McKenna?" Belton asked.

"I'd say about nine-thirty." I checked my watch which had survived its dip in the pool, then removed my cell phone from its clip and flipped it open. Not so lucky there. God, I hadn't called Nora. And now I really didn't want to call her, not after this.

Belton was scribbling an awful lot in his notebook considering I'd only answered one short question. I stretched forward, trying to read his words upside down, then jerked back when he raised his head.

"What's your relationship to the deceased?" he said.

"Didn't have one," I said. "I never met the woman."

"Okay. So your business with Carmen Messina was–"

"I'm a private investigator."

"Is that right?" His gaze fell to the logo on my wet T-shirt.

"And process server." I pulled out the soggy subpoena. The pages tore in half when I unfolded them. Not that they mattered anymore. I removed the ten-dollar bill and placed the paper face up in front of Belton. "I came to serve this subpoena."

For good measure, I pulled a wet business card from my other pocket and slid it over to him.

He glanced down but didn't seem too interested.

"You came to serve the subpoena and ended up in the back yard?" His eyebrows lifted in question.

"She didn't answer the doorbell," I said.

"So you came in the back gate, saw her, and–" He stopped when he noticed me shaking my head.

"The gate was locked. When we–that's me and the neighbor, Mr. Doyle–realized something was wrong, I went over the fence."

His eyebrows inched up a fraction further. "Fence is six feet tall."

"Uh-huh."

"You call for help first?"

"No."

"Why not?"

"I didn't think there was time."

"You thought you could be a hero?"

"I don't appreciate your cynicism," I said. "When someone's in trouble, I don't stand around and watch. I take action. Don't you?"

"Sure," Belton said. "Because I'm trained to take action."

"Who says I'm not? I've worked as a lifeguard."

"Is that right?"

"Yes, that's right. At the River Oaks Country Club." As soon as the words were out, I cringed. Name-dropping's a habit of Mother's I try to avoid. Not to mention more than fifteen years had passed since my teenage lifeguarding days.

Belton looked up from his notes. "You see a lot of accidental drownings there?"

Personally I had no problem with his use of the word "accident," but for George's sake I said, "Do you always assume drownings are accidents? What if–"

"Do me a favor," Belton said, cutting me off. "Leave the investigating to us. Now, tell me more about this subpoena." He leaned forward and glanced over the papers. Since the style of every divorce begins "in the matter of the marriage of," the nature of the case was obvious. "What's Carmen Messina's connection?"

"She worked for the parties." I explained about Nora and Serenity in the City. "From what I understand, Carmen cut hair at the spa."

"Must be good money in that." Belton glanced around the spacious kitchen before looking at me. "I'll need Mrs. Litchfield's name and phone number."

"Why?"

"For my report," he said. "Some facts become

important later, some don't."

"So you suspect foul play?" I said.

"Didn't say that," Belton said. "Just give me your client's name, please ma'am."

I gave him Nora's information, then asked, "Will a crime scene unit be coming in?"

"Hardly." Belton rolled his eyes. "You have any idea how many of these drownings we see every summer? Damn depressing, you ask me, and it's only May."

He turned to the window and lifted the curtain. The backyard crowd had begun to thin. When a paramedic shook out the folds of a white sheet, my shoulders sagged.

"Looks like we're about to wrap this up." Belton let the curtain drop back into place and stood. "I need you to come to the station sometime tomorrow. Sign a formal statement." He handed me one of his cards, then opened the door.

I got up and stuck his card in my pocket along with the ten, but didn't move to leave. "Now what? What about the nephew? Shouldn't we call someone? His parents?"

"We'll handle things here," Belton said. "And you'll handle that statement tomorrow, right?"

Clearly being dismissed, I nodded and walked out.

Somehow it felt wrong to leave, though I had no reason to stay. George was nowhere in sight as I trudged through the gate. Two police cars and an ambulance crowded the driveway. Trey Salinas paced alongside the vehicles, taking deep drags on a cigarette. I walked over to him even though he wore a stay-away expression. He sported a small hoop in a pierced eyebrow that I hadn't noticed earlier, and he wore a black T-shirt bearing a glittery gold Serentity in the City logo.

"I'm so sorry," I said.

"Yeah." His tone sounded accusing, like he doubted my sincerity.

"Is there anything I can do to help? Are you gonna be okay?"

He stopped pacing and exhaled smoke in my direction. "You did enough."

I told myself the kid was hurting, lashing out at the nearest person. But George Doyle hadn't trusted the kid even before Carmen's death, and I wondered why.

"The police have asked me to come in and make a formal statement about what happened. So, your aunt stayed home sick today?"

"How would I know? I'm not her babysitter."

"You talk to her today?"

"No." His clipped tone gave me the impression they never talked.

"You've been here all morning?"

"What's it to you?" He glared at me.

If the kid always acted this way, I could see why George didn't like him. "Thought maybe you saw something," I said. "Were you here when she got in the pool?"

"You think I'm some freakin' pervert? Watching the old lady run around butt naked?"

"I didn't say that."

"Well, I wasn't here."

"Where were you?"

"Working."

I glanced at his shirt, then looked him in the eye. "You get that from Carmen?"

The kid grunted. "Woman never gave me a damn thing."

"You work at the spa then."

He blew out a breath. "Yeah."

"Are you a hairdresser?"

"Shit no. I'm nothin' but somebody's bitch. All day long. Go here, do that, kiss my freakin' butt."

His cell phone rang, and he turned away from me to take the call. A wave of sympathy for Trey washed over me. The poor kid probably took orders from Nora, and I knew what that was like. But it wasn't my place to deal with him or to make sense of what had happened here.

I headed for my pickup, fully convinced the day couldn't get worse, but then a red Volkswagen Beetle pulled to a stop at the curb behind a fire truck. Maggie Robbins, gossip columnist extraordinare, climbed out. She spotted me instantly.

"Corie, yoo-hoo." Maggie gave me a finger wave. "I thought that was your truck parked out here. What's going on?"

I groaned aloud.

*I want you to make it clear,*
*Tell me what you're doing here.*
*I don't like you spreadin' dirt,*
*Don't want no one gettin' hurt.*

# CHAPTER 3

What had I done to deserve all this bad luck in one morning? God, I hate the way reporters exploit tragic situations – one of the reasons I never went to work for my dad's newspaper. But Maggie didn't strike me as the type to sit around listening to a police scanner. Her specialty is the social scene, rumors involving the Who's Who of Houston. Which too often includes my family.

So what was she doing here at Carmen's house? And where were the police when you needed them? I checked the HPD squad cars. No officers in sight. Weren't they supposed to keep nosy reporters away from scenes like this?

Maggie headed my way, high-heeled sandals clopping up the concrete drive as she took measured steps, restricted by the narrow skirt of her off-white business suit. Traffic had slowed out front. Cars merged left to go around her VW and the emergency vehicles. Drivers gawked in our direction. Runners stopped on the jogging path, watching the house.

"Must be a slow news day," I said when Maggie came within earshot. "This isn't your normal beat."

"I was in the neighborhood." She eyed my wet clothes. "You get caught in a sprinkler?"

I wanted to stick my tongue out. Maggie and I butted heads all though college. Then, as my luck would have it, she ended up moving to Houston. I had felt sorry for her last year when she'd been the victim of what everyone thought was a drive-by shooting, but that didn't mean I had to like her.

"If you must know," I said, "I tried to save a woman's life. Unfortunately, I was too late. She drowned."

"Oh, no." Maggie looked at the house, then back to me. "Who? Not Carmen?"

"You know her?"

Maggie put a hand to her forehead. "She can't be dead."

"Sorry," I said, compassion edging to the forefront. "She is."

"I can't believe this." Maggie's naturally rosy complexion had paled. "How'd it happen?"

"I don't know. She was already in the pool when I arrived."

"God, this is terrible." Maggie began pacing, five clip-clops of her sandals to the right, then five to the left. "Poor Carmen. She always seemed in great health considering she had to be, what? Mid-forties, you think?"

"I don't know, but I'm sure there will be an autopsy."

"Right." She stopped walking and pinned me with a stare so intense I figured she could see right into my brain. "What were you doing here?"

I backed away, palms raised to her. "Hey, I can't talk about confidential business."

"Give me some credit." Maggie propped her right hand on her hip. "It's no secret Wade Alexander is handling Nora Litchfield's divorce, or that Carmen and Jack Litchfield used to be an item. So you're here because of the case, right?"

I'd thought that Harris County's district clerk had changed their procedures to keep new family law cases confidential for thirty days. Maggie no doubt had a 24-7 gossip hotline, but she wasn't getting any additional tidbits from me.

"Happened to be in the neighborhood, huh?" I said. "I knew your showing up was no coincidence. You wanted the dirt about the Litchfield divorce. Tell me, Maggie, does poor Carmen's death give you an even bigger scoop?"

I looked away, seething, and when I turned back to Maggie her eyes were tearing.

"That's not why I'm here," she said. "Everybody knows Jack Litchfield has had a string of women since Carmen. I came because she contacted me."

"Carmen did? When?"

"Yesterday. Called my office out of the blue. Requested an appointment."

"With you? Here at her house?"

"Yes."

"Why?"

"I don't have to tell you anything either." She made a face.

"Maybe not. But I'm sure the cops will want all the juicy details."

Maggie looked toward the backyard, then at her car, like she was considering making a quick getaway.

"How did you know Carmen?" I said.

"How do you think?" Maggie huffed. "She was my hairdresser."

"Oh." Those dark roots probably needed coloring every other week. But why would Carmen want to meet with Maggie here at home?

"Did she want to talk about Jack?" I said.

Maggie shrugged. "All she said was she needed to tell someone about her situation. She sounded awful. I agreed to come over. God knows she's listened to me plenty over the years."

One of Belton's cronies came through the gate then, and Maggie took off after him, whipping an ID from her pocket. So much for the five-minute grieving process. She gave the officer a thousand-watt smile and identified herself. Maybe she hadn't come for a scoop, but she was getting one anyway.

I nibbled on my lower lip. Wade wasn't going to like it if the Litchfield divorce got press coverage. Reluctantly, I followed Maggie.

"Wait out front if you must," the cop was telling her as I approached. "Belton might make a statement after a while."

She turned around, and her expression registered surprise that I hadn't taken off.

"Sticking around to get a story for Daddy's paper?" she said.

I opened my mouth, outraged. Carmen's death might warrant a notice in tomorrow's edition of the *Houston Globe*, but how dare Maggie put me on her level. Luckily my brain kicked into gear before I said what I was thinking. Telling Maggie off would have the opposite effect of what I wanted.

I forced a smile. "I'd appreciate your keeping the Litchfield case out of the news. There's no reason my being here needs to be reported."

"True." Her eyes narrowed. "I'll keep that in mind. Maybe we can make a deal."

"What kind of deal?" I didn't like the sound of that.

"I'd like to do a pre-event story about the Denim & Diamonds Gala your mother's chairing this weekend. You get me the guest list, and I might be able to keep the Litchfield divorce out of the papers."

"That's blackmail," I said. "Besides, you're well aware I don't keep up with Mother's social calendar." I didn't give a damn about what the press termed "another Olivia Poole extravaganza" on a good day and certainly not today after discovering Carmen's body.

"See what you can find out," she said, "I can keep quiet about Nora's case for a couple of days. I'm gonna go call this in." Maggie turned and flounced toward her car.

I wanted to tell her to stick it, but leaving without further comment seemed a wiser idea. Seconds later, I was driving down the street, eager to put the bad chain of events behind me. Suddenly I realized somebody had to break the news about Carmen to Nora Litchfield. Ugh. I sure hoped that somebody wasn't me.

***

I arrived at the office just past noon and took the stairs to the second floor. Bypassing my McKenna Investigations office, I entered the law firm of Alexander & Glover through a back door. Reba Hofstetler, Wade's full-time legal secretary and my part-time songwriting collaborator, stood at her desk with several three-ring binders open in front of her. She busily inserted numbered tabs and pages from a stack of copies into the binders. Her blonde curls were held back in a rhinestone clip, and she wore one of her trademark country-western outfits, complete with fringe and turquoise-studded buttons.

I could see Wade in the glass-walled conference room caty-corner from Reba's desk. File boxes lined the top of the long mahogany conference room table. A tall redhead stood next to him, their shoulders touching. Wade spoke animatedly, pointing to a document he held before her, but the woman didn't appear to be paying a bit of attention to the page, just smiling demurely at him.

"Who the hell is that?" I said, and Reba jumped.

"Jeez Louise, you about scared the pants off me," she said, following my gaze. "Her? That's Jennifer Simon, client going to trial today. And if you're thinking she's hot for Wade, guess again. More like boiling."

"That's disgusting." Jealousy shot to the surface as I watched the woman close her hand over Wade's and tip her head toward his. "Has she no pride?"

Wade seemed oblivious to the woman's come-on, but that didn't keep me from wanting to yank her out of the room. Good thing I trusted Wade. Our relationship was growing, steady and sure, and I couldn't see a floozy client changing that.

"Don't know about pride," Reba said, "but she doesn't have a lick of sense. Listed quarterly trips to some Lake Tahoe retreat under necessary living expenses."

"Hey, everybody deserves a little R&R," I said. "I'm sure the Judge will appreciate that."

Reba turned, laughing, and did a double-take when she caught sight of me. "You going for the grunge look these days? Doesn't suit you. By the way, where've you been? Nora Litchfield's been callin' here like a teenager tryin' to win concert tickets on K-I-L-T."

I ran my hands through my hair and pulled back the unmanageable tangle of damp curls. "Why's she calling here? I said I'd call *her* when I was finished." I dropped the hair and looked down at my phone. "Oops. Forgot my phone's dead." I'd have to add phone shopping to my to-do list.

"Convenient," Reba said. "So why aren't you finished? What's the hold-up?" She snapped the rings of one notebook shut and picked up another section of copies.

My stomach felt queasy, thinking about what had happened. "Because Carmen Messina is dead, that's why."

Reba dropped the papers. "No way."

"It's true. She's dead."

A door opened, and we turned toward the conference room.

"Reba, those trial notebooks about ready?" Wade said, "I'm almost out of time."

"Close." Reba grabbed the copies.

Wade crossed to her desk, looking lawyerly in a well-fitted charcoal suit and a medium blue shirt that matched his eyes. He met my gaze, his expression a blend of curiosity and concern. "Sounded like you said somebody's dead."

Reba and I looked at each other.

Behind Wade, the redheaded client had moved to the conference room doorway, gazing after him like a lovesick cow. Judging by the tight skirt and revealing blouse she wore, Wade must have skipped giving her the speech about appropriate courtroom attire. Or she hadn't paid attention if he had.

"Can I have two minutes?" I asked him in a low voice. "It's urgent."

Wade gave the client a back-in-a-second gesture and followed me to his office.

"What's up?" He gave me a quick kiss in passing and went to his desk to pick up a fresh tablet.

I closed the office door. "Well, Jack Litchfield has been served," I said. "That's the good news."

He looked up. "And there's bad?"

I gave him a shortened version of what had happened to Carmen.

"That's a damn shame." He came over and tipped my chin up. "Are you okay? You don't look so hot."

That was probably an understatement. I hadn't checked a mirror since going into the pool. "I'm fine."

"Good." He touched my cheek, brushing my hair back from my face in a gesture I found endearing. Then he checked his watch. "I have no problem working the case around this turn of events, but Nora won't take it well."

"I'm sure she won't. I already feel sorry for the cop who breaks the news."

Wade's head jerked up. "Nora's name came up with the cops?"

"Well, yeah," I said. "I *was* there to serve a subpoena in her case. Cop asked for her name and number."

Frown lines creased Wade's face.

"He asked about lots of things," I said. "If you're worried that Jack's affair with Carmen will make them take a look at Nora, don't. That's ancient history. And I believe Nora when she says she doesn't care who Jack sleeps with, so long as it isn't her."

"She needs a heads up, though, before the cops call or

show up on her doorstep."

"I guess you're right," I said. "So how soon can you let her know?"

"Can't." He slid a pen into the inside pocket of his jacket. "I need you to fill her in. I'm due in court at one."

Damn, yet another phone conversation with that woman. "Okay," I said with a sigh. "You're the boss."

"Love that attitude." Wade grinned. "Go by the spa, would you? Nora needs special handling. Information like this should be delivered in person."

*I don't see the attraction,*
*Of all the polishing and preening.*
*Me, I'm into action,*
*And things that have more meaning.*

# CHAPTER 4

My official title may be private investigator but usually I'm more of a glorified go-fer. I'd fallen into the business by doing favors for Wade and my late husband, David, when they were law partners – filing papers with the court, making deliveries, interviewing witnesses. Things sure had changed over the years. Wade and his ex-wife, Laura, had helped me over the rough spots after David's death–murder actually, which we didn't realize at the time. Then Laura shocked everyone by divorcing Wade and remarrying two months later. Somewhere along the way I'd taken some classes, and after a stint working under well-known Houston PI, J. J. Riley, set up my own shop.

I enjoyed PI work, but visiting Serentity in the City Spa on West Gray sure didn't feel like an official PI assignment. Maybe a male investigator would enjoy coming here for some girl-watching, but the place held no attraction for me. I don't even like getting my hair cut, which is why I wear it long and every six months or so pop in at a strip-center salon that takes walk-ins.

I pulled into the spa's parking lot and bypassed the valet, snagging the nearest spot despite his scowl. Was he frowning at my choice of parking space or his lost tip? Maybe the fact that I had the audacity to park a pickup between a Jaguar and a Mercedes?

Too bad.

I jumped out, ignoring him as I headed for the entrance. At least keeping busy would take my mind off Wade spending the afternoon in court with that flirtatious client. But

I wasn't looking forward to seeing Nora Litchfield which, even without bad news to deliver, held about as much appeal as an IRS audit.

Inside the spa, I stood still for a moment as my eyes adjusted from the bright outdoors. My stomach knotted as it struck me that Carmen would never again come through this entrance. I wondered if she'd been happy here. Life at the spa would irrevocably change as soon as everyone learned about her death. I wanted to turn around, make believe it never happened, save them all the grief.

Instead, I waited until I could focus more clearly on the cheery reception area, done in vibrant colors with bright abstract prints adorning the walls. Tropical plants surrounded a large fountain built into the corner. Rattan seating held throw pillows in vivid primary colors. A young woman was seated and filling out forms attached to a clipboard.

Several customers browsed in alcoves displaying beauty products, and a perky young brunette stood behind the island check-out counter, ringing up a customer's purchases. A sign stood on the counter, advertising today's special in loopy script–a "Day of Beauty" for a mere four hundred dollars. Jeez. What was the regular price?

No one was paying attention to me, so I headed straight for the teak door that separated the lobby from the rest of the place and pushed through, immediately intercepted by a statuesque blonde who smelled like she'd bathed in cologne. She moved forward, edging me back into the lobby and pulling the door shut behind her. In a white pantsuit accented by a colorful scarf, she looked like she'd stepped off a modeling runway – except for the frown.

"Are you here for the interview?" she said, taking in the Gap capri pants and T-shirt I'd changed into before leaving the office.

"Interview? No. I came to see Nora Litchfield."

"Do you have an appointment?" Her expression said I wasn't fit to enter this high-dollar establishment much less expect an audience with the owner.

"No, but she'll see me." I handed her a generic business card – the one with my name and phone number only.

"Mrs. Litchfield can't be disturbed," she said. "Perhaps I can help you with something. I'm Haley Winter, the spa manager."

"When she learns I'm here, Mrs. Litchfield will want to be disturbed." I forced a smile. "We have personal business."

"It's highly unusual for her work day to be interrupted by personal matters," Haley said. "I can certainly give her a message that you stopped by."

Did she think I was a salesperson or what? Not knowing how much the staff knew about Nora and Jack's relationship, I didn't want to tell this snippy woman the reason for my visit. I reached to my waist and unclipped my cell phone. She didn't have to know it wasn't working.

"Don't bother. I have Nora on speed dial. Why don't I just call and tell her I'm in the lobby and that you won't let me in?" I poised my index finger above the phone's key pad.

Haley looked at me like I was a zit on a smooth, milky complexion. "That won't be necessary. Wait here."

Feeling smug, I joined the browsers and began sniffing tester bottles to occupy myself.

Two hoity-toity types in cleavage-boasting tops were deep in conversation, talking about every little detail of somebody's wedding last weekend.

"What did you think of that hideous shade of green Brooke chose for her bridesmaids?" said one, holding her hands with fingers outspread to protect her new glossy pink manicure.

"That wasn't the worst part," said the other, making a face. "The cut of those dresses didn't do a thing for those two overweight friends of hers."

I bit my tongue to keep from asking how much plastic surgery the woman speaking had endured to enhance her own figure. Inane gossip was exactly what I hated most about places like this. What business was it of theirs, anyway, if a bride wanted her bridesmaids to wear green? I picked up a jar of face cream and turned it over out of curiosity. Three hundred eighty-five bucks! I replaced the jar carefully. I'd stick with my Dove soap, thank you very much.

"It is dreadful, though, about the burglary," said the other woman. "That diamond tiara was handed down through four generations of brides and it's worth a fortune. Jan only left the house long enough to get her weekly massage and when she got back, it was gone."

The friend sighed. "No one's safe anymore. If I know Hugh Martin, there'll be hell to pay at the next community association meeting."

My interest perked up. I knew the Martins. They lived on my parents' street. Seemed like this was the second time I'd heard about a recent burglary in the River Oaks area. I wanted to know more about this theft the two women were talking about, but the grouchy manager was back, beckoning me in her direction.

"I'll show you to Mrs. Litchfield's office." She shoved the teak door open, not holding it for me, and I hurried to slip through. My rubber-soled sandals squeaked on the marble floor as I entered the sanctuary of beauty makeovers. Yuck. The potent odors of chemical solutions and hair sprays lurked under the aromatherapy scents, threatening to cause a killer headache.

Ahead of me, plants and more rattan seating lined the wide hallway. Some women waited here for their appointment or maybe the next phase of their Day of Beauty. A couple of them peeked over the tops of magazines – *Vogue* and *Oprah* – looking me over. It seemed wrong that these nosy twits were going on with their trivial routines while poor Carmen lay dead. The knot in my stomach tightened.

I made a sharp left and followed Haley down the corridor. She reached a door with Nora's name engraved on a brass plate and rapped twice before opening it. Then she swept an arm, gracious as Vanna White displaying a prize, for her boss's benefit I guessed, and stood aside for me to enter.

Nora sat behind a modern black-and-chrome desk, pushing folders and loose papers into a pile. We'd met once before, the day Wade introduced us, and she had on even more makeup than she'd worn that day. Her glossy coral lips were so full I suspected she had lipliner tattooed outside the natural lip line. She punched the power button on her flat-screen computer monitor, turning it off, and removed her half-moon glasses, dropping them on the desk.

"Thank heavens you're here. I've been calling." She swept sleek tawny bangs back off her face and nodded toward the door, dismissing the manager. The door clicked shut behind me.

"Sorry." I lifted the hand holding my phone. "My phone's not working." The news I'd come to tell her sat on the tip of my tongue, burning to be delivered, but I couldn't make myself say it.

She rolled her brown eyes, highlighted with shimmery taupe shadow. "Have a seat. Did you serve Jack?"

"Yes. Right after we talked."

I plopped into a cushiony visitor's chair and couldn't avoid noticing my reflection in the mirrored office wall behind Nora. Gross. My face, devoid of makeup, looked anemic. My hair had dried into its natural frizzy waves and expanded to three times the usual volume.

"Good." Nora's rigid expression relaxed. She had fifteen years on me, but her complexion was smoother than mine. Probably the result of those expensive miracle creams she sold out front.

"How did he take it?" she said. "Any comments?"

I described Jack's overly dramatic reaction to receiving the papers. "He was angry, that's for sure."

"What does *he* have to be angry about? I should be angry, putting up with him all these years and supporting his hare-brained investment schemes." She blew out a breath. "He's crazy if he thinks I'm dropping the divorce. I want this case over and done with as soon as possible."

"I can certainly understand that," I said.

"Did you serve Phyllis?" Nora sat back, her attention turned to a loose button on her lightweight floral-print jacket.

"No. I was, uh, detained." After what I'd been through, the secretary's subpoena would have to wait until another day.

Nora looked up and her thin eyebrows drew together. "I thought you were going straight to Jack's office after you served him."

I tapped my fingernails on the chair arm. "I decided to serve Carmen first. I went to her house."

"And?"

"Something terrible has happened."

"What?"

"Carmen died this morning."

"No." Nora pushed away from the desk. "That can't be true."

I had delivered this news to far too many people

already. Denial was a common reaction. "I'm sorry."

"She told me she was sick today, but I didn't think it was anything serious." Nora stood, the hem of her jacket catching on a desk drawer knob. She yanked it loose. "What happened?"

"I don't know the details yet. The police are investigating."

"The police?" Nora's eyes widened.

"Yes." I related the morning's events as Nora paced the office.

"This is dreadful," she said. "Then they don't think it was an accident?"

"No one knows at this point."

"Good heavens, poor Carmen." Nora sat on the visitor's chair next to me, dropping her head into her hands, massaging her temples. "I can't believe this. Poor Trey, that sweet boy."

Sweet? She must know a different Trey.

"The clients," she went on. "They'll be devastated."

I hadn't thought that far ahead. Carmen probably had a slew of regulars. Mother talked about the woman who cut her hair all the time, and I could imagine her distress if anything happened to Diane. Serenity Spa would undoubtedly have some depressed clients when they learned that Carmen had given her final haircut.

I placed a tentative hand on Nora's shoulder. "I know it's a shock."

"Yes." She drew a few deep breaths, then sat up and focused on me. "Did you mention Carmen's subpoena to Jack?"

"No, of course not." I withdrew my hand. "Why?"

She shook her head, looking away. "Nothing. It's silly."

"What?" I said.

Nora began wringing her hands. "I hope Jack didn't have anything to do with this."

I hesitated, remembering his red-faced fury. "You mean with what happened to Carmen?"

Nora stood and started pacing again. "Forget I said that. I shouldn't have said anything."

"Do you have reason to believe Jack would hurt Carmen? I thought they were friends."

Nora whirled to face me. "I said forget it."

My back stiffened. "I'm the one who pulled Carmen's body from that pool this morning and tried to save her life. By all appearances, the woman drowned. But if you think Jack was involved, I want to know why. Why did the thought even cross your mind?"

Nora's lips quivered. "If Jack suspects we could get information about his business dealings through Carmen, who knows what he'd do? You said yourself he was very angry." She stared at me, her gaze unwavering.

I couldn't see Jack jumping into his car as soon as I left him and rushing out to murder a woman, but what if he'd been at Carmen's house earlier in the morning? No one knew how long Carmen had been in that pool.

"Jack did seem irrational," I said. "Maybe you should tell the police your concerns."

"No, no." Nora shook her head. "I overreacted, that's all. My husband is secretive and controlling, but he's not a killer. Please, don't mention this to anyone."

She walked around the desk and opened a drawer, pulling out a tissue to dab her eyes. "Now if you'll excuse me, I need to make a list of Carmen's clients and decide on the best way to let them know what's happened."

"Of course."

I got out without promising to keep quiet about her husband's behavior. If there was even a remote possibility he'd hurt someone to keep his financial secrets, the man needed to be locked up. I intended to find out more about Jack Litchfield's true colors. And I knew the perfect place to begin gathering information.

*Tell me all that you have heard,*
*Every bit and every word.*
*If he's dangerous as they say,*
*She should keep out of his way.*

# CHAPTER 5

Black clouds darkened the afternoon sky, a daily occurrence lately. As I headed down Shepherd Drive, raindrops pelted my windshield and lightning streaked the sky. Traffic slowed to a crawl. Streets flood quickly during Houston's heavy rainstorms, so I was thankful I didn't have far to go.

I pulled off of Lazy Lane into my parent's cobblestone driveway and parked behind the house next to a row of crape myrtles by the pool. Mother would be surprised to see me since I usually spend more time declining invitations and dodging her calls than talking to her. But she was my best source for getting the scoop on anyone in the country club set and that included the Litchfields. I checked the rearview and realized she'd have a fit when she saw I'd been out in public looking so bedraggled. Nothing new.

Thunder rolled in the distance. I climbed out to make a run for the back kitchen door and noticed Mother beckoning frantically to me from the study's French doors.

"Corinne Elizabeth, get in here."

I veered in her direction and shook my head like a dog emerging from a bath before stepping over the threshhold.

"Goodness gracious." Mother shut the door and stepped back to get a better look at me. "I was on the phone and couldn't believe my eyes when I saw you traipsing through this downpour. Don't you own an umbrella?"

"Guess I wasn't thinking." And what's a little rain compared to jumping into a pool fully-clothed?

She looked at the water dripping onto the hardwood floor.

"Mother, I need to talk to you about–"

"Where did you get those shoes?" Her eyes locked on my feet. You'd think I'd sprouted reptilian claws.

I looked down. If I admitted picking up the sandals at Payless she'd go off on a tangent. "Can't remember. Now, do you know–"

"Wait right here." Her lavender silk pants swished as she walked toward the hallway and called, "Ruby, help please. We need a bath towel."

Jeez. Couldn't I even ask her a simple question? I dutifully stood in place and got my first good look at the room, usually picture perfect. Boxes and packages of all shapes and sizes were stacked in corners and covered the desk top and coffee table. Next to the sofa stood a statue protected by bubble wrap.

"What's all this stuff?" I said.

She turned, waving a hand. "Oh, things I've rounded up for the gala's silent auction Saturday. I'll show you later. First, let's get you out of those wet clothes so you don't catch your death of cold."

"It's May, Mother. People don't catch their death of cold in May. I'm fine."

I started to ask about Jack Litchfield, but the phone rang and she walked over to the desk to pick it up. Ruby came in, her daffodil yellow shirt brightening both her mahogany complexion and the room in general. She carried a tray of brownies in one hand, a plush mint green towel in the other. She'd worked for Mother nearly twenty years, and sometimes I thought that glow about her might be the aura of sainthood. She held out the towel, but I grabbed one of her double-fudge brownies first, shoving the whole thing in my mouth.

"Girl, you sure know how to get your Mama's goat, drippin' on her floor."

"These are to die for," I said, talking around the chocolate.

Ruby grinned. "Glad to know I haven't lost my touch. What've you been up to?"

"Attracting trouble as usual."

"I know that's the truth," she said.

I shook out the towel, kicked off my cheap sandals, and began drying my feet and legs. "Where's Dad? I haven't heard from him in a couple of days."

"New York City. Won't be home til Tuesday. Looks like you got a whole pan of brownies to yourself." As I reached for another square, Ruby left the room to get me a glass of milk.

I wrapped the towel around my waist, walked over to the coffee table, and lifted a box lid. Inside was a large crystal bowl bearing a Waterford label.

"We'll be moving everything around three on Friday," Mother was saying, "So if you're running late you can take the painting directly to The Briar Hill Club. I so appreciate your generosity."

She hung up. "Your Uncle Lewis. He's donating his original Batiste. You remember? That painting of the harbor hanging in his library. They're redecorating, and Sherie never liked his nautical decor."

I had no idea what painting she was talking about, but I nodded. "Sounds expensive."

"It's a donation, Corinne. A write-off. And proceeds from the auction are going to a good cause."

As always. Mother seemed to have donated her life to fund-raising lately, which was okay by me. Meant she had less time to try running my social life.

"All of your fund-raising activities benefit worthy causes," I said.

"Then why won't you volunteer?"

I sighed. "Because I don't want to. That's not me. It's never going to be me."

"Well, I don't see why not. You don't *need* to be working, especially not putting yourself in the middle of dangerous situations."

Why had I allowed the conversation to head down this path? I was like some mindless animal, falling into the same trap again and again. "Mother, I enjoy my job and it's not dangerous–"

"Wait just one minute." She marched over to stand in front of me, wagging an index finger in my face. "Joyce Adams' daughter is a Vice President at Johnstone Financial Advisors. *Her* job is not dangerous. Muriel's Katie is about to start work as a corporate attorney for Fulbright & Jaworski. No danger there." She tapped a shoe on the wood floor. "How can you stand here and tell me your job is safe when you begin your day confronting a maniac like Jack Litchfield, then pull a dead body out of a swimming pool, and end up in a police interrogation?"

I stared at her, dumbfounded. "How could you possibly know this?"

"I have ways."

"My cases are supposed to be confidential," I said. "You are absolutely incredible, and I *don't* mean that in a good way. You have a police scanner in here or what?" I jumped off the sofa arm and paced in a circle, looking around the room.

"Corinne, stop."

"Was it Maggie Robbins? Has she already been on TV telling all?"

"You know I don't watch television," Mother said. "It's very simple, if you'd calm down and listen to me."

"I'm listening." I stared at her, my face feeling heated.

"Carmen Messina was Muriel's hair stylist," she said. "I'd just hung up from talking to her when you arrived. She had an appointment today and they didn't reach her in time to cancel."

I plopped into a chair. "Oh."

"Muriel saw you at Serenity Spa, as you were leaving, and naturally she asked what you were doing there."

"Naturally."

Mother silenced me with a look. "Don't be snippy. She knows you avoid those places like the plague."

This was actually making sense. "You're saying everyone at the Spa knows all of this?" Every last sordid detail?

"I don't know. Muriel talked directly to Nora."

Who was I to keep the Litchfield's divorce case confidential if Nora herself went around blabbing to everyone?

"Okay, let's back up a bit," I said. "Why do you think Jack Litchfield is a maniac?"

"Well, I don't know him personally."

"Tell me what you've heard about him."

She eyed me suspiciously. "Why?"

I debated on how to answer that one, decided on the truth. "Because Jack Litchfield does seem a little off, okay? I need to know what people are saying about him. This is important."

"I knew your job was dangerous," Mother said with an all-knowing smirk.

"Will you please stick to the subject?"

"Okay. Let me think." She sank into the sofa and crossed her legs. "I hear a lot, doesn't mean I know for a fact."

"Understood."

"I'm sorry I upset you, it's just that I worry."

"I know."

"So if I tell you what I've heard, you'll forgive me?"

"Yes."

"And you'll come to the dinner party tomorrow night?"

She was too much. "What dinner party?"

"I left you a message days ago."

My subconscious had a way of blocking out undesirable messages. "This isn't another one of your setups, is it?"

She folded her arms over her chest, looking offended. "You asked me to quit matchmaking, and I've quit. Doesn't keep me from wishing you would reconsider Clay Mitchell. He is quite a catch, and some other lucky–"

"Mother, please."

"Okay, okay. I assure you the dinner party is no setup. And I expect only eight people. I know you don't like crowds."

What she *didn't* know was that Wade and I were dating. Not that she disliked Wade personally, but Mother had unreasonably high standards when it came to prospective son-in-laws. She'd never had one good thing to say about my late husband, and I wasn't ready for my relationship with Wade to be held under her scrutiny.

"I'll think about it," I lied.

"Good." She clapped her hands together as if the whole matter was settled.

"Jack Litchfield?" I prompted.

"Lord knows why Nora waited this long to divorce the man," she said.

"What makes you say that?"

"Why, the poor dear is doing all the work, keeping the spa running like a well-oiled machine, and what's Jack doing?" She gave me a pointed look.

I shook my head. "I don't know. What?"

"Not much, that's what. He lounges around the country club all day. Spends money like it's water. But that's not the worst part."

"What is?" I figured she was about to fill me in on Jack's flings with younger women–nothing Nora hadn't already told me.

"The corrupt business dealings, of course," Mother said.

I sat up straighter. "What are you talking about?"

"Jack Litchfield has been seen at Tony's with Nicholas Brandt on more than one occasion," she said, as if that explained everything.

"And?"

"He's obviously doing business with Brandt."

"I thought nobody knew where Nicholas Brandt got his money," I said. Brandt had become a hot topic when he and his daughter moved into the heart of River Oaks several months before, mainly because no one knew a thing about the man. Now all of a sudden he was corrupt.

"Where have you been?" she said. "On the surface he's Mr. All-American Businessman. His company is putting up public storage facilities in every neighborhood. But I hear he associates with some shady characters."

"What are you trying to say?"

"There's talk he might be a money launderer."

Jeez. Jack Litchfield in cahoots with a money launderer? I reminded myself that Mother was a reporter of gossip, not necessarily fact. But I'd suspected from the start there was more to Jack's behavior than anger at being served with divorce papers. If he was into money laundering, he could be a dangerous man indeed. Then again, maybe he was running from danger. Or maybe Carmen knew about the money laundering–knew too much–knew something that ended up getting her killed.

Before leaving, I made Mother swear to keep my questions about Jack Litchfield to herself. In exchange she extracted my promise to attend the Denim & Diamonds Gala on Saturday. I got the raw end of that bargain.

Halfway down the street, I remembered the deal I'd made with Maggie Robbins. No way was I turning around to go ask Mother about the gala guest list. If Maggie asked again,

I could make up some names. I munched on another of Ruby's brownies I'd snagged on my way out, ignoring the falling chocolate crumbs.

When I got back to the office, people had already begun to check out for the day. The parking lot under the building was half empty, but Wade's car sat in his reserved spot. We had made dinner plans earlier, but I needed to send a quick e-mail to a client first.

I took the back stairs to avoid a wait at the elevators. When I opened the stairwell door on my floor, I heard bumping and thudding that sounded like somebody moving furniture. Then I neared my closed office door and realized the noise came from inside.

I turned the knob but the door was blocked by something and only opened an inch.

"Hey, what's going on in there?" I pounded my fist on the door. "Open up."

"Call the cops, Corie."

The shout came from inside. Wade.

Damn. I couldn't take the time to go find a phone. Instead, I put my shoulder into the door and shoved hard. Whatever was blocking it moved enough for me to see Wade's body sail across the room and smash into my bookcase.

"Wade!" I squeezed through the opening and ran to him, nearly knocked over myself by the burly intruder who whizzed by me on his way out.

*I need to have my space,*
*So don't come to my place.*
*And stay out of my face,*
*Or I'll be on your case.*

# CHAPTER 6

The stairwell door slammed as I knelt next to Wade. He lay crumpled against the bookcase with the dazed expression of a boxer down after the first punch.

"Dammit." He tried to stand on wobbly legs. "Got to stop that prick."

"Too late. He's gone." I put my hand on his shoulder. "Take it easy."

Wade's legs caved, and he sank back against the shelved books behind him. His chest heaved, and his breathing sounded ragged. Not surprising for a lawyer accustomed to dealing in verbal blows rather than physical ones.

"Call the cops. He can't get away with–"

"Who the hell was that?" I said.

"No idea. But–"

"Did you get a good look at him?"

"Not good enough."

I grabbed a tissue from my purse and pressed it to blood trickling from a cut on his right brow. "You okay?"

"I'll live." He held the tissue in place, and I moved my hand.

"Can I get you something? Water?"

He shook his head.

"What on earth happened?" I pushed aside CD cases that had spilled from the bookcase and sat cross-legged in front of him, crowding him so he'd have to sit still. I reached out and finger-combed his hair into place.

"Judge recessed early," he said. "On my way back to my office, I stopped to tell you something."

"And the guy was in here?"

He nodded. "I heard a noise, figured it was you, but the

door was locked and you didn't answer. Seemed funny, so I used my key."

I looked around the office. Tablets and pens had been swept off my desk, chairs overturned, drawers pulled out. Good thing I scan and save my confidential client files on the computer rather than keeping loads of paper around.

"Wonder what he was looking for?"

Wade shrugged and winced at the movement.

"You really are hurt."

"It's nothing. Hazards of my first fist fight." He rotated his head from side to side, testing his neck. "Guy was behind the door when I swung it open. Tried to slip by me. If I'd let him go, my head might still be attached to my body."

The thought of the stranger hitting Wade made me more angry than the trashed office.

"Did he say anything?"

"Nope. Tried to bulldoze past me, but I grabbed his shirt. He started swinging. You know the rest."

"Maybe he was some guy off the street looking for cash," I said.

"Don't think so. Check the computer."

From where Wade sat, he had a direct line of vision to the CPU under the desk. I turned around to check it out and saw the CD burner drive was open.

"You leave it this way?" he said.

"Uh-uh." I stood and walked to the desk. "But my computer's locked and everything's passworded." I moved the mouse and the screen came to life, showing the log-on screen.

"See," I said. "No problem. He didn't get in."

"Or he got in, copied what he wanted, and got back out," Wade said. "I'm just glad you weren't here when he showed up."

I closed the CD drive and dropped into my chair. "I'm calling the cops."

I dialed nine-one-one, figuring they would take their time since there was no immediate threat. When I finished the call, I watched Wade limp toward the overturned armchair that had blocked the door.

"You need a doctor. If we didn't have to wait for the cops to show, I'd take you to the emergency room right now."

"Not necessary." He righted the chair and sat down,

then loosened his necktie and undid his top shirt button. Dark chest hair poked out.

"You sure I can't get you some water?"

"I'm *fine*," he said, his brow wrinkled. "Have you taken on any new cases lately?"

"Nothing besides Litchfield," I said. Most of my work was related to Wade's cases, though independent clients hire me from time to time.

"That's what I was afraid of."

"You think Jack Litchfield is behind this? I don't have anything he would want."

"He doesn't know that." Wade dabbed at his cut, checked for blood and came up clean. He tossed the wadded-up tissue into the wastebasket that had miraculously remained upright during the scuffle.

"Why do I get the feeling there's more to this divorce than I've been told?" I said.

Wade gave me a palms-up. "Nothing withheld intentionally. Thought we'd get the papers served before moving on to the next phase."

"Which is?" No doubt another phase of Nora calling me regularly. I got up and closed the office door, then went back to my chair.

"Nora thinks Jack may have been hiding money."

"What a shocker," I said. "Don't all your female clients accuse the husband of hiding money?"

"Common complaint," Wade agreed, "but Nora pinpointed some withdrawals from joint accounts. She wants us to trace the money."

I raised my eyebrows. "Isn't that what forensic accountants are for?"

"When the opposing party produces documents like he's supposed to, yes, but we don't expect Jack to cooperate. I'm surprised Nora didn't mention this."

"Probably wasn't thinking about paperwork after she learned what happened to Carmen." My mind drifted to what I'd heard from Mother about Litchfield and Nicholas Brandt, but Wade didn't like gossip. If I could get some facts about their relationship, then–

Wade leaned into my line of vision and waved a hand. "Are you listening?"

"Sure. You said we need to trace the money."

"Right. Nora was convinced Carmen knew what Jack does with the cash. Now that she's gone, we'll have to count on what the secretary can tell us."

"Uh-oh." I dropped my head back and stared at the ceiling.

"What?"

"Phyllis Keene's subpoena is still in my truck. I'm sorry, but after what happened–"

He put up a hand. "Tomorrow then. Can you serve her first thing?"

I nodded, then said, "Nora insinuated that Jack might be involved in Carmen's death."

Wade said, "Can't say the thought didn't cross my mind."

"Seriously?"

"The guy's a hothead. Makes lousy decisions."

I stood and picked up the CD cases. "If Jack is so intent on keeping the money a secret that he'd kill Carmen, maybe it's a good thing I didn't serve Phyllis Keene yet. Maybe she's safer if I don't serve her at all."

"With Carmen gone, Phyllis's testimony is doubly important. And I don't really believe Litchfield had anything to do with Carmen's death. Besides, we're the only ones considering this to be homicide, am I right?"

"So far."

"Let's hope it stays that way." Wade got up and walked over to me. He grabbed my hand, brought it to his lips, and kissed my fingers. "Not every day I have a beautiful woman come to my rescue."

I moved closer and nuzzled his neck. "In a real rescue, I'd have arrived before you got hurt and kicked that punk's ass. He'd be in jail as we speak. You call this a rescue?"

"Close enough." Wade wrapped his arms around me and kissed me, a deep satisfying kiss that almost erased Litchfield from my mind. But what about the intruder? I broke off the embrace and stepped back.

"Let's say Jack hired the guy to search my office–for what?"

"Don't know," Wade said. "Nora e-mailed me a list of witnesses, notes about their connection to the case, that kind of thing. Could be what he was after. Just a guess."

"But *you* got the e-mail. If Jack knew about that and wanted a copy, why wouldn't he wait until the firm locked up for the day and break into *your* office?"

"I don't know." He checked his watch. "And right now we're both wrapped too tight to think straight. Why don't we revisit this tomorrow?"

"Good idea." I bent over to pick up my purse, then remembered my call to nine-one-one. "Hope those cops hurry, 'cause I'm starved."

Wade snapped his fingers. "Damn. That's what I came to talk to you about. I'll have to take a rain check. New client meeting tonight." He checked his watch, then hurriedly rebuttoned his shirt and straightened his tie.

"We could eat late."

"Don't think so." He shook his head apologetically. "Complicated case. No telling how long I'll be."

"Oh, okay." I needed a good night's sleep more than a heavy meal anyway. "Why don't you go on? I'll buzz your office if the cops need to talk to you personally."

He shook his head. "The meeting's not here."

"Oh." I shrugged. "Then I'll play it by ear."

"You're the best. Lock the door behind me till the cops get here." Wade kissed my cheek and was out the door.

Instead of a quiet evening with my favorite guy and a hot meal, I ended up snarfing pizza while fending off pissed-off cops who kept asking me why the main witness had skipped. By the time I reached home after nine, I could barely drag myself over the doorsill.

My black Lab, Midnite, met me at the door, acting her bouncy, over-excited, and hungry self. I don't like to keep her waiting so long, but Kit, my on-call dogsitter next door, wasn't home tonight. Good thing I had a doggie door installed so Midnite could take breaks as needed on days like this.

"Hey girl, bet you're ready to eat." Before I could finish the sentence she was at the pantry door fixing me with her what-are-you-waiting-for look. I went straight to her food bin and scooped out her supper.

"Mom's had a rough day." I opened the refrigerator and reached for a Coke, saw the White Zinfandel and poured that instead. I chugged a half-glass of wine, then checked my answering machine. No blinking red light. That was just fine since the majority of my messages are from Mother. I'd already had enough of her for one day. My first glass of wine took the edge off, but after a long, hot shower I moved on to the second.

I found a rerun of *Pure Country* with George Strait–the next best thing to working on my own lyrics. I was too wiped out to be creative tonight anyway. I settled into my over-sized recliner to watch the movie for the umpteenth time. Midnite curled up beside my chair and went to sleep. I pulled a fleece throw over me and relaxed for the first time all day.

An obnoxious buzzing interrupted my nightmare about an Olympic-size swimming pool filled with dead bodies. I reached over and felt for the alarm. No luck. My eyes felt glued shut. What was that noise? Finally, I managed to pry an eye open and saw Arnold Schwarzanegger as *The Terminator* on the television screen. Midnite pranced around my chair, whimpering. I ratcheted the recliner up a notch. Damn. The phone was ringing.

I jumped up and hobbled stiffly into the kitchen to grab the receiver. "Hello."

"Is this Corie McKenna?" The man sounded agitated. Before I could answer, he went on. "It's George Doyle. Someone's in Carmen's house."

My eyes opened a little wider. Doyle. Carmen's neighbor. "Mr. Doyle. I'm not sure I understand. What's the problem?" I peered at the kitchen clock. Three-fifteen a.m.

"Someone's in there right now," he said.

"Well, Trey lives there–"

"It's not Trey," he interrupted. "Kid drove off in Carmen's BMW early this afternoon. Right after the reporters left. He hasn't come back. Someone broke in. There's two of 'em."

"Mr. Doyle, I don't remember giving you my number. How did you find me, and why are you calling me now?"

"You're a private eye, aren't you? Got your card right here. Seemed like you cared about Carmen. If I'm wrong–"

"No, I did care. I mean, I do care, but you need to call the police."

"Called 'em already," he said. "You hear any sirens? They'll take their sweet time, and by then these jerks will be gone."

He had a point. "I understand what you're saying, but I don't know what I can do."

"Well if you're not coming, then I'm going over there and stop 'em myself," he said. "Thought you might help, but if not–"

I was standing now, reaching for my shorts. "I'm on my way. Please don't do anything 'til I get there."

I hung up the phone and dressed quickly.

On my way out the door, I patted Midnite's head. "Watch the house, baby. Too many break-ins going on lately."

In less than five minutes, I was in my pickup and speeding down the street. My conscience couldn't allow the elderly man to walk into a burglary on his own, even though I wasn't sure what either of us could do to stop the thieves from getting away.

The coincidence of Carmen's house being burglarized less than twenty-four hours after her death bothered me. It was possible that the burglars had heard about her drowning in the news and decided to take advantage of what they hoped was now an unoccupied house. So why couldn't I shake the nagging suspicion that this break-in was linked to the woman's death?

*Why did they show up here*
*On the very night she's gone?*
*There's more to this I fear,*
*Even so, I hope I'm wrong.*

# CHAPTER 7

The wee hours of the morning might be the only time Houston traffic isn't congested. I speculated about the drivers of the few cars I passed. Shift workers headed to or from their jobs? Exhausted parents driving around with their sleepless baby? And here I was, on my way to help an elderly man apprehend burglars. Crazy.

Now would be a good time to have that handgun I'd briefly considered buying after an episode last fall when I'd borrowed Reba's. Too bad I had decided against the purchase. I groped in the storage compartment between the bucket seats, found my canister of chemical spray, and stuffed it into my pocket. Better than nothing.

I reached Carmen's neighborhood in record time. After parking on a side street, I sprinted down the bayou's jogging path until I was directly across from her house. No police in sight yet. Both Carmen's and George's houses were dark, their driveways empty. The night was quiet except for the periodic whoosh of traffic noise coming from the 610 Loop. I stood behind some oleander bushes, watching Carmen's place for a minute before crossing the street for a closer look.

I was on the sidewalk when a narrow beam of light moved past a window near the front door. Yikes. I ran around the hedge separating Carmen's yard from George's and hid on the opposite side. Footsteps approached from behind, and I dropped to a crouch. I pulled the spray from my pocket, my finger poised on the nozzle.

"Don't shoot," came a frantic whisper. "It's me–George."

"God, you scared me." I let out my breath. "How long since you called the police?"

"Too long." He moved toward Carmen's. "C'mon. We can see through the back window."

Against my better judgment, I followed. If we were lucky, the police would show up before we did anything foolish. I sure didn't want the burglars to get away, but how to stop them? We didn't know what kind of weapons they carried. I had my spray and George wielded a long black flashlight, which he wisely kept off for now.

The back gate was unlocked. George opened it slowly, and we tiptoed across the deck and moved into a flower bed to hunker under a window. I inched up until my eyes were above the sill. Carmen had wood shutters, but they didn't meet very well and through the crack I saw a shaft of light darting around a bedroom.

The guy holding the light was dressed in a black long-sleeved turtleneck and dark pants. He wore a stocking pulled over his head and gloves. An identically-dressed partner entered the room, picked up a jewelry box, and dumped its contents onto the dresser. The first guy shined the light over the pile while the other shuffled through the jewelry, then inspected the box itself before dropping it on the floor.

"What are you gonna do?" said George.

"I don't know," I whispered. "Have any brilliant ideas?"

"Not a one."

Inside, sheets were yanked off the bed, pillow cases turned upside down and shaken as if treasures were expected to fall out. One of the guys lifted the mattress as the other skimmed the light underneath. Did they think Carmen was one of those people who didn't believe in banks? I half expected them to pull out a knife to slash the mattress, but they turned to the dresser drawers instead, emptying them onto the bed and methodically looking through every item.

"We have to do *something*," George said.

"Well, we're not going to barge in there. Be serious. Ever seen *Butch Cassidy and the Sundance Kid*?"

He nodded.

"Maybe you could find their car," I whispered. "Get a plate number. I wouldn't recognize any strange vehicles in the neighborhood, but you might."

"Good idea. Here, take this. I have another one in the

house." He handed me his maglight, then crawled from our hiding spot and disappeared into the blackness. When I turned back to the window, it was dark. George had only been gone for a minute when the back door opened on squeaky hinges. I ducked behind the shrubbery.

The thieves emerged from the house, each toting a suitcase. I felt stupid holding my spray canister, as if it could help. The burglars ran alongside the swimming pool, and the taller one went over the back fence like a trained athlete. Damn. They were going to get away. Impulsively, I grabbed a brick from the flower bed's border and flung it into the fence. Anything to stall them.

"Freeze, you slimeball!" I hollered as the brick whacked the fence. I flicked on the flashlight and pinned the second guy in its beam.

He might have hesitated for a split second, and my heart seemed to stop. I was a sitting target here behind the damn light. But the guy didn't even turn around, running instead to the fence and throwing his suitcase over first before disappearing after it. About that time George came running through the gate holding another flashlight.

"What happened?"

"They're gone. Over the fence. I'll get my truck and–" Before I could finish we heard tires squeal and a car sped away.

"Gosh damn," George said.

We walked over to the fence and shined our flashlights on the cedar planks.

"Look at this." George pointed to a nail protruding from the fence slat. A few black fibers clung to its head.

"Don't touch that," I said. "We'll show the police. I don't suppose you spotted their car."

"Didn't get that far. Went in for pencil and paper, to write down license numbers, you know. And the light." He held up his flashlight. "Just came back outside when you yelled."

The man looked depressed, like all this was his fault. I patted his shoulder. "That's okay."

He hung his head. "Sure wish we had caught those jerks. They mighta been the ones who killed Carmen."

Earlier, George had thought Trey was involved. This

burglary had changed his perspective and even though we didn't officially know Carmen's death was a homicide, I was thinking along the same lines.

"Let's go see what those sons of bitches stole," he said, taking off toward the house.

"Wait." I hurried to keep up with him. "We shouldn't go in there."

George didn't hesitate. He barged through the back door, which had been left standing open. I entered right behind him.

"Don't touch anything," I said.

"I know that." He flicked on the kitchen light switch with his elbow. "C'mon."

I hesitated for a second, then figured what the heck. We moved through the house and picked our way around the piles of Carmen's belongings strewn across the floor. I took mental snapshots of each room though I had seen a "before" image of only the kitchen.

I went back there now to compare the room to what I'd seen before. All the cabinet doors stood open. A set of white stoneware dishes with pastel flower borders remained in neat stacks. White porcelain pots and pans had been shuffled in the bottom cabinets, handles sticking out so that the doors wouldn't close. The pantry was a mess, all cans shoved to the side, the boxes emptied. Cereal, crackers, and uncooked spaghetti littered the floor. Frozen popsicles lay scattered on the counter top, the box thrown aside.

The silverware tray was empty. The drawers of the built-in kitchen desk were pulled out and held only a few pens and pencils.

I caught up with George in the master bedroom—the room we'd been peering into from outside. Puffy pillows lay on the floor, their shams removed. The flowered chintz bedspread edged in lace was crumpled into a pile along with lace-edged sheets and pillowcases. The mattress rested diagonally across the box spring.

"How dare they destroy Carmen's house," George said, his fists clenched. "Look at her beautiful things, thrown around like trash."

I was still having trouble believing this could be a random burglary. "Do you know if Carmen had any enemies?

Anybody giving her trouble lately?"

"No one besides the kid," he said, his voice rising. "And I wouldn't be surprised if he had something to do with this."

"Calm down. Let's not assume. Remember, there were two guys."

"I'm calm enough." Despite his statement, he paced the bedroom floor and stepped around Carmen's undergarments and nightgowns from an emptied drawer. "Kid could have brought a friend with him."

"But why would Trey steal what he might end up inheriting?" I said.

He gave me a look. "Carmen wouldn't leave anything to that twirp. She didn't even like him."

"So why was he living here?"

"I'm not sure. Came here a month or so ago. He was supposed to look for his own place, but I don't think he ever tried. Kid has an attitude."

And you don't? I didn't say what I was thinking, asking instead, "Does Carmen have other relatives?"

"A brother, Trey's dad. Lives in New Braunfels. Name's Ruben Salinas."

"You've met him?"

"No. He called me, asked for some recommendations about the funeral. He'll be here later today. Seemed an okay sort, better than the kid."

I wasn't all that interested in Carmen's brother. The jewelry strewn over the dresser had captured my attention. I wondered how the burglars had decided in the dim light that it wasn't worth taking.

"This stuff looks pretty nice to me. Why would they leave it?"

"That's not all," he said. "Left that antique flatware in the dining room."

"Interesting."

He walked out, and I followed him into the dining room where he stopped in front of the china cabinet. He pulled out the center drawer and picked up a fork, turning it over in his hand.

"Carmen has had me over for dinner on occasion." He swallowed hard. "I remember how happy she was the day she found these pieces at an estate sale. I'm glad those sons of bitches didn't get them."

"Were you and Carmen–" I hesitated, unsure how to word the question, but George caught my meaning.

"No, no." His complexion reddened. "She was neighborly, checking up on me, fixing me dinners, ever since my wife passed on last year."

"Oh, I'm sorry."

"Carmen helped me through some tough times," he went on. "Nothing romantic about it. She already had more men interested in her than one woman could handle."

He made that statement with an air of disapproval, but I sensed this wasn't the best time to ask questions along those lines. I walked into the kitchen and stopped in front of the desk. "No paper anywhere," I said.

"Paper?" George stood beside me and looked around.

"Where are her bills? Receipts? Junk mail?" I pointed to the desk. "All the drawers have been cleaned out. I don't see a bit of paper."

"Hadn't noticed," he said.

I scratched my head and wondered how others would view this burglary. I could imagine Nora Litchfield blaming this on Jack like she did everything else. Which might not sound that farfetched. What if Carmen had kept a journal detailing her love affair with Jack? Details her married lover would want to keep secret.

A noise in the other room startled me. Assuming the police had arrived, I walked into the hallway. Something hard and cold pushed against my back.

"What the hell are you doing here?"

The slurred voice sounded familiar. "Is that you, Trey?" I got no response and took that as a yes. "Mr. Doyle called me. There were burglars in the house. I came to help."

"Yeah, right." He shoved his weapon into my back, hard. I bit my lip and thought about the spray in my pocket, but I didn't trust making a move to get it out.

"She's telling the truth, kid. Put the gun down." George to the rescue.

The hard metal against me moved away.

I rotated slowly. Trey was holding a rifle, and George had fooled the kid into thinking the butt of his flashlight was a more serious weapon. I took the rifle from Trey, wondering if he always carried the weapon with him.

"Where you been, kid?" George asked. "You have anything to do with this mess?"

"No way, old man," Trey said. "I've been at a friend's house, drinkin'. You think I wanna hang out here all day after seein' that dead broad?"

George grabbed Trey by the throat with his left hand and raised the flashlight in his right. "Don't you talk about your aunt that way, you disrespectful juvenile delinquent."

"Police, freeze!"

The three of us did as instructed. I could only guess what an unusual picture we presented there in the hallway and what they might do with us – a drunk young man being assaulted by an older man with a flashlight and me holding the rifle–all in the middle of a house ransacked from end to end.

*You want me to what?*
*Tell me you're not serious!*
*Must have heard you wrong,*
*Or maybe I'm delirious.*

# CHAPTER 8

Several hours later, the patrol officers who answered the burglary call released us, and that was only after they talked to Sergeant Belton. He confirmed everything that I'd told them about events at Carmen's house the day before was true. I didn't bother to mention the guy who had broken into my office. That event seemed irrelevant to the investigation at hand anyway, and they'd have kept me even longer.

I finally crawled into bed around seven a.m., feeling fortunate to have escaped arrest. I mean, who gets interrogated by the police three times within twenty-four hours? I fell asleep with Johnny Cash's "Folsom Prison Blues" running through my head.

The phone woke me again just before ten, and I was only slightly coherent when I said "hello."

"How's my favorite daughter?"

I was his only daughter, and I wasn't in the mood for his old joke. "Hey, Dad. Ha ha."

"You don't sound yourself," he said. "What's wrong?"

"Oh, nothing." I sat up and ran a hand through my hair. He'd only worry if he heard the whole story. "Just sleep deprived lately. How are you?"

"Great. The Big Apple is crisp and cool, a pleasant relief from sweltering in Houston." A familiar sound came over the line, and I knew it was his ever-present lollipop tapping against his teeth. I could picture Dad lounging in a luxurious New York City hotel suite sucking on a Tootsie Roll Pop.

"Sounds nice."

"Sorry I woke you honey, but I need a favor."

I stretched. "Sure, what's up?"

"I'm here 'til Tuesday morning," he said. "And I'm concerned about your mother."

"Why? Did something happen?"

"No, but I'm hearing an awful lot about burglaries in the area. Pete Stein on my staff is dubbing these criminals the River Oaks Banditos."

Little did Dad know I had witnessed two break-ins myself. "I hadn't heard that," I said. "Do they think the Mexican Mafia is involved?"

"I don't think the cops have any idea who's behind this, but you know Pete. Always looking for a gimmick."

"Right," I said. "How many burglaries are we talking?"

"About a dozen over the past two months. The pace is picking up and the police are seeing similarities. Up 'til now nobody's been hurt, but Joyce Adams came home early yesterday afternoon and caught them in the act."

Joyce lived two streets over from my parents. "That's awful. Is she okay?"

"She's fine," he said, "but the episode scared her pretty badly. And she can't help with the ID–said they wore something over their heads."

Stockings, I thought. Just like those two I saw.

A phone rang on Dad's end, and he began talking faster. "Here's the deal. I need you to keep an eye on your mother. She's got the gala coming up. No matter what anyone tells her she won't keep a low profile."

"No, she won't," I agreed.

"It's asking a lot, I know," he said. "But I'd feel better if she wasn't alone."

"You want me to move in while you're gone?" I gulped.

"Just do what you can, okay?" he said. "Have to run. I'm meeting with the *Times* editor in five minutes."

"I'll take care of Mother," I said. "Don't worry."

"Knew I could count on you. See you soon."

Dad clicked off. I moved the receiver from my ear and stared at it before hanging up. Midnite stood beside the bed, her chin resting on the mattress, solemn brown eyes watching me.

"Do what you can, he says. I've just sentenced myself

to torture."

I scratched Midnite behind the ears, wondering what Dad would say if I hired a bodyguard for the job. But I knew why he'd asked me. Mother wouldn't stand for being "guarded" by a stranger. I'd have to be inconspicuous about it or she'd send *me* packing.

I sighed. Dad had entrusted me with this important task, so now I'd have to follow through on my promise to attend the gala. Instead of obsessing about the problem I jumped up and headed for the shower. First on today's agenda was phone shopping. I'd grown so accustomed to being in constant contact that I couldn't imagine doing without the cell phone, even for one day.

Before leaving the house, I called Reba at the office and left her a voice mail message about where I was going. I didn't expect to spend much time choosing a new phone–probably something smaller, lighter. I was totally unprepared for the range of options demonstrated by the Asian salesman at the phone store in Rice Village. The more models he showed me, the more confused I became.

"I'll take one of these." I picked up a small blue phone, cutting off his sales pitch.

He picked up a red phone instead and thrust it at me. "But with this model you get the same features, *plus* the ability–"

"I want this one." I backed away from his outstretched arm and bumped into someone.

"Nice shot, lady," came from behind me.

I turned around to see what the problem was.

The man behind me wore a white Ben Hogan cap. He held a phone in one hand, a Starbucks cup with no lid in the other. Coffee had splashed on his U.T. orange golf shirt and dripped from the cup onto his ostrich boots.

"I'm so sorry," I said.

The salesman said, "I'll get something to clean that up" and hurried away.

I pulled a tissue from my purse and offered it to the man, but he wiped the bottom of his cup with a hand and dried the hand on his Wranglers. "Forget it."

I stooped to dab at the blotches of coffee on his boots. "Leave it," he said, backing away. "Just watch where you're going next time."

"Excuse me?" I stood, staring him down. I had hoped today would be better than yesterday. So far it wasn't, and I wasn't in the mood to take any grief off of this cowboy, or golfer, or whatever the hell he was.

"If I'm not mistaken, you were the one crowding up behind me," I said, "not to mention bringing a beverage into a store without a lid. So don't go pinning all the blame on me."

He stared back with grizzly bear brown eyes that looked mean until they crinkled at the corners.

"Are you laughing at me?" I said.

"Not me, ma'am." He tipped his cap. "You have a good day now."

He turned and walked out, and as I watched him go I couldn't help but notice his athletic build. He was so tan I wondered if he played golf professionally.

Then the salesman was back, clutching some wet paper towels. When he saw the man had left, he dropped the towels on the floor and used his foot to swipe them across the spilled coffee.

"Let me tell you about our special rate plans, this week only," he said.

I put up with another pitch, insisted on the blue phone and on keeping the plan I already had, then exercised patience during the check-out process. Finally, I headed out of the store armed with my phone, a charger, a belt clip, and a manual which I might or might not ever read.

It was noon by the time I arrived at the office. I plugged the new phone into the charger, then found Reba in the law firm's kitchen eating a Subway Cold Cut Combo, one of her favorites. Shredded lettuce and bell pepper strips scattered as she bit into the fat sandwich.

"Yum. That looks great." My stomach growled, a reminder that I'd skipped breakfast.

"Help yourself," Reba mumbled around the food. She pointed to the counter, then swallowed the bite before explaining. "Picked up lunch for the mediation in the conference room. These are leftovers."

"You sure?" I went to the counter and checked the clear plastic bag that held three sandwiches. "What are they?"

"One like this, two turkey."

Turkey sounded too healthy. I chose the other Cold Cut Combo and grabbed a bag of potato chips. "Heard anything from Nora today?" I said, already knowing the answer.

"Lord, yes." Reba put her sandwich down and wiped her mouth with a napkin. "Has documents for Wade, some she claims you'll need to do something with. Sorry, but I tune that woman out after five minutes. Every conversation's the same – blah, blah, blah. She's expecting you to come by the spa today before five."

"Isn't that peachy?" I took my food and a Coke to the table and sat in the chair across from Reba. "My favorite place."

"Girl, this is one reason I say we should pack up and head for Nashville."

"Don't start." Reba was like a broken record when it came to her hopes for our country music career.

"How about American Idol? You could show those people something. Everybody would vote for you, and you'd be recording your first CD by Christmas."

"You're assuming that I *want* to record a CD." I took a bite of my sandwich and washed it down. "Not everyone is meant for stardom."

"Well, it'd be a helluva lot better than where I'm sittin' every day of my life, typin' my fingers off." Reba fiddled with a dangly beaded earring.

"You must be having an unusually bad day," I said. "I thought you loved working for Wade."

"Yeah, Wade is great." She pushed the scattered lettuce into a pile. "But can you believe that bitch is back, that she even has the nerve to show her face here?"

It was clear yesterday that Reba didn't like Wade's client, but today she sounded downright hateful. "What's the big deal?" I said. "You shouldn't let Jennifer bother you. Ignore her."

"Jennifer? I'm talking about Laura." Reba picked up her fork, loaded with lettuce, opened her mouth, then froze. She raised her eyes slowly to meet my gaze.

I put my sandwich down. "What do you mean Laura?"

"Uh-oh." Reba stuffed lettuce into her mouth and chewed slowly, ignoring my stare.

"Laura who?" I asked.

She swallowed. "Laura Payne."

"What about Laura Payne?"

"Jeez Louise, why don't you just shoot me? Sometimes a person should be shot for their stupidity."

She started to get up, but I grabbed her arm. "Sit."

She obeyed, pouting. "Damn Wade. He said *he* was gonna tell you."

"Tell me what?" I stared at her. "Or maybe I don't want to know."

"It's not that bad," she backpedaled. "Just his bitchy ex-wife is back in Houston and ready to divorce lover-boy."

I let go of Reba's arm and sat back. "She's divorcing Payne?" Laura's affair with Drew Payne had begun while she was still married to Wade.

Reba nodded. "And guess who she's hired to handle the case? That oughta be a conflict of interest, don't you think?"

I didn't answer. The fact that Laura Alexander Payne wanted a divorce didn't bother me nearly as much as Wade's cancelling our dinner last night to meet with his newest client.

"I can't believe he didn't tell you," Reba said.

"Oh, he told me part of it. He said his new case was complicated."

*I know he was hers before,*
*How I wish that didn't matter.*
*But it does, my heart is torn,*
*And my whole world may shatter.*

# CHAPTER 9

I left the office, sandwich uneaten. Reviewing my mental to-do list, I headed downtown. Funny how meeting with the police seemed more desirable than meeting with my own client, but Nora's impatience wore on me. And right now I was digesting the news about Wade's ex being back in Houston. Why would she ask him to handle her divorce? And why hadn't he told me he was meeting with her? It's not like they never talked. They had two kids to raise, for Pete's sake. So why the big secret?

At a red light on Memorial Drive, I punched radio buttons restlessly, settling on 93-Q. Shania Twain was singing. *Don't freak out until you know the facts–relax–don't be stupid.* Sounded like good advice. I already had too much to fit into this day. Why add useless speculation?

In record time I was in and out of the police station. I had expected to be there for hours, but the cops had been right. All I had to do was sign my statement. No fuss. No surprises. No more excuses to avoid Nora, so I headed for West Gray.

Serenity Spa was busier today. Probably women preparing for a weekend full of social engagements. I entered the crowded lobby, hoping I wouldn't run into the ill-tempered manager again. She was nowhere in sight, and I hurried toward the cash register to ask for Nora. The check-out girl wasn't perky today. Her shoulders shook with sobs as two other employees with their backs to me tried to console her.

One of them turned around, sensing my presence, and I was surprised to see the glossy brunette ponytail belonged to a man. He wore a fluorescent lime shirt with multi-colored polka dots over tight black leather pants that seemed far too hot for our weather.

"May I help you?" he said with a thin smile.

"Yes." I gave him my name and explained that Nora was expecting me.

"So sorry." He gave my hair a once-over as he spoke. "She just began an interview. But do wait." He leaned closer to me and lowered his voice. "I saw the applicant come in, and she doesn't have a prayer."

I indicated the girl behind him who was still crying. "Is she all right?"

"Give her a little time. She'll be okay. Just had some bad news." He turned to the computer and clicked to a screen that looked like the appointment calendar. "If you'd like to have a seat, I'll–"

"This have anything to do with Carmen?" I said.

He looked up from the computer, and I noticed his eyes were teary. "Yes. Did you know her?"

"Not really." Something about his friendly demeanor made me go into the story of how I'd found Carmen in the pool.

"Carmen was such a dear." He wiped at his damp eyes. "At least I thought so. That's why I'm so shocked to find out she was murdered."

"You know that for a fact?"

He leaned close again and spoke quietly. "One of my clients works for HPD. She knew I was beside myself about what had happened. Called me this morning." He stepped back, inspecting me from different angles. "You really need to do something with that hair."

I straightened and put a hand to my head. "I don't think–"

"A teensy trim would make a world of difference." He held his thumb and forefinger about an inch apart.

He had brightened at the prospect of fixing my hair, and I wanted to know exactly what he'd heard about Carmen. He might tell me more given enough time. Hmm. "Do *you* cut hair?" I said.

"I'm one of the best."

"If you had time right now, I'd go for it." I shrugged. "But you're probably booked."

He checked his watch and pursed his lips, then glanced at my hair again. "I have a client coming in soon, but I make exceptions for emergencies. Come on back."

My curiosity meter was hitting the top by the time the shampoo girl had finished with me and escorted me back to the hair stylist, who had introduced himself as Zachary. I sat in his swivel chair, wondering what had possessed me to go this far.

Zachary discussed his plan to rid me of my dead ends. When he paused to catch his breath, I jumped in.

"What did your friend tell you?" I adjusted the purple cape over my knees as he combed through wet strands.

"What friend?"

"The friend at HPD," I prompted. "About Carmen?"

"Oh, yes. Now, no names." He picked up his shears. "You didn't hear this from me."

I nodded agreement.

He placed a hand on his chest and took a deep breath as if gathering his courage to discuss the disturbing topic. "Carmen's autopsy is already done, and she didn't drown. She was smothered, then dumped in the water. Oh, my poor dear."

I turned and put a hand on his arm. "I'm so sorry." Although I had suspected as much, the news made me shiver. "Do they have any idea who did it?"

He blinked away tears, then took another deep breath and began cutting my hair. "Not one. You know, you are going to love your hair with this extra weight gone."

I looked at the hair falling into my lap, pieces nearly three inches long. Yikes. But it *had* been unmanageable lately, so I didn't object. "What do *you* think? Why would anyone want to kill Carmen?"

He stopped snipping and screwed up his mouth. "I have no earthly idea. We've worked together for a couple of years now. Carmen's been moody lately, but then who wouldn't be after working a job like this as long as she did?" He resumed cutting. "Not everyone is as agreeable as you are about their hair. I mean, they'll come in and say they want it dyed blonde. Two weeks later they've changed their mind and insist on auburn. They won't take no for an answer, then when their hair looks fried, it's all our fault."

I imagined a disgruntled client killing Carmen as revenge for a botched haircut. Stranger things have happened.

Zachary sectioned off my hair and clipped a portion up

out of his way. "My latest fiasco is Brynley Mulloy. Darn, did I let that name slip?"

I grinned. "I didn't hear any name."

"Sorry, but some people cannot be tolerated. You don't know Brynley, do you?"

"No, but I can sympathize."

"She's threatening to sue the spa over some shampoo she bought from us. Can you imagine? Claims her hair is falling out now. See your doctor, Brynley, is what I'd like to tell her. Maybe you have a thyroid problem. Sorry, I'm getting carried away."

"Long as it's not with your scissors."

"We're almost done here," he said, sobering. "Staying busy helps keep my mind off Carmen."

"I understand. Listen, Zachary, you're trusting me to keep your confidence. Can you return the favor?"

"Sure."

"I'm an investigator working on Nora's divorce. We thought Carmen might have some information about Jack that we could use. What's the story with those two? What was their relationship?"

Zachary removed the clip and combed out my last section of longer hair. "That affair is ancient history. Carmen put up with Jack's crap, excuse the French, for too long. They were still friends, but that's the extent of it."

"Haven't heard much good about Jack Litchfield," I said.

"Because there isn't any." Zachary stooped and pulled on the ends of my hair to make sure each side was the same length. He reached for a tube of styling gel.

"You think Jack ever talked business with Carmen?"

Zachary chuckled. "That man would talk business to a fly. To hear Jack tell it, he's always on the verge of the biggest and best deal of the century."

"Back when the affair was going on, what was Nora's reaction?"

He squirted gel on his hands, rubbed them together, and began applying it to my hair. "Nora is married to her work," he said. "Nora wouldn't know–"

"Nora wouldn't know what?" The voice bounced over the partition.

My head jerked up. Zachary jumped back, accidentally pulling my hair as Nora Litchfield walked into the cubicle.

Zachary's complexion turned a rosy pink. ""Nora!" he said, "I was telling Corie here you wouldn't know what to do without fabulous clients like her."

Nora eyed me. "I didn't know you were a client."

"This is my first time," I said. "Not the last, I'm sure."

"I've been waiting for you." She tapped the face of her watch with a crimson fingernail. "We need to talk. Zachary, are you almost through here?"

"Ten minutes," he said, "and I'll bring her to your office."

She left, and he dried and styled my hair in eight minutes flat. "You look marvelous." He handed me a mirror. "What do you think?"

My hair looked pretty darn good, and I wondered what Wade would think about the new style. "I like it, but no time for oohing and aahing with your boss waiting. How much do I owe you?"

He waved a hand. "Forget it. This little trim was my pleasure. Consider it a thank-you gift. For trying to save my friend." His eyes grew watery again, and he pointed the way to Nora's office.

I smiled and handed him my business card. "Nobody's going to get away with this murder," I told him. "You hear anything that might help catch her killer, report it to the police. You want to talk, give me a call."

I headed down the corridor to Nora's office, thinking I should go ahead and pay for the cut. She probably conducted an audit every night to make sure her employees collected their fair share. Not paying attention, I turned a corner sharply and was nearly mowed down by a woman in a red dress. Our eyes met before she rushed on. I was about to knock on Nora's door when I remembered where I'd seen the woman before.

Phyllis Keene, Jack's secretary. She looked a lot different from the last time I'd seen her. The hair was shorter. Maybe she'd had a makeover, but I was almost positive it was her. Damn, her subpoena was in my truck. Maybe I could catch her. I turned and sprinted toward the lobby. The place was still crowded, but I caught sight of Phyllis's red dress going out the front door.

I raced across the lobby and hit the door running. I put up a hand to shade my eyes from the sun and saw Phyllis nearing a black Mercedes. "Excuse me," I hollered, "Ms. Keene?"

The woman turned around, saw me, then picked up her pace. Her clothes were so different from the inexpensive, almost frumpy, dresses she'd worn on those days I'd stopped by Litchfield's office trying to serve him with the divorce petition. The flashy dress went with the new car. She'd been driving an old Buick Regal the time I'd seen her in the Greenway Plaza parking garage. I ran toward her.

"Ms. Keene, you work for Jack Litchfield, don't you?"

She glanced around the parking lot and opened her car door. "You've mistaken me for someone else," she said before sliding into the car seat.

"You *know* Jack Litchfield," I continued. "Let's not play games. You and I have talked at his office."

Her stare was frosty. "I have no idea who you're talking about. If you'll excuse me, I have an appointment to keep."

"I'd be glad to make an appointment to talk with you," I said to her slamming door. Phyllis Keene revved her engine and sped out of the parking lot, narrowly missing a valet attendant who jumped out of the way. He wisely stayed out of my path when I jumped in my truck and took off after her.

*Don't run from me girl,*
*I know that you lied.*
*Your mind's in a whirl,*
*But there's no need to hide.*

# CHAPTER 10

I sped down the street, trying to keep the shiny Mercedes in my sights. Keene ran a light at the West Gray and Shepherd intersection. I stopped, not willing to test the brakes of the UPS truck barreling toward the light from the other direction. What was I doing anyway? Nora would not be a happy camper when she found out I'd left the spa before our meeting. But I couldn't ignore Keene's odd behavior. Why would she deny knowing Jack Litchfield? She'd even denied her own name. That was plain weird.

Keene got caught at the next light, so I was able to spot her before she took a right off Shepherd onto West Alabama. I followed, staying back far enough so she wouldn't notice me. After about a mile I had a hunch where she was going and sure enough she pulled into the parking garage for the Greenway Plaza high-rise where she worked.

"Gotcha," I said aloud.

I'd spent a lot of time in this building during my pursuit of Jack Litchfield. Talk about getting caught in a lie. Phyllis Keene was going to the office of the employer she'd claimed she didn't know. What was up with her?

Phyllis pulled into the contract section of the garage, and I found a spot in visitor parking. I watched her race across the garage toward the building. The full skirt of her dress danced around thin calves as she disappeared into the corridor that crossed between the garage stairwell and the elevator.

I waited a few seconds, then hurried after her, nearly colliding with a janitor coming out of the storage closet next to the stairwell. I missed him, but rammed into the mop handle extending from his rolling bucket. The bucket tipped enough for water to slosh out over the tiled walkway. I lost more time as we apologized, each of us assuming blame for the incident. By then, I'd lost sight of Phyllis, though I figured I knew exactly where she was going.

When the elevator doors opened on the seventeenth floor, I turned toward the office of Litchfield Enterprises. The lobby was dark. I peered through the leaded glass on the door. Tried the knob. Locked. So where was Phyllis? She was really starting to aggravate me. I walked down the side hall to the office's back door. I had tried getting in this way once before, hoping a sneak attack on Jack might work. The door had been locked then, and it was locked now.

Damn. I didn't think Phyllis was sitting inside in the dark. Maybe she'd stopped at the ladies' room. I went down the hall and found the restroom empty. I returned to the front door and stood there for a few seconds before turning to the dentist's office across the hall. I'd come to this building so often the receptionist waved a greeting when I entered their lobby. I asked if she'd seen Phyllis.

"Nope. Nobody's been over there for a couple of days."

"Is that unusual?"

"I would say so," the woman said. "They kept to themselves, but this is the first time since I've worked here that the office has been closed."

I thanked her and left. In the hallway, I stabbed the elevator's down button repeatedly. Maybe Phyllis was visiting with a friend. I'd sit and watch her car till she came back. That sounded like a good plan, but when I reached the parking garage the Mercedes was gone.

Now what? I stared at the empty space for a moment, more curious than ever about why the woman felt the need to run from me. Maybe for the same reason Jack had avoided being served. An urgent enough reason to close the office and go into hiding?

I reached for my cell phone automatically before remembering it was still plugged in at the office. I went back inside in search of a pay phone and found one on the lower level. Maybe Nora knew something about why the office of Litchfield Enterprises was closed. I dug out some change and placed a call to the spa, asked for her, and prepared myself for a tongue lashing.

Haley Winter answered and addressed me in a chilly

tone that matched her name. "Mrs. Litchfield is not available. You were due to see her earlier, and she was *very* upset to find you'd left."

"Couldn't be helped," I said. "An emergency came up, and I'll explain to Nora when I get there. I should be back within twenty minutes."

"Don't bother. She's not here."

Jostling sounds came over the line, then a man spoke. "Corie? Zachary. Listen, I think Nora's in trouble."

"What kind of trouble?"

"Hold on a sec."

Zachary may have covered the mouthpiece, but I could hear Haley reprimanding him for talking with me about Nora's private business.

"This isn't an Action News bulletin," he told her. "I'm speaking confidentially to someone who has Nora's best interests at heart. Right, Corie?"

"Of course. What's going on?"

A door slammed on his end.

"Finally," he said. "Got rid of that witch. Anyway, my friend Lynda overheard Nora on the phone. Office door was shut, but Nora was shouting. Talking statements and withdrawals, that kind of thing, so Lynda figures it's either a bank or an accountant on the other end. Next thing we knew, Nora lit out of here calling Jack names I never heard come out of the lady's mouth before. It's like she was breathing fire."

"You sure she wasn't talking to Jack?"

"Oh, I don't think so. He won't return her calls. That's one reason she's so hacked."

"But you're saying this is unusual behavior for Nora?"

"I'm saying I only saw Nora lose her cool once before, last week, but that was tame compared to today. This divorce business is sending her over the edge."

"What do you think she's gonna do?"

"All I know for sure is ol' Jack better watch himself. Right about now Nora makes that woman who cut off her husband's, ah, you know, look like a lamb."

"I'll try to find her," I said. "What's she driving?"

Zachary described Nora's champagne-colored Lincoln Navigator and said she'd been gone about twenty minutes. I hung up and ran to my truck. If Nora hadn't talked to Jack lately, then there was only one place she might expect to find him – and I was the fool who'd given her the address where Jack had been house sitting. I tore out of the parking garage, headed for Tanglewood.

My imagination went wild on the way there. Too many divorce cases ended with murder. I'd heard stories of people shooting, stabbing, even running over their spouse with a car. Nora Litchfield wasn't my favorite person, but I didn't want her doing something stupid and ending up in jail.

It was nearing five o'clock and I knew traffic in the Galleria area would be impossible so I bypassed the worst of it by cutting through side streets. Short-cuts always seem like such a good idea but usually end up taking longer than the ordinary route, and today was no exception.

When I finally turned onto the street where Jack's friends lived, I spotted Nora's Navigator and pulled up behind it. On other days when I'd been here, I hadn't seen any neighbors. Today women and children were out front, all staring in the same direction. Nora stood on the porch, and I heard her shouting obscenities as soon as I opened my door.

"Nora," I yelled, "come over here. We need to talk." She didn't even turn around.

"I'm not leaving, you son of a bitch," she hollered, beating her fists on the door. "Not until you come out here and face me like a man. You can't steal from me and get away with it."

This wasn't the Nora Litchfield I knew. I stayed by the truck, watching to make sure she didn't have a weapon. I didn't remember if my can of chemical spray had ever made it back into my purse, and even if it had I didn't want to use the stuff on Nora. From the corner of my eye I saw a gray-haired woman in a turquoise house dress crossing the street.

"You know her?" she said.

"Yes, I'm afraid so."

"Want me to call nine-one-one?" She pulled a portable phone from her pocket.

I put up a hand. "No, please. I don't think that will be necessary. She's going through a nasty divorce."

The woman nodded. "Suspected it might be something like that, but if she's lookin' for the fella who watched the house for the Gibsons, she's out of luck."

"Why is that?"

"He's gone."

"Are you sure?"

She raised her eyebrows like she couldn't believe I would doubt her.

"Did you see him leave?" I said.

"Yes. I was out front watering my begonias when he threw a suitcase into that little sportscar of his and took off."

"What about the Gibsons? Are they home from their trip now?" If they were inside, they had probably called for police already.

She shook her head. "Not yet."

"Thanks for the info. I'll calm my friend down and get her out of here then, no harm done. Right?" I walked toward Nora, not waiting for the neighbor's reply.

I stopped a few yards from the porch. "Nora, Jack isn't here. Let's go."

She kept pounding on the door and yelled, "Jack, get your sorry ass out here this minute."

I moved closer and raised my voice. "He's not here. The neighbor saw him leave."

She pounded some more.

"Nora, you're making a scene. You don't want the police involved."

"I don't?" She turned around, a crazed expression on her face. "They need to lock up that miserable excuse for a husband." Her hands were balled into fists, the knuckles on one hand scraped and bleeding. Dirt smudged the front of her light gray slacks.

"Whatever he's done, that's not the answer. Come on, let's go."

"The s.o.b. stole my money. He belongs in prison." She turned and resumed her attack on the door.

The last thing I wanted was another session with the police. I grabbed her by the shoulders and gave her a little shake.

She whirled. "Don't you touch me!"

I didn't back down. "For God's sake, let's get out of here. You can talk this out with your attorney."

She glared at me. "This is not some petty little matter."

"I'm sure it's not, but Jack has left and we need to do

the same before the neighbors complain."

"*I'm* the one who's worked night and day to build the business while he's out schoomzing and wasting money." She brushed hair out of her face. "*I* make all the decisions, I do all the work. We wouldn't have anything if–" Her voice cracked and she began to cry. She covered her face with her hands and sagged against the door.

I dared to touch her again, putting a hand on one shoulder. I looked up and down the street, saw that some people were still watching. The elderly woman stood in her front yard, holding her phone.

This was crazy. "Nora, tell me. What exactly did Jack do?"

She looked up, studying me for a second through mascara-streaked eyes. "The son of a bitch withdrew over two million dollars from the bank."

I gulped. "But he can't do that. There's a restraining order."

Nora's laugh sounded more like a cackle. "Jack doesn't care what's written on some damn piece of paper. The money's gone."

"The money is *not* gone," I said. "It's community property, and he'll have to answer for what he's done." A sick feeling was building in the pit of my stomach. Two million dollars. The closed office. Jack could be on his way out of the country for all we knew.

"Let's go talk to Wade before these people have the cops after you."

This time mention of the police made Nora take notice. She lifted her head and looked around as if she'd just awoken from a bad dream. "Okay," she said.

Nora was too shaky to drive, so I commandeered the Navigator and left my pickup behind. At a red light, I borrowed her cell phone to call Wade. Reba picked up the call, but not until the fourth ring. I'd already figured her reluctance to answer came from seeing Nora's name on caller ID.

"What are you doing on Nora's phone?" she said when she heard my voice.

"Long story," I said. "I'm with her, and she needs to see Wade immediately. Is he available?"

"For you, maybe." Reba lowered her voice so Nora

couldn't hear. "He's been edgy all afternoon, tryin' to reach you. Think he's feelin' bad for not tellin' you about Laura?"

"That can wait," I said. "Nora has an emergency, and I'm bringing her there now."

"Okey-dokey. I'll break the news."

We disconnected, and I glanced at my passenger. She was leaning back, her eyes half closed, but her neck muscles were taut and her fists still clenched.

There wasn't going to be a better time, so I told her about my afternoon, beginning with Phyllis Keene and ending with my trip to Jack's office. "Looks like your husband has closed his business."

"Business." Nora snorted in disgust. "Jack set up that office to create the illusion of being in business."

"Why would he do that?"

"To play the influential businessman in front of his friends, of course," she said. "Working out of the house or the spa simply didn't create the right image, so let's waste money on leasing commercial office space."

I didn't blame Nora for her sarcasm. She wasn't a likeable woman, but I felt sorry for her. Anyone would be testy after having to put up with the likes of Jack. I had only come face-to-face with the man one time, and that was enough for me.

"I want to hire you," Nora said abruptly.

Just when I thought I was nearly through with the case. "This is a matter for the courts. I'm sure Wade will file some sort of emergency motion right away and ask for an expedited hearing."

"What good will that do? Jack hasn't made an appearance in the case yet. And he has the money."

"Maybe the bank can–"

"I want *you* to find that man," she said. "You found him once, you can find him again. I don't care what it costs. Just find that son of a bitch."

*He took the loot, then he split,*
*She found out and threw a fit.*
*He cleaned her out, now he's gone,*
*Might have planned this all along.*

# CHAPTER 11

By the time we arrived at the law office, Nora had regained her composure. She went straight to the ladies' room to clean herself up. Reba was hanging around out of curiosity which was a good thing since Wade would probably need her help to get documents ready for the court. She looked eager to hear the gory details about Nora's sudden emergency, but before I could say one word Wade dragged me to his office and shut the door.

"Look, Corie, we need to talk. I'm sorry–"

"Later. You need to focus on Nora's problem right now. Let me tell you–"

"Wait." He put up a hand. "I'll do that, but first I need to explain about last night." He placed his palms flat on the desk and leaned forward, pinning me with his intense blue eyes.

I felt the involuntary tug on my heart that always occurred when he looked at me this way, but I didn't want to acknowledge the power he had over me right now. We had business to tend to. I wanted to blurt out what Jack had done, but first I wanted to hear what Wade had to say, so I waited.

"You changed your hair," he said. "I like it."

"Thanks."

"About my new client." He cleared his throat. "It's Laura."

"I know."

His eyebrows shot up.

"Reba mentioned it." I shrugged. "She thought I already knew."

"You *should* have known. I mean, I was going to tell

you."

I crossed my arms. "I can see how her name slipped your mind while you were making excuses for not having dinner with me."

"Oh, hell." He picked up a pen, rolling it between his fingers. "It's just, oh I don't know. I'm sorry. Guess I didn't want you to get the wrong idea."

"*Not* telling me gave me the wrong idea." I hesitated, then said, "What's going on between you two?"

"Nothing. She wants me to handle her divorce, that's all."

"Have you forgotten that I *know* Laura?"

"What's that supposed to mean?" He dropped his pen on the desk.

"Your ex *always* has an agenda," I said, "and she came to you for more than legal representation."

He frowned. "Well, that's all she's getting."

He sounded too defensive. I didn't say anything, just nodded my head. He came around the desk, looking contrite, and put his hands on my cheeks, forcing me to look directly into his eyes. His cologne smelled sexy, and I fought the urge to melt into his arms.

"I don't want Laura," he said. "I want you."

He seemed sincere, yet I couldn't help but wonder if he was working to convince himself. Their kids were part of the equation, too. Laura would use them to her advantage.

"Okay. Good." I gave him a quick peck on the cheek and started to pull away, but Wade was faster. He caught me in his arms and kissed me deeply, a kiss that tingled down to my toes.

When he released my mouth, I had to catch my breath. Wow. I hated leaving this piece of business unfinished. But Reba was probably out there with her ear to the door. And Nora was waiting.

"That was," I hesitated, searching for the right word and not finding one, "*very* nice."

"You're telling me," he said.

I pulled back to look up at him. "I hate to ruin the mood, but now you'd better focus on Nora."

His shoulders sagged. "What's happened?"

"Jack took two million out of their account."

Wade dropped his hands and raised his eyes to the ceiling. "Dammit."

"And his office is closed." I told him about Phyllis Keene. "I wouldn't count on her showing up for any hearing."

He sat down, suddenly all business, and pulled his chair up to the desk. He grabbed a tablet. "Did Nora tell you which bank?"

"No."

"I'll appear in court first thing tomorrow," he said, scribbling some notes, "see if I can get an emergency hearing. Maybe subpoena the bank. If we can trace the money, the judge will grant an order to freeze the assets." He looked up. "You have any good news?"

I shook my head. "Sorry, fresh out. Just be glad you're not me. The hunt for Jack is back on."

"Says who?"

"Nora wants me to find him no matter what it takes."

"Let me talk to her. I'll explain this is in the court's hands, not hers."

"I'm sure she'll find that comforting."

"Seriously. Can't you hold off? I don't think she ought to see him right now. Not after what he's done."

"You think she'd do something to him?"

"More like he might hurt her if she starts throwing a fit."

"Good point. Okay, I'll hold off for a little while." I walked to the door. "Let me know how that discussion goes over and if you need me to serve the bank subpoena."

"Sure," Wade said. "See you later?"

I hesitated, my hand on the doorknob. I could purposely monopolize his every free moment or give him time to think about his options. My chest felt constricted. "I need to go by Mother's house tonight."

"Maybe you should take me with you," he said. "Isn't it time you told her about us?"

"Not tonight. Soon." Maybe.

I left Wade's office and ducked down the side hallway. I'd had my fill of Nora today, and I wasn't in the mood for chit-chat with Reba. I stopped at my office, grabbed my phone, and attached it to my belt before heading out. Belatedly, I remembered I didn't have wheels, so I called a taxi

and killed some time storing numbers in the new phone until
it arrived. Thirty minutes later, I finally reached my truck.
Between my promise to Dad and what I'd told Wade about my
plans for the evening, I felt obligated to stop at Mother's
before heading home.

Driving through the heart of River Oaks, I wondered
what kind of thief would have the audacity to target a
neighborhood like this where the homes were no doubt armed
with state-of-the-art alarm systems and where a security patrol
made continuous rounds. An overly confident one, I'd say.

I pulled into the circular drive at Mother's and parked
behind a Cadillac that belonged to her friend, Muriel
Townsend. Having Muriel here might keep Mother from
brushing me off when I began my safety consciousness pitch.
I didn't expect the front door to be locked, and sure enough it
wasn't. I barged in, ready to spout off the Top Ten Ways To
Avoid Becoming a Burglary Target.

"Mother?" I crossed the entry hall toward the brightly-
lit formal living room. "You need to keep your doors–"

I froze as conversations halted and a half-dozen people
poised around the room turned to stare at me. Damn, I'd
forgotten the dinner party. Most of the guests must have
parked behind the house. I closed my eyes for a second and
took a deep breath. With several women in the room, the place
smelled like the fragrance counter at Neiman's. Didn't they
ever hear the expression less is more? I opened my eyes,
looked around the room, and forced a smile.

Mother had redecorated earlier in the year, changing
the wall color from deep burgundy to a medium khaki much
more to my liking. The old heavy floral upholstered furniture
was gone, replaced with off-white pieces over a colorful
Persian rug. The place felt younger, an extension of Mother's
personal quest for everlasting youth. She wasn't in sight, but
Muriel approached me.

"Corinne, how nice to see you." She gave me a big
hug, then stepped back and couldn't help herself from glancing
down at my cotton shirt and chinos. "Your hair looks lovely."

I smiled and reached up reflexively. "Didn't expect
Mother to have company."

"She'll be thrilled to see you." Muriel took my arm and
led me across the room where she introduced me to the group

which included her husband and other friends whom I'd met from time to time over the years.

"You remember Kaitlyn," she said, indicating her daughter.

"Oh yes." How could I forget? The stuck-up young attorney forced a smile before turning her attention back to the very attractive blond man standing beside her.

"And this is Lucas Turner," Muriel said. "Lucas is an absolutely stunning tennis player."

Did she mean stunning in ability or stunning to look at in his tennis duds? I suspected both. Kaitlyn was nearly drooling over the man, but he was looking at me. He gave me a dazzling smile as he extended his hand. Lucas Turner had a penetrating gaze that made me feel like a butterfly pinned to a posterboard. Not entirely unpleasant, but somehow unnerving. I had to make a conscious effort to break eye contact. Jeez.

"What's new in the PI business?" said Muriel's husband. "Been on any stake-outs lately?"

I turned to him, grateful for the disruption. "Same old, same old. Not the exciting work you might imagine."

"You're too modest, dear." Muriel shook a finger at me. "Corinne's working on the 'Hairdresser Murder Case'."

"Who told you that?" I said, playing along. Wouldn't hurt to know what these people had heard on the subject.

"If there's any news at the spa, Muriel knows all about it," answered her husband. "But that story is going around the country club, too."

I shook my head, not believing this. "You're telling me the men at the country club are discussing Carmen Messina's death?"

He cleared his throat. "Well, more about Jack Litchfield getting the boot from Nora than anything else, which leads to talk of his various indiscretions, then on from there. You know."

"Right." I put a hand on one hip, trying to look casual. "What's up with Jack anyway? Have you seen him around?"

The men exchanged glances, shrugged, shook their heads.

"He hasn't been himself," Muriel's husband said. "Heard he had some financial trouble, but I haven't seen him around the club in weeks. Odd. Used to hang out there every day."

"Huh," I said. Not good news for me.

"Maybe somebody popped him, too," said one of the other men.

"Oh hush," Muriel said. "Don't joke about such things."

I felt sure Jack Litchfield was alive and kicking somewhere – with the two million. I wanted to ask more about him, but the conversation turned to the weekend's silent auction. I made a beeline for the kitchen, entertaining thoughts of slipping out the back door before Mother saw me. If only I hadn't made that promise to Dad.

I pushed through the swinging door, and Ruby looked up from putting her finishing touch on a row of dinner salads. "Well lookie here. Didn't expect to see you tonight."

"Didn't expect to be here, but Dad's worried about Mother. Asked me to keep an eye on her while he's gone."

Ruby grinned. "Lucky you."

"Smart aleck." I sniffed the air appreciatively. "Yum, something smells scrumptious."

"One of your favorites." She handed me a glass of wine. "You stayin' for dinner?"

Ruby's cooking was hard to pass up, and I might find out something useful about Jack if I stayed. I swirled the wine in the glass. "Guess so, as long as you have enough."

Her expression said that was a dumb question. "I have plenty, 'cept I don't know if your Mama will let you up to the table in that outfit."

"Hey, her guests have already seen me, and they don't give a hoot what I'm wearing." I slid onto a bar stool across the granite counter from her. "All they want to do is gossip about me working on the hairdresser murder case – which by the way isn't true."

Ruby pulled a tray of dinner rolls from the oven, and I inhaled the warm, yeasty scent.

"I heard 'em talkin' about that woman," she said.

"I don't know where they get their information." I took a sip of wine. "The Houston Police Department wouldn't appreciate me getting involved in a homicide."

"Why do your Mama's friends think you are?" She

lined two bread baskets with forest green napkins and began filling them with rolls.

"They're experts at jumping to conclusions. I happen to be working on a divorce case for the dead woman's boss, and they've translated that into me working on the murder investigation."

"Gossip makes their world go 'round," Ruby said.

"It's like whisper down the alley," I said. "You ever play that game?"

Ruby nodded. "Back in grade school."

"By tomorrow night, their version will say I'm holding important evidence about the victim that will lead police straight to the killer." I took another sip of wine, rolled it around my mouth before swallowing. "Um, this hits the spot."

The door swung open behind me and I looked up, expecting Mother. It was Lucas Turner.

"Oh, hi." This man was movie-star material with his crisply-cut blond hair and gray twinkling eyes. Not someone to hook up with dull, corporate attorney Kaitlyn Townsend.

"Anything I can help with?" He flashed one of those brilliant smiles.

I swear Ruby blushed. "Help yourself if y'all need more wine," she said, motioning to bottles on the counter.

"Got you covered." He left with two bottles.

Ruby stared after him, watching the door swing back and forth several times before she spoke. "I swear, that man sets my heart to racing."

I giggled at her unexpected comment and didn't stop. Tired and feeling strung out, I couldn't remember the last time I'd had a good laugh. Ruby joined in and we were giggling like a couple of eight-year-olds when the door opened again. This time it *was* Mother. I put a hand on my chest, trying to get control of myself. "Hi."

She stood in the doorway, looking flamboyant in a lavender dress with rows of ruffles bordering the skirt. She inspected me silently for a moment. Then she walked over and gave me a kiss on the cheek, making sure she didn't get too close, as though the casualness of my attire might rub off on hers.

"Your hair looks very nice. You actually went to a salon?"

"I did," I said. "Will wonders never cease?" I'd only drunk a few sips of wine, but it had me feeling silly.

"There's no need for sarcasm," she said. "I wish you had called me back to let me know you were coming. I've left several messages for you today."

I touched my new phone. "Sorry. I was phone-less most of the day and very busy. Forgot all about your dinner party until I walked in."

"Then why are you here?"

It wouldn't do to tell her Dad asked me to check up on her. Why *was* I here? "You wanted me to get involved in volunteer work, right?"

She looked skeptical. "Yes."

"I could make some free time the next couple of days. You need some help with the silent auction?"

In the background, Ruby coughed and I fought to keep a straight face.

"Of course." Mother beamed. "We'd love for you to help. That's one of the reasons for this dinner party, really a psuedo committee meeting is what this is. We're all working on the auction plans." She turned to Ruby. "Give us five minutes, then begin serving."

"Yes, ma'am." Ruby winked at me as Mother took my arm and guided me into the other room, chattering all the way.

*** 

What I had intended as a short visit turned into a couple of hours. During dinner I put in my two cents about safety precautions during the auction. The men assured me they had already addressed security issues and that I shouldn't worry, so maybe I'd needlessly involved myself in the whole mess.

I stayed through dessert, but it was clear the committee wasn't finished discussing every facet of the upcoming event in agonizing detail. I made my excuses and headed home. The wine had loosened me up, a nice change from the stress of the past couple of days. Kaitlyn had relaxed quite a bit by the end of the evening, too, and I wondered if she'd be spending the night with Mr. Movie Star. I thought about Wade and wished that I *had* brought him with me. Keeping our relationship a secret now seemed ridiculously immature, and I promised myself to rectify the situation as soon as possible. So what if

Mother tried to run our relationship, our social life, my business, and Wade's practice? We were grown-ups. We could handle her.

It was a little after ten when I pulled onto my street, and my relaxed mood vanished. The flashing lights of a West U police car brightened the trees in front of my place. My house lights were all turned on. I pulled to a stop at the curb and jumped out. Kit, the twelve-year-old from next door, stood in the driveway.

"Corie!" The girl's dark hair sailed behind her as she raced toward me.

I met her halfway. "Are you okay? What happened?"

She didn't need any coaxing to spill her story as she dragged me to the house and in through the back. I reached the kitchen doorway and stopped. I grabbed the door frame, my knuckles white.

The place was ransacked–drawers and doors standing open, food from my pantry dumped out on the floor.

"Oh, no. Where's Midnite?"

Obviously, the dog hadn't been in here or she'd have gobbled her way through the spilled Rice Chex if not the flour and dry macaroni.

"It's okay," Kit said. "She's at my house."

"Thank God."

I looked around the room, thinking I'd be freaking out right now if not for the calming effect of that wine. But beneath the calm my mind worked furiously.

My house was a wreck. Just like Carmen's.

*My world is upside down,*
*I feel like leaving town.*
*Sure wish someone would confess,*
*To causing this whole mess.*

# CHAPTER 12

A police officer burst into the kitchen, one hand gripping his holstered weapon. A fringe of dark hair surrounded his bald egg-shaped head and his name tag said S. Ramirez.

"Is this the lady you saw?" he asked Kit.

"No," Kit said with a boy-are-you-dumb roll of her eyes. "This is Corie."

I approached the officer, my hand extended. "Corie McKenna. I live here."

Ramirez gave me a once-over as he shook my hand. "You got some identification?"

I bit back a wisecrack. "My ID's out in the truck," I told him, then looked at Kit. "What lady is he talking about? You told me you saw a burglar."

"I did," Kit nodded. "It was a lady."

"With the stocking pulled over her head, how could you tell?"

This time the eye roll was directed at me. "You're not gonna like this," she warned.

I gestured for her to get on with the explanation.

"Midnite and I were over at my house," she said. "I was doing homework. But if Mom came home, well you know how she feels about dogs, so at nine I got up to bring Midnite back here."

"And your mother is *still* not home?" I said. One of these days Jean Thompson would hear exactly how I felt about her galivanting around the city like she didn't even have a daughter.

"Not yet," Kit said. "Anyway, I looked out the window

and saw a light over here, and I knew it wasn't you 'cause you always call me the second you get home if Midnite's not there."

"That's true," I said.

"So I left her at my house," Kit went on, "and I sneaked in through the back and stopped at the bathroom to listen." She pointed toward the powder room off the hallway between my kitchen and living room.

"Wait a second," I said, raising my voice. "You're telling me you came into this house while there was a stranger inside?"

"That's what she's tellin' you." Ramirez shook his head. "And she left the dog instead of bringing it along for protection."

"I didn't want her to start barking or something," Kit said.

Ramirez said, "Girl watches too many cop shows, you ask me."

I grasped Kit's shoulders. Her lack of fear during potentially dangerous situations worried me. "Don't ever do that. How many times have I told you–"

"I know, I know," Kit said. "But I wasn't sure it was a stranger. Could've been Mr. Alexander. So I waited to see. Then all of a sudden she came rushing past the bathroom and I smelled her."

"You *smelled* her?" I looked at Ramirez.

"Girl claims her teacher wears some strong cologne and this perp had the same scent," he said.

"Yeah." Kit nodded eagerly. "Ms. Carson sprays her yucky cologne every day after lunch, gives me a major headache. That's what I smelled. Then she was gone. I waited a while before I came out and called the police."

"You're sure this woman was alone?" I said.

"Positive."

"You see this kind of vandalism much in burglaries?" I asked Ramirez and pointed at the floor. "I mean, why empty boxes of food?"

"You talk burglary, they're in and out," Ramirez said. "One, two, three. Grab the TV, the DVD, the computer, electronic gizmos, some jewelry, then scram. That's not this."

"So what *is* this?" I walked over to peer into the living

room. Kit came and stood beside me. Magazines and pillows were strewn around, but my flat screen TV and DVD player hadn't been touched.

"More like a search," Ramirez said. "You keep lots of money here?"

"Almost none," I said.

"Prescription drugs?"

I shook my head.

"Illegal drugs?"

"God, no," I said, offended.

"Just doing my job," Ramirez said. "Got to ask all the pertinent questions."

Footsteps pounded down the hardwood stairs, and I let out a little yelp.

"It's cool," Kit said. "That's his partner."

A tall black officer came into view. "More of the same up there." He eyed me. "You the owner?"

I nodded and introduced myself.

"You can make a report on what's stolen, if anything," he said. "You still got your electronic equipment. Some jewelry might be missing."

"I don't have much jewelry," I said.

"Looks like the perp spent some time going through your desk," he said. "Any idea what she was looking for?"

"No clue." I turned back to the kitchen. "But maybe this has something to do with the case I'm working on."

"Case?" Ramirez said.

"She's a private eye," Kit said.

"Hoo boy." Ramirez grimaced.

"Why don't I make a pot of coffee," I said, "then we'll all sit down and I'll tell you what I know. After we get Kit safely home, that is."

"Aw, c'mon," Kit said. "I always miss the good parts."

***

As it turned out, Kit didn't miss much. I was convinced that the break-ins at my house and Carmen's were somehow connected to her murder. The cops didn't see it that way. Ramirez had managed to get in touch with Belton who reported they were focusing on Carmen's nephew as their key murder suspect.

After the officers left, I made sure all the doors were locked before getting out a dust pan and broom to clean the kitchen. Midnite nosed around, snarfing some of the cereal and pasta scattered on the floor as I swept around her. I got up the bulk of the food and dumped it into the trash as I blinked away tears. This incident had me angry and scared, and I wasn't sure which emotion held first place. I threw the broom down and went to the phone to call Wade.

No answer. Maybe he was in the shower. I sure didn't want to spend the night alone. Looking around the house, I decided I didn't want to spend the night here, period.

I stooped next to Midnite. "What d'ya say we surprise Wade? You wanna go?" She perked up immediately at the word "go." I threw a change of clothes into an overnight bag, and we left the house within minutes.

Life on the road, in my truck, felt safer but I kept checking the rearview to make sure no one was following us. Being the victim of a crime made me feel terribly vulnerable, isolated from the rest of the world. Thank God I had Wade to go to.

I cracked the window for Midnite to stick her nose out and adjusted the A-C. I punched radio buttons, skipping past commercials, searching for something upbeat. Alan Jackson's Chattahoochee fit the bill.

Maybe I could forget about this horrible night if I did what the song suggested – sit down by the river, or Bayou in my case, and make a pyramid of empty beer cans in the pale moonlight. Trouble was I didn't want to forget – I wanted answers.

My brain struggled to find logic in a seemingly illogical series of events. Two home break-ins, valuables left behind. Same M.O. Carmen's home vandalized the very night of her murder. My office intruder.

I didn't care what the police thought. These incidents were connected. And Trey Salinas as the perpetrator didn't sit right. The kid acted surly and uncooperative, but I didn't think he'd murdered his aunt. I couldn't imagine why he'd send some woman to break into my house.

"Then there's Jack," I said to Midnite. "You never met the guy, but he's very weird. And now, very rich."

But did Jack have a motive for murder? It was hard to imagine Nora's scenario of him killing to keep his financial secrets quiet. But what if Carmen knew Jack was about to take the two mill and threatened to blow the whistle?

"Now that sounds like a motive," I said, "but it still doesn't explain the break-ins."

I wondered again if Carmen kept a journal and if Jack would care if she had. But even so, why would Jack think I had it? Bottom line was, I needed to find out more about Carmen and Jack before I could guess at motives.

Midnite turned away from the window with an expression I interpreted as Mom-are-we-there-yet?

We were heading down Westpark toward the new Riverside Condominium complex where Wade leased a three-bedroom unit. The condo association wasn't thrilled about having large dogs on the premises, but Midnite was well behaved and so far management had ignored her periodic visits.

In spite of the fact that all the units looked alike, Midnite ran straight to Wade's place when I opened the truck door. She stood uncharacteristically still outside his door with her head cocked and tail wagging.

I grabbed my overnight bag and headed across the parking lot. She was too cute. I leaned over to pat her on the head, then stood to punch the doorbell. When I heard voices inside, I pulled my hand back.

Maybe the kids were here. If they were, I'd ditch my plan to spend the night. But If Wade saw the overnight bag he'd insist I stay, so I'd have to put the bag back in the truck before I knocked. I turned my head, placing my ear closer to the door.

I knew that voice, and it didn't belong to any child. My shoulders stiffened. I backed up and stood under the porch light where I could see my watch. It was after twelve.

Midnite began whimpering.

"Shh, baby." I patted her head and stepped off the porch into the flower bed. I squeezed past a prickly bush and moved to the window.

The vertical blinds were twisted to a three-quarters closed position. I moved left, then right, and peered through the slats. When I spotted them, my breath caught.

Laura and Wade stood at the living room's wet bar, shoulders brushing, each holding a wine glass. Wade's back was to the window, but I had a good view of Laura. She looked different than the last time I'd seen her – carefree, seductive. She was laughing, and with a toss of her head long blonde hair cascaded down her back. She wore a sundress that exposed plenty of cleavage, and her skin looked like she slept in a tanning bed.

I couldn't breathe. My heart was beating so fast I felt like I was going to die. I closed my eyes. A person could only take so much in one night.

"C'mon, baby, let's go."

Midnite looked confused.

"Come." I grabbed her collar. "I've got to get out of here."

Back in the truck, I twisted my key in the ignition, fighting tears. Now what? I sure couldn't face my house after this. I grabbed my phone and punched in Reba's number.

"You still up?" I said when she answered.

"Does a pig like to slop in the mud?" She laughed, amused with herself. When I didn't respond, she sobered. "What's the matter?"

"Midnite and I need a place to crash. Please. Can we come over?"

*You didn't know her very well,*
*Even though you thought you did.*
*There are stories I can tell,*
*Many things that she kept hid.*

# CHAPTER 13

Early the next morning Midnite and I went outside to walk with Gidget, Reba's yellow Lab mix. They lived on a two-acre tract in a suburb southwest of Houston, property awarded to Reba in her last divorce. The fenced back yard was perfect for dogs. Pin oaks and pecan trees shaded the property, and a small barn housed the instruments and other equipment for The Stetler Girls, her C&W band – the band she regularly hounds me to join. I'd rehearsed with them a few times just for fun and filled in once for their lead singer. Despite Reba's nagging, I didn't plan my involvement to go any further.

The dogs stayed well ahead of me, in squirrel hunting mode, sniffing the grass and stopping periodically to inspect tree branches for any sign of movement. Watching Midnite play with Gidget usually brings a smile to my face, but not today.

I couldn't erase the image of Wade with Laura from my mind. It was still hard to believe what I'd seen. He and I were so good together, so happy, so compatible. I thought we were best friends. Now this. Did he want to reconcile with Laura or was he screwing around behind my back for old time's sake? I scooped up a dead tree branch and kept walking, slapping the stick against my thigh.

What made me more angry than anything was that Wade didn't have the balls to talk to me about the situation. Was he planning to string both of us along? I lifted the branch and slammed it against a thick tree trunk. The wood split into three pieces, the shock of the blow reverberating up my arm.

Damn. Damn. Damn.

I had made several laps around the fence line,

attempting to work off some frustration, by the time Reba emerged from the house with steaming coffee mugs. She placed them on the patio table and sat in a cushioned chair. I left the dogs to their play and tromped across the lawn to join her. She was dressed for casual Friday in a slim denim skirt and matching vest over a red T-shirt.

"You look rough," she said. "You sleep at all?"

"Not much." I ran a hand through my tangled hair as I settled into the chair beside her. We'd stayed up until two, and I'd told her all about the break-in. Nothing about my short visit to Wade's condo.

"Why don't you go back to bed? Grab a couple more hours."

I picked up a mug and blew on the hot coffee. "Can't."

"Why not?"

"Too busy."

"You're a woman of few words this morning. Want to explain why *I* had the pleasure of your company last night?"

"If you'd seen my place, you wouldn't be asking." I sipped the coffee. "Nobody would want to spend the night there."

"Uh-huh." Reba gathered her hair into a ponytail, fastened it with an elastic band, then covered that with a decorative band of multi-colored beads. "Not that I mind. Gidget and I love havin' you two over. Been a while, huh?"

"Guess so."

"What'd Wade think about your place being searched?"

"Haven't told him yet."

"And why not?"

She was fishing for the real reason I'd come to her instead of Wade, but I didn't want to talk about it. "He worries too much," I said.

"That's our Wade. Matter of fact, after Nora left the office last night he mentioned she wants you to find that s-o-b husband of hers. He doesn't like it."

I stiffened. "I don't take on jobs based on whether or not Wade *likes* them. Nobody asked for his stamp of approval."

"Whoa, girl." Reba laughed, but it was forced. "He doesn't like to think about you bein' in danger, that's all."

"Like this was *my* choice. One day I'm serving papers,

no big deal, then I'm suddenly in the middle of God knows what."

I got up and paced the patio. Mooning over Wade wasn't going to help anything. I needed to focus on finding the link between Carmen's death and the break-ins.

"I really believe that if I hadn't gone to Carmen's house the day she died my house wouldn't have been broken into," I said.

"So what does that tell you?"

I laid out the various motives I'd come up with for Jack Litchfield wanting to get rid of Carmen. "If that man is somehow tied to her death and the break-ins, I'm going to nail him."

"How? Sit Jack under a bright light and torture him till he spills his guts?"

I stopped pacing and gave her a look. "Not right away. I'm going to focus on Carmen first. Find out who her friends were, what she did in her spare time, what made her tick. Getting to know the victim better could lead to the answers I'm looking for."

"Sounds like a plan," Reba said.

*** 

I took Midnite home, then headed for Carmen Messina's neighborhood. Driving across Beechnut during rush hour turned out to be a bad idea. The light at the Loop was flashing yellow and traffic inched along. I made use of the delay by calling Ruby to ask if she knew someone I could hire to put my house back in order. Facing that disaster was too much in addition to everything else on my mind. I should have known she'd offer to do the job herself, and I agreed on the condition that she not mention anything to Mother.

When I pulled up at Carmen's, I noticed George Doyle outside working in his flower bed. He was meticulously picking weeds from the monkey grass border, and I wondered if he was competing for Yard of the Month. The slam of my truck door caught his attention. George stood slowly as I approached and shook out the kinks in his legs. He removed his gardening gloves and dropped them on the grass next to a small spade. We said our hellos, and I asked him if Carmen's brother had arrived yet.

"Yeah, he's here." George slapped at the dirt on the

knees of his dark green work pants. I guessed the brother hadn't made a favorable impression.

"That his truck?" I pointed to a faded blue Chevy in Carmen's driveway.

"Yup."

"Is there some problem?"

"Yeah, there's a problem." George frowned. "I don't like the man. Now I understand why Carmen wouldn't talk about him, wouldn't even mention his name."

"You seemed to like him well enough when you talked to him on the phone," I said.

"Changed my mind. Ruben Salinas is a cold fish – not even upset about losing his sister." George glared at Carmen's house.

"There's been a new development," I said, hoping to take his attention off Salinas. "I'd like to ask you some questions if you have a minute."

George shook his head as if waking himself from a dream in which he was pummeling the brother. "Huh? New development, you say?"

"Yes. Could we sit down?" I nodded toward his front porch. "I love your swing."

"Used to be my wife's favorite spot," he said, leading the way.

We settled on the wide oak swing, and George mellowed a bit with the swaying motion. I told him what had happened at my house and that I was searching for connections.

"Do you know Jack Litchfield?" I asked for openers.

"Carmen worked for a Litchfield," George said, "but her boss was a woman."

"That's right. She worked for Nora Litchfield. I'm asking about Nora's husband, Jack."

"She complained plenty about work," he said. "Long hours, low pay. Carmen worked like a dog for that woman, brought in lots of customers."

"I'm sure she did. But I think Carmen liked Jack much more than Nora. I think they were friends."

"I don't know about that," George said.

"Maybe you've seen him around here. He's about five ten, one seventy, reddish hair, skinny legs."

George's face screwed up. "If you're saying Carmen messed around with a married man, you're wrong."

I may as well refer to her as Saint Carmen where George was concerned. He wasn't going to be much help.

"What about men in general? Did Carmen date?"

"Used to. Kept to herself mostly. Spent some time with me. Nothing romantic mind you."

Like I'd think they had something going. He wished.

We swang silently for a minute, then George said, "Something was eating at her."

"You don't know what it was?"

George nodded toward Carmen's house. "Him, probably."

I turned to see Trey and an older man coming down the sidewalk. "Which one are you talking about?"

"The kid," George said.

"I assume the man's her brother?"

"Sorry excuse for one."

"Be right back," I said. "I need to talk to him for a minute."

I left George and hurried across the lawn toward the father and son who were about to climb into the Chevy. "Mr. Salinas?"

Salinas looked at me, one hand on the open truck door, and waited. Trey got into the passenger side and slammed his door. His father was a small man, a head shorter than me, wearing worn Levis and a plaid short-sleeve shirt. A blue cap bearing the red-and-white Purina logo covered most of his gray hair. I introduced myself and we shook hands.

"Pleased to make your acquaintance, ma'am," he said quietly. "I understand you tried to save Carmen, and I appreciate that."

No sign of the callous man George had described.

"I was hoping we could talk," I said, "but if you're busy I can come back later."

"We won't be stayin' in the city long," Salinas said. "I need to get my boy back to New Braunfels where he belongs."

Trey snorted, but Salinas paid no attention. I wondered if the police had cautioned the kid to stay in the area.

"Carmen worked for a client of mine," I said. "I need to find out more about her relationship with a man named Jack

Litchfield. Do you happen to know him?"

Ruben Salinas removed his cap and ran a hand through his thinning hair. "I wouldn't know my sister's friends, Miss McKenna. It is over twenty years since I saw Carmen. She wouldn't have anything to do with us."

"Don't blame it all on her," George barked.

I jumped, surprised that the older man had come up behind me.

"George, please." I motioned with a hand for him to back off.

Salinas looked at George with sad eyes. "That's how she was. Carmen didn't like our small town. She always said the only excitement around was the Guadalupe River when it flooded and since she hated water, she wasn't stayin'. Didn't seem to matter she was leavin' family behind, too. She took off and never looked back."

"You really haven't seen her in more than twenty years?" I said.

"Twenty-two come October," Salinas said.

"And she hated water?" I said. "Kind of odd that she'd buy a house with a pool if she hated water."

"That's what I thought," Salinas said.

"Duh," Trey said. "She didn't own the place."

We turned to him. Trey stared back, wearing a smug expression. Today there were two hoops dangling from his pierced eyebrow.

"How do you know that?" I said.

"You think I'm brain dead?" Trey said. "She was always moaning about paying the rent. Like she was flat broke. Wouldn't give up a dollar if my life depended on it–"

"Trey, that's enough," Salinas said. "You were taught to respect your elders."

"Why should I respect–"

"That's enough!"

I jerked at the harsh reprimand, but kept my eyes on Trey. He made a face behind his father's back.

"Do you know who your aunt paid the rent to?" I asked him.

George said, "House was bought by some corporation after the original owner passed on."

"Some redheaded dude came over to collect one night,"

Trey said.

Sounded like an apt description of Jack, though neither Nora nor Wade had mentioned the Litchfields renting to Carmen.

I watched the kid for a second. If looks could kill, his stare would have struck all three of us dead by now. He wasn't my problem, yet I didn't want to see him blamed for something he didn't do.

I backed up and lowered my voice. "Mr. Salinas, could I have a word with you in private? Just one minute, then you can go."

He closed the truck door.

"I assume you know the police consider your son a suspect."

He nodded and said, "They're wrong."

"I agree with you." I noticed the flicker of surprise in his eyes. "I'm trying to help, but Trey isn't helping himself."

"My son is a troubled young man," he said, "but it's not what they think."

"I'm not sure why the police suspect him," I said, silencing George with a look. "Trey told me he was working at the time your sister died."

"He was. Made a run out north to the airport to pick up a delivery for his employer. Tells me he does that kind of thing often."

"Maybe they have his signature. Something to prove he was that far away at the time of her death."

Salinas was shaking his head. ""He got to the airport and there was no package. Some kind of mistake with the airlines."

George said, "Ever consider the kid might be lying?"

Salinas' glare could have sliced diamonds. "Are you saying my boy is a murderer?"

"Maybe I am," George said.

Salinas made a move toward George, but I jumped between them, my hands out, trying to keep peace.

"I'm sure the police will check with Trey's employer and clear up his alibi," I said. "Jack Litchfield is a more likely suspect in my opinion."

Salinas tore his gaze away from George. "Who is this Litchfield?"

"A friend of Carmen's. Actually, her boss's husband."

"She was having an affair with this *friend*?" Salinas said.

"Carmen wasn't like that," George said. "You didn't know her."

I put a hand on George's shoulder to quiet him down. "Actually, I've heard from more than one source that they *did* have a relationship at one time." I turned back to the brother. "I didn't mean to offend you by bringing up her relationship with a married man."

"Offend me?" Salinas smirked. "If what you say is true, not much changed about my sister in the past twenty-two years."

A new image of Carmen formed in my mind – twenty something, bored with small-town life, sleeping with married men.

"We think they broke off their affair some time ago," I went on, "but from Trey's description he might be the owner of this house."

"I assume he has money," Salinas said.

"Plenty," I said.

"I'm sorry to remember my sister this way." Salinas gave George a pointed look. "But Carmen would lay with any man, make that *every* man who came along and had something to offer her. She was a self-centered little fortune hunter who *never* cared about family. That's what started all this trouble."

Before I knew what was happening, George had sprung past me and grabbed Salinas by the shirt, shaking the smaller man like a rag doll.

"You son of a–"

Salinas caught George with a quick left hook, and the old man crumpled at my feet.

*Maybe I should just move in,*
*Seems like I'm always here.*
*But with you I never win,*
*Our end's in sight, I fear.*

# CHAPTER 14

"Doyle didn't know Carmen." Salinas straightened his shirt. "Only thought he did."

He glanced down at George, shook his head, and opened his truck door. Trey had slid over on the bench seat to peer out the window at George, his eyes wide with obvious surprise that his father had decked the other man. When he noticed his father's expression, he jumped back to the passenger side without saying a word.

Salinas climbed in the truck and calmly started the engine, then backed out and drove away.

George was moaning and holding his jaw. I tried to give him a helping hand, but he wasn't interested. He stood, brushed himself off, and stomped toward his house as if nothing had happened, probably more embarassed than anything.

The man looked like he wanted some space, and who was I to stand in the way? I had enough on my plate without worrying about grown men who acted more like children.

Couldn't say that the trip over here was a waste. I <u>had</u> learned more about Carmen's personality. I just didn't know if the new information would be of any help.

I went back to my truck and turned on my cell phone to call the office and check messages. There were four from Nora Litchfield, her tone raised to a more urgent pitch in each one.

"Have you found Jack yet?"

"I hope you're putting other work aside to find Jack."

"Why aren't you making progress? It's a simple thing I've asked you to do."

"I need you to call me immediately. I'll pay a higher rate if that's what it takes. And I still have those documents you need to pick up."

Happy Friday.

I disconnected, sighed, and headed for Serenity Spa.

\*\*\*

Hanging out at the Spa was getting to be a daily occurrence, one I could do without. The place was supposed to be relaxing–except I wasn't getting the seaweed wrap, the aromatherapy or the foot massage. I was getting Nora.

At least I knew my way around now, and I hoped to slip in and reach Nora's office without any interference. I was halfway through the lobby when I noticed Haley Winter standing near the fountain. She wore lime green today and with her frigid expression she reminded me of a frozen margarita. She was talking with a man who looked familiar for some reason I couldn't put my finger on.

I detoured around the shelves of beauty products to check out Haley and the man from a different angle. He was medium height with a brawny build. His brown hair had a freshly-cut-and-styled look about it. He held a white cap in one hand, twirling it around his pointer finger as he talked. I picked up a bottle of moisturizer and tipped my head, pretending to read the label as I squinted across the room to see what was written on the cap.

Ben Hogan. A golf cap.

I put the bottle down. He was the guy from the cell phone store yesterday. Small world. I'd bet his grin and those dimples worked miracles with most women, but Haley didn't look impressed. Guy should count his blessings, you ask me. I took advantage of the diversion to dart through the double doors into the salon. I figured the chemical odors were starting to grow on me since I didn't gag this time.

Nora wasn't in her office, and I stood in the doorway for a moment trying to decide what to do next when I heard a cheery voice behind me.

"Back so soon?"

Zachary approached, holding a cardboard box filled with perm rods and an assortment of hair potions. He stared at my hair the way he had the day before.

I had a classic case of bed head–half flat, half frizz. I

attempted to fluff up the flat side. "Sorry, I've neglected your masterpiece. But I don't have time to mess with hair when Nora calls."

"She can be a time zapper." Zachary smiled. "At least we got rid of those dead ends. With your looks, who pays attention to the hair anyway?"

"Thanks." I smiled at the compliment and looked down at his box. "You're not leaving, are you?"

"Leaving Serenity? Goodness, no. Nora offered me Carmen's station. Much better location. All I have to do is get my gear moved."

"Need a hand?"

He shrugged. "No thanks. I'm using time between appointments, which at the moment is just about up. You say you need Nora? She's in the supply room. Last door on your left."

He disappeared around the corner, and I reluctantly headed down the hall. Helping him move would have been lots more fun.

The windowless supply room was lined with glass storage units like those used to lock up expensive cologne and condoms at the local Kroger's. I'd like to think the spa clientele were above petty theft, but having seen some of the price tags on the products sold out front I couldn't blame Nora for keeping the stuff locked up tight.

She stood in the middle of the room, knee deep in boxes from a recent delivery, with her back to me. She picked up one box and set it on top of a stack, then expertly slit the packing tape with a razor knife. She pulled one bottle from the box and turned it over to read the back before placing it on a shelf. She referred to a packing list and looked inside the open box, her head bobbing as she counted.

In a melon-colored silk pants outfit, Nora wasn't exactly dressed for this job. Was she such a control freak that she couldn't even trust her employees to unpack boxes? This was the sort of thing Trey could do for minimum wage.

I walked in behind her and peeked over her shoulder into the box. "What you got there?"

Nora jumped, slapping the box flaps closed as she turned to glare at me over the top of her reading glasses. "You are supposed to be focusing on my case, not on my business.

If this is how you treat all your clients, I'm surprised you have any. To completely ignore my calls–"

"I didn't come over here to be insulted," I said, in no mood for her condescending attitude.

She stared at me, open-mouthed. Before she could respond, I went on. "If we're going to continue working together, we need to set some ground rules. You can't assume that because you don't see me I'm twiddling my thumbs."

"I expect you to keep me informed."

"Do you have new information to give me?" I asked.

"No, but–"

"Well, I don't have new information for you either. Must be because we just saw each other late yesterday afternoon." I made a point of checking my watch. "And it's only nine-thirty in the morning." I closed my mouth, suddenly regretting my outburst. Nora didn't have a calm temperament, and she *did* have a knife in her hand.

She stood with the rigid posture of a soldier at role call, her lips pursed.

"I know you're upset about the money," I said, softening my tone. "Anyone would be. If you want me to continue working on your case, I will. If you don't, tell me now. But I can promise you won't find anyone more devoted to finding out what the hell is going on." My eyes strayed to the knife.

As if she knew what I'd been thinking, she retracted the blade. "What makes you say that?"

"Because I'm positive your case and Carmen's murder are connected somehow."

Nora's pencilled eyebrows lifted in disbelief but she waited for me to go on.

"Whoever ransacked her house the night she died has also ransacked my house. Jack might have the answers I'm looking for, and I want to find him as badly as you do."

Nora hesitated, and in the change of her expression I imagined her mind as a train rushing full speed down a track, then having to slam on the brakes and back up. "That's ludicrous," she finally said. "First of all, I should have never insinuated Jack's involvement, though I certainly wouldn't mind seeing him behind bars. And there's no telling how many burglaries take place every single night in a city this size."

"These were no ordinary burglaries," I said. "Someone's searching for something."

"And you think it's Jack?" Nora tapped the closed knife against her leg.

"At this point, I'm just trying to fit pieces together."

Nora shook her head. "I don't buy it."

"Do you know if Carmen had any enemies?"

"Enemies? Of course not. People loved Carmen."

"How about Trey? What kind of employee is he?"

"He's a fine employee," Nora said. "Very helpful. Polite."

"Is it true that he went to Intercontinental Airport the day Carmen died to pick up a delivery?"

Nora repeated the same story I'd heard from Ruben Salinas, then said, "These questions are totally irrelevant to my case. This is not what I'm paying you for."

"If you don't mind, I'll decide what's relevant to the investigation and what's not. That is, if you want me to continue working for you."

Nora slapped the knife down on top of a closed box. "Yes I want you on the case. But I'm not paying you to investigate what happened to Carmen."

"I have to follow where the trail leads, Nora. Do you know who owns the house Carmen and Trey live in?"

"No. Why would I?"

"Because I think Jack owns the house. Carmen was paying him rent."

"What?" Nora's knees went slack, and she lowered herself to sit on top of a box. "He bought real estate without telling me? That bastard."

"I need to research the property ownership," I said. "Carmen's neighbor says a corporation bought the place. Assuming it was Jack's company, you'll need the details during your divorce settlement."

"Assuming we reach that point," Nora said. "Assuming that you ever do your job and find my husband."

\*\*\*

I left the spa, relieved that I'd unleashed my frustration in front of Nora. Maybe she'd be easier to deal with from now on. I could only hope. I loaded the box of financial documents she'd given me into the back seat and headed for the nearest

Denny's. Nothing jump-starts a day like the fat-filled, sugar-induced high of their Grand Slam breakfast, complete with pancakes, gobs of maple syrup, and a giant orange juice.

I ate with the passion of a carb addict who'd spent a month on the Atkins diet, giving myself permission to quit thinking about the case for a few minutes. The waitress was a pleasant middle-aged Hispanic woman who didn't even blink when I asked for a regular Coke after finishing off the O.J. If I expected to get anywhere on this case, the caffeine jolt might help.

The restaurant was noisy and fragrant with the scent of bacon and strong coffee. I looked out the window as I worked on the last of the pancakes. A slight breeze ruffled the shrubbery outside the window. I stabbed another bite of gooey pancake and let my gaze drift across the parking lot.

A young couple with a toddler strolled over to a Suburban, and I watched as they went through the ordeal of strapping the squirmy child into a car seat. Next to them, a man sat in a navy blue Jeep Cherokee that he'd backed into the parking space. Almost as soon as my gaze reached him, a newspaper snapped up in front of his face. I watched for a few more seconds, but only a white cap was visible over the top of the paper.

The weird sensation that overcame me took away my appetite. Or maybe my stomach had finally caught up with the huge quantity of food I'd already ingested. I turned back to my plate, pretending to be interested in the food. This could simply be a guy reading the paper, but I didn't think so.

I kept my head down, absently swishing pancake chunks around in the syrup pooled on my plate. After a minute, I adjusted my position so that I could glance outside without being obvious. The newspaper was still up. The Jeep's front license plate bracket was empty.

The waitress had already left my check. I dropped a couple bills for a tip, then headed for the checkout. I nearly threw my money at the cashier and burst out the door into the sunny parking lot. The Jeep was gone. Squinting, I looked left and right.

Traffic on the street running alongside Denny's was congested by a construction crew that had blocked off one lane. The guy couldn't have gotten very far. I hurried to my truck and stood on the running board for a better view, my gaze moving down the line of traffic, then to the outdoor parking lot of the office building across the street. The lot was about three-quarters full, and the aluminum shades people propped in windshields to protect their car interiors from the sun glared back at me as I scanned up and down the rows.

There.

I spotted the Jeep parked at the end of a row. Its blue roof stuck out above the other vehicles the same way I had towered over my classmates back in the third grade.

Gotcha.

*He's followed me all over town,*
*This time I'm gonna run him down.*
*Get ready now, hold on tight,*
*I'll nab him if it takes all night.*

# CHAPTER 15

I clenched the steering wheel to keep my hands steady as I pulled out onto the congested street. Even without seeing the guy closer, I knew his cap had the words Ben Hogan scrawled above the brim. So he had already been on my trail yesterday morning. Maybe longer. But why?

I wanted to drive straight up to the Jeep and ask the jerk who was he and why he was sticking his nose into my business, but he probably wouldn't sit still for that. If the guy wanted a confrontation, he wouldn't have left the Denny's lot when he saw me get up from my table. Besides, I had another plan.

Counting on him continuing to follow me, I headed in the general direction of my office. Once I got through the construction, traffic spread out and I spotted the Jeep in my rearview mirror about five cars back. At the next light, I punched Reba's direct line into my cell phone and put the phone on speaker so I could keep both hands on the wheel.

"I need a big favor," I said when she answered.

I explained briefly what was going on. Reba jumped at the chance to help, and we hung up.

About three blocks from the office, I parked in one of few spaces in front of a ladies' hosiery outlet on Bissonnet. The Jeep cruised by and pulled into a lot on the opposite side of the street. I climbed out and headed into the store, swinging my purse and whistling, pretending I didn't have a care in the world.

Inside, I said hello to the middle-aged clerk who was hanging packaged socks on a row of pegs. She halfheartedly offered me assistance and seemed glad when I declined. Two older women were looking at pantyhose, deep in a discussion about which brand led the market in control tops. I glanced out the front window. The guy was still in the Jeep. Probably wouldn't follow me in here. I stole another look at the clerk, then went straight to the rear of the store and out the back door.

In the alley behind the strip center, Reba was already waiting in her Suburban. She grinned at me as I climbed into the passenger seat.

"Girl, what did you do this time?" She handed me a scarf and a pair of sunglasses.

"Wish I knew." I used the scarf to cover my hair, knotting it at the nape of my neck, and put on the glasses. I told Reba about seeing the same man yesterday at the phone store and again this morning.

She drove out of the alley and made a loop around the block, coming back onto Bissonnet from the other end.

"Hey, what are you doing? I said I'd drop you back at the office." I planned to use Reba's Suburban to turn the tables on this guy.

"No way. I want a piece of the action." She whipped into the lot of a gift shop where we had a good view of the Jeep and shifted into park.

"What about your job?" I glanced at my watch. "It's not even your lunch hour. And I have no idea how long this might take."

"Ask me if I care."

Reba was a free spirit in many respects, but she was always conscientious when it came to her job. "What's going on?" I said.

"I've lost a little respect for the boss," she said. "Let's leave it at that."

"Laura?"

"Bingo." Reba sat up straighter. "Hey, your guy's moving."

We watched the man get out of the Jeep and head across the street toward the hosiery shop.

"Impatient, isn't he?" I said. "Couldn't even sit fifteen minutes."

"Ooh-la-la," Reba said. "Nice jeans. I could put up with a little impatience for that–"

"The guy is stalking me, for God's sake, and you're

acting like you want to take him home."

We watched as the man stepped up to the store entrance, looking somewhat reluctant before he finally pulled open the door and went inside.

"He's pretty hot, you ask me," Reba said.

"I didn't ask." I dangled my pickup keys in front of her face. "Here, take these. I'm driving the Suburban. You can take my pickup after we're out of sight."

"Nope."

"C'mon Reba. What's up with you?"

Ignoring me, she flipped up the console lid and pulled out a pair of binoculars. "You get his plate number yet?"

"No." From where we sat, we had a side view of the Jeep. She handed me the binoculars.

"Keep these handy, 'cause we're gonna be behind this bad boy soon."

"You're serious."

"Can't think of a better way to spend an afternoon."

I blew out a breath. "You are such a hardhead. At least let me drive. You don't have any experience at surveillance."

"Excuse me?" Reba raised her eyebrows. "I have more experience following men than you'll ever know."

I couldn't help laughing at that. I didn't want her getting involved in whatever was going on here, but the man was already back and jogging toward his Jeep. I sighed. At least if Reba drove I could make some phone calls. And I did feel less edgy with her for company.

"We're on the move." Reba waited until the Jeep made a left on Kirby before following. I thought the man was headed for my office, expecting to find me there since it was so close, but he continued south on Kirby and drove right on through West University Place.

When I was able to get the Jeep's license number, I put in a call to Erin, the law firm receptionist, and asked her to log onto a public data service Wade subscribed to. Within seconds, she was reading me information about the mystery man which I jotted into my notebook. I thanked her and hung up.

"Jeep's registered to a Mark Allen Gentry, lives in the First Colony area, Sugar Land."

"My neck of the woods," Reba said. "He live alone?"

"Cut that out," I said. "Assuming this is our guy, there's

nobody else listed at that address, but you don't want to be involved with someone like this jerk."

"You think our guy is Gentry?"

"Brunette, brown eyes," I continued. "Six-one, one ninety-five."

"Sounds like him."

"Yeah, it does." I punched in the number for the Spa and asked for Haley Winter, hoping she'd be in a decent mood for answering questions.

She wasn't what I'd call friendly, but Haley didn't seem to have a problem talking to me. Maybe she only got testy when I was in her face, trying to interrupt the boss's work day.

"Yes, there was a man here earlier this morning fitting that description," Haley said, after I'd given her a rundown of Gentry's clothes and physical appearance.

"What did he want?"

"I think he came in for a haircut," Haley said. "Then on the way out he asked for Jack."

"Did he say why he thought he could find Jack at the spa?" I said.

"No. He said something casual like hey, is Jack in today?"

"Oh," I said, disappointed.

"I think he said they were working on some business deal together."

"What kind of deal?"

"He didn't specify."

"If they were working together, he'd have Jack's office address," I said.

Haley's voice turned a notch cooler. "I know that, and I said as much. But he wanted to know when I'd last seen Jack, asked if Nora had information on where he might find Jack today. Obviously, he doesn't know the situation."

"Obviously," I said. "Did he leave a card?"

"No."

"Had he ever been to the Spa before?"

"Not since I've been here. I'd have remembered."

Her tone went all mushy with that last statement. For Haley Winter that said a lot. I didn't get the big attraction to this guy.

I hung up and turned to Reba.

"Gentry's looking for Jack Litchfield," I said.

"Join the club," Reba said. "Hey, I think he's turning off. Is that his blinker?"

I leaned to the right, looking around the vehicles that separated us. "I think so."

We had covered five or six miles and were now on the south end of Kirby. The Jeep turned in at the entrance to a small office complex. A pile of broken bricks and debris alongside the building said this was new construction. The pristine sign out front announced Master Tile, Madge Meadows – Bridal Consultant, and held four vacant slots.

"Go on to the Quik Stop." I indicated the convenience store on the other side of the new building. "Looks like you need some gas anyway, right?" I pulled out my credit card and dropped it in her lap. "Use this, and wait right here. Understand?"

"I don't think you should go in there," Reba said. "Why don't we call somebody?"

"And tell them what?" I clipped my cell phone to my belt and jumped out. "You don't think Mr. Hot Stuff would be dangerous, now do you?"

"Well?" Reba chewed on her lower lip. "Probably not."

"I'll just look around a bit. He'll never know I was here, and I'll be back in a flash."

"You'd better be."

I gave her a thumbs up and crossed the parking lot. I came up beside the building and looked around the corner. I felt silly. No one was in sight. I hesitated, decided this was no big deal, and went in through the center door.

An atrium garden sat in the middle of the lobby, surrounded by a fountain that paled in comparison to the one at Serenity Spa. This one had a delicate shooting spray and the slight trickling sound that's meant to make people feel serene but only makes me feel like I need to go to the bathroom. Several corridors branched out, spider-like, from the lobby.

I held onto the door, letting it close slowly so there'd be no noise. I took off my sunglasses and hooked them on the neck of my shirt. My tennis shoes were silent on the gray marble floor as I approached the first hallway to my right.

No sign of activity down the long freshly-painted white corridor.

I went back to the lobby, headed for the next hallway, and froze when I heard voices.

"About time you showed up," a man said, sounding none too friendly.

"Got here as fast as I could," said another male voice. Was it Gentry?

"Not fast enough," said the first guy.

A door slammed. My heart thudded so hard I was sure somebody would hear me.

Everything went dead quiet. I waited for a full minute, knowing I should turn around and get out of here. I had a bad feeling about this place, but no way was I quitting now.

Curiosity carried me to the mouth of the next corridor. I held my breath and peeked around the corner.

Potted plants and artwork adorned this leg of the building. No Gentry in sight, but two other men dressed in black pants and white shirts flanked a door near the end of the hallway. Ramrod straight, they stared ahead at the blank wall across from them.

But it wasn't their body language that captured my attention. My eyes were riveted on the ominous, jet black Uzis in their hands.

*They're comin' after me,*
*Look now, can't you see?*
*Swear I don't know why,*
*But I'm gonna run and hide.*

# CHAPTER 16

My feet felt like someone had super-glued my tennis shoes to the floor. I had seen weapons like that in movies, never in real life. What kind of mess had I fallen into this time? I wanted to know what was in that office and why the goons with guns were guarding it, but I wasn't stupid.

I pried one foot up and took a step backwards.

Just get out. Quickly. Quietly.

Two more steps.

I pivoted, and my shoe screeched on the marble floor. I froze, waiting, but nothing happened. They hadn't heard me.

The new cell phone bleeped.

I fumbled, trying to disengage the phone from the waistband clip. I popped it off, and flipped the top up. I didn't know how to turn the thing to vibrate only.

"What are you doing now?" Reba's urgent whisper transmitted over the phone.

Damn that walkie-talkie feature. The men couldn't have missed that.

I did remember which button to punch to talk back. "Stay outside. Quit talking." I flipped the phone shut and race-walked back the way I'd come.

Another bleep. "Something's wrong," Reba said. "What happened?"

I couldn't believe her. I clasped the phone in my hand, like that would shut her up.

"Girl, are you there?" Louder.

Footsteps clapped in my direction. Not running, but walking plenty fast. I judged the distance between me and the front door. I wasn't doing anything wrong, but running away felt smarter and safer.

"Hello?" came over my phone. "Can you hear me?"

I darted across the lobby, past the fountain. I could hear the footsteps clearly over the trickling water when Reba said, "Answer me."

I threw the damn phone into the water. Too late to head for the front door. They'd see me for sure. And do what? Shoot me? I wasn't sticking around to find out. I ran to the first corridor, skidded around the corner, and raced headlong down the pristine hallway. I came to a white door with a small oblong window about eye level, and without taking time to look inside twisted the knob and burst through. An automatic ding-dong sounded. I closed the door quickly and caught my breath as I looked around.

The room I'd entered was spacious and empty save for a stack of large pink plastic storage containers and an eight-by-ten floral carpet of the Home Depot variety. A second door led into an interior office. Strains of "The Wedding Song" emanated from speakers mounted in corners near the ceiling.

What was that sickeningly sweet smell?

I was trying to decide what to do when a thin, busty woman tottered into the room on high-heeled, pointy-toed shoes. Bleached blonde hair and a pastel plaid pantsuit contrasted with the woman's leathery tanning bed complexion and her dark-framed glasses. Her smile was straight out of a teeth whitening commercial. She held an armful of Modern Bride magazines.

"Tiffany," she said, doing a head-to-toe assessment of me in one glance. "You're early, aren't you? But that's okay. Come right in. I know you're excited. And we have so much to decide, don't we?" She placed the magazines on top of a storage container and beckoned with one finger for me to follow her.

I started to protest, but wasn't sure what I'd say. That I'd unfortunately attracted the attention of her gun-toting co-tenants?

"You must be the bridal consultant," I pulled the scarf off my head and shook out my hair. "Miss Meadows?"

"Call me Madge, hon. We're going to be the closest of friends over the next six months. This is the most glorious time of your life, isn't it?"

"You might say that." God, I hated people calling me "hon." That high-pitched, breathy voice of hers could wear on my nerves, too, but I didn't want to leave her office right now. I could play along for a little while, until those men went back to minding their own business.

To Madge's credit her smile never dimmed, despite her expression telling me I'd need a ton of work to fit into the blushing bride mold. She led me into her office, where I identified the overpowering odor. A crystal vase holding a huge arrangement of pink-and-white day lilies occupied the desk corner. Poster-size bridal portraits lined the walls, separated by two solid panel doors. Cushiony side chairs were covered in deep pink crushed velvet. Draperies of heavy maroon brocade, with elaborate swags fringed in gold, decorated the windows. Gross.

"Excuse my disorganization." Madge plucked a pink glossy pocket folder from a stack on a side table and handed it to me. "As you can see, I'm not quite through moving in. Give me a week or so and my showroom will be all set up next door, but we didn't want to put you off any longer, did we?"

I looked down at the folder with the phrase "Your Special Day" centered on the cover, Madge's loopy script logo below. I noticed her bare left hand and wondered if she'd ever had a special day of her own. She motioned for me to have a seat, then walked around to her side of the desk.

"In there you'll find everything your heart desires for a perfect wedding," she said, "from the dress to the cake, flowers, musical selections. You *have* started shopping for the dress, haven't you?" She peered at me over the top of her glasses.

This was about to get complicated. "There's been a misunderstanding," I said.

"Don't tell me somebody's already getting cold feet." Madge put a hand to her cheek. "Everything will be fine, hon. All brides get the jitters, but never fear. I have the perfect cure." She smiled, apparently waiting for me to ask about the cure.

Instead, I said, "How long have you been working as a consultant?"

"Sixteen years, come September. You'll find references in the back of your packet. But your friend Cathy recommended me, didn't she?"

"Just curious," I said, skirting the question. "This seems like a very interesting job. And this is a nice building, too. Looks brand new." Maybe she knew something about the other tenants.

"It is," Madge said.

"I have a friend who's looking for space to lease," I said. "Do you know if this building has anything available?"

"Well, my showroom is going to be over here," she said, pointing to one of the panel doors, "but the space on the other side is up for grabs."

"Do you like this location?"

"Oh, yes," she said. "Now, I like to begin by reviewing my twenty-four step program. All the necessary ingredients for your perfect day." She pulled out a pink sheet of paper. "But first we need to discuss my retainer, don't we?" She turned the paper around so that I could read it and pushed her ballpoint pen across the desk. "If you'll sign this contract and make your check out as indicated, we can begin."

"Are the other tenants nice?" I said.

A frown creased her forehead. "Excuse me?"

"The other people in the building. My friend is very particular, and very social, too."

Madge sat back. "What's this all about?"

"Sorry," I said. "I just know my friend. She'll be asking me if the people here are friendly, what types of businesses they're in, things like that. I know she'll love that you're here. Actually, she'll probably hire you. She's recently engaged and it seems like *all* of her friends are getting engaged, too."

Madge's smile reappeared. "This is an excellent location, and I'd be happy to meet with her.

"And you like the other people in the building?"

"Oh yes," Madge said. "The people at Master Tile are very friendly, and Nick's men are very well-behaved."

"Nick?"

"My boyfriend. He owns the construction company. They build those Store-'N-Stuff places. He owns them, too." She beamed like a proud mother.

"How impressive," I said.

"His workers are real gentlemen," she said, "not the typical construction crew types. So far I'm the only female proprietor in the building, but I like being close to Nick. Plus, there's that huge Bridal Mart down the street."

I started to ask more about Nick, but a sharp rap at the office door interrupted me, followed by the bell indicating the door had opened. Madge looked past me.

"Johnny," she said, removing her glasses. "I'm with a client. Excuse me a minute, hon. Johnny works for Nick." She tottered toward the door. I turned slightly and saw the visitor's white shirt and black pants. No sign of a weapon, but my heart rate sped up anyway. I opened my pink folder, pretending to study a list of musical selections inside.

The two of them stepped into the other room. I wanted out of here.

I jumped up, dropping my folder, and tiptoed to one of the doors. Opened it. A storage closet lined with shelves holding wedding-related pamphlets. No exit. I checked the next door. Locked.

I went to a window and lifted the godawful heavy drapes. A fixed sheet of glass, no latches. I lifted the second set of drapes. No different. I turned, the rubber of my tennis shoe catching on the drapery fabric. I yanked my foot away.

I was over-reacting, spooked. There was no good reason why I shouldn't simply walk away, but I didn't want to take any chances.

I ran back to the desk and pulled open the top drawer. Yes! I grabbed a ring of about ten keys and went to the locked door. Holding the other keys to keep them quiet, I jabbed one at the lock. No good. I tried another.

The outer door ding-donged again.

I heard muffled voices, then Madge's raised tone. "Tiffany? Well, if you're Tiffany, then who is–"

The third key fit. I twisted the knob, removed the keys and took them with me, disappearing through the door and locking it behind me. I turned around to a room packed with stacks of boxes and a row of nude mannequins. The room was unfinished–studded walls, no ceiling.

 . I dropped the keys on top of a box and sucked in my stomach to squeeze through a tight space between boxes and a blonde mannequin. We were about the same height and bumped shoulders on my way through. She swayed, setting off a chain reaction of mannequins toppling into each other like dominoes.

Damn. I pushed through, jumping over falling limbs and boxes on my way to the front of the unfinished space. The door on the hallway side had a keyless deadbolt latch. I flipped it open and hit the hallway running, never looking back.

Reba was still at the Quik Stop, pacing next to her Suburban. "Why didn't you answer me? I was worried sick."

"Get in," I yelled.

"What's the matter?"

"Just get in." I practically leapt into the passenger seat, and she ran around to her side and jumped in.

"Well, what did you find out?" she said.

"Nothing much." I watched the office building, feeling better behind the truck's dark tinted windows. No one was chasing me.

"I still have no idea what Mark Gentry is up to. Maybe we can park across the street and wait till he comes out. Keep trailing him."

"Too late for that," Reba said. "He took off five minutes ago. Thought about following him, but I couldn't leave you here. Especially when you wouldn't talk to me." She looked at the empty clip attached to my waistband. "Where's your phone?"

"It was a *very* bad time to talk," I said.

"And?" She gave me a palms-up.

"You wouldn't shut up, so I threw the damn thing away."

"Threw it where?"

"The phone's a goner." My expression must have told her to drop the subject.

"So now what?" she said.

"We may as well head back to the office."

"Okey-dokey." Reba shifted into drive, pulled out, and took a left on Kirby.

"The trip was definitely worth it even if he got away," she said. "I met this really hot guy in the parking lot. Reminded me of one of those Village People in his hard hat and T-shirt."

How could she be thinking about picking up men at a time like this? "Don't you ever quit?"

She stuck her tongue out at me. "You never know when Mr. Right will come along. We hit it off. He even gave me his home phone number." She pointed to a business card on the console.

I looked down and read the card. Brandt Construction. An additional number scrawled in ink. I picked the card up.

Brandt. Madge's boyfriend Nick.

Nicholas Brandt.

The suspected River Oaks money launderer.

*Time keeps slippin' by,*
*And I don't know why*
*This woman is so hard to find,*
*She'll cause me to lose my mind.*

# CHAPTER 17

"Why are you so bent out of shape about this Brandt character?" Reba asked after I filled her in on what had happened inside the building.

"Maybe it was his goons with the Uzis," I said. "Or could be the fact that Mother says the guy is a money launderer."

"Where'd she hear that?"

"She didn't say."

"Interesting country club chit-chat," Reba said. "But since when do you believe your Mama's gossip?"

She had me there. "It's possible Jack Litchfield and Brandt are in cahoots somehow."

"Why would either of them care to follow you?"

"Good question."

"Maybe Jack's still ticked off about you serving him the other day," she said.

"Why would he bother with me when he's got two million dollars to think about?"

"Men are psycho. Sometimes there's no good explanation."

"Nora will be the psycho one if she doesn't get the money back," I said. "If I'm lucky, I'll figure out why Gentry is following me in the course of finding her husband."

Reba dropped me at my truck, and I followed her back to the office. Pulling into a parking space under the building, I noticed Wade's car wasn't in its assigned spot. Just as well. I didn't feel like a confrontation with him right now. The thought of him with his ex-wife still stung like an open wound.

We took the stairs up to the second floor, our small

concession to the concept of regular exercise. I suggested Reba give her hard-hat friend a call later, see what she could find out about Brandt in casual conversation. Meanwhile, I would continue my search for Phyllis Keene–the one person who might give me a lead to Jack.

Upon entering my office, I conducted a careful inspection. I assured myself that everything was precisely as I'd left it, then sat down and checked my voicemail. Zachary had left me a message, claiming he had something to show me. He left his cell number and asked me to stop by the spa if I had a chance. Ugh. I'd already been there one too many times today. I made a mental note to call him later, then began an internet search for information about Jack's secretary.

I found two different apartment addresses for Phyllis Keene and jotted down both along with her phone number next to Zachary's. I stuck the note in my shirt pocket, debating between going out to check the addresses or trying to call the woman. My phone rang before I made up my mind. It was Ruben Salinas.

"The police say is okay we start cleaning up Carmen's house," he said. "We will donate much to charity, but I was looking to be sure my sister did not have a will. No matter what the past, I would abide by her wishes."

"Of course," I said, curious where he was headed with this.

"First I want to apologize for my bad behavior," he said. "I should not have hit Mr. Doyle."

You can say that again.

"Forget about it," I said. "We all reacted badly. Now what was it about Carmen's will?"

"I did not find any will, but I *did* find her bank statement very interesting."

"Oh?" The burglars hadn't gotten all of Carmen's paper after all. "Where did you find a bank statement?"

"She had unopened mail in her car. My sister made some large deposits, Ms. McKenna. I do not know where she would get this kind of money."

Salinas hadn't seen Carmen in twenty years, so why *would* he know anything about her finances?

"That is why I called you," he went on. "Maybe this has something to do with the man you asked about."

That was a thought–Jack might have siphoned

community property money to Carmen to keep it from Nora. "How much money are we talking?" I asked.

"Two deposits. Ten thousand dollars each. Both in the past month."

Hmm. I scribbled the figures on my notepad. Even before Jack took the two million Nora had suspected he was depleting their assets, but Salinas' find was small potatoes for the Litchfields.

"Does Carmen have a lot of money in the bank?" I said.

"Less than fifteen thousand total now," he said. "From her checks, I can see she spent plenty in department stores."

"I hope you'll tell the police," I said. "This might be important."

"Already have," he said. "Just thought you would like to know, too."

"Yes, I appreciate the call."

I asked Salinas for the dates of each deposit and jotted them down. He gave me his home phone number in New Braunfels, and I promised to let him know if his information became important to my case.

I hung up and dragged out the documents Nora had given me the day before. It would be interesting to see if Carmen's deposits matched withdrawals from any of the Litchfield bank or brokerage accounts. Everything was meticulously organized and it didn't take me long to scan the transactions on the most recent statements from each account against the dates mentioned by Salinas.

I didn't find any ten thousand dollar withdrawals or withdrawals that added up to ten thousand. The Litchfields used automatic teller machines often, but unless Jack was taking two hundred dollar cash withdrawals and saving them up until they reached ten thousand before giving them to Carmen, the money in her account wasn't related to them.

So where did the woman get that money?

I doodled on my notepad, drawing circles around the deposit dates. A knock startled me, and I looked up to see Mother's friend Lucas Turner, aka Mr. Movie Star, in the doorway. He looked even more yummy today in a white shirt and jeans than he had at the dinner party. He held a sheaf of papers in one hand.

"Hi," I said, feeling tongue-tied.

"Hello yourself." He dazzled me with a smile.

"Can I help you?"

"Don't mean to interrupt." He moved into the office and settled in a guest chair. "I have the agenda here. Thought I'd drop off your copy."

"Agenda?"

Lucas laughed at me as I sat there in a fog. "For the gala. I understand you volunteered to help out with security."

"Oh, that." I sat back in my chair. "Sorry. I have a lot on my mind. The gala. Right."

"You still planning to be there?" he asked.

"Of course." I flipped my hair behind my ears in an attempt to make myself more presentable. "Big day's almost here, huh?"

"Tomorrow." He handed me a sheet of paper. "If you're too busy, I'm sure we can handle things just fine. Working on a murder investigation outranks any gala."

"The police are handling Carmen Messina's murder investigation," I said. "I can assure you, my involvement is quite accidental."

"Must be stressful," he said.

"Extremely."

"You were engrossed when I walked in." He glanced at my notepad. "Total dedication. I admire that."

"I'm not sure dedication is the right term," I said, laughing. "Trying to unscramble the confusion might be a better description." I scanned the agenda. The auction items were being moved to the country club at three tomorrow afternoon.

"Bet you could use a break," Lucas said. "Want to grab some lunch?"

I looked up, surprised, and started to say no. I shouldn't be hungry after that huge breakfast, but in times of stress my stomach becomes a bottomless pit.

"I don't want to step on Kaitlyn's toes," I said.

"I have no commitment to her." He beamed another smile. "What do you say?"

Guilt hovered over me for a full two seconds. But hey, Wade was the one off doing God-knows-what with Laura. Why should I sit around and mope? I shrugged. "Let's go."

\*\*\*

We took Lucas's red Porsche which he obviously

enjoyed driving well over the speed limit. The man was into appearances, as were most of the men who hung in Mother's social circles, and he suggested we eat at Grotto on Westheimer. I wasn't exactly dressed for lunch at the trendy spot, but didn't let that bother me. I enjoyed my seafood salad and the people watching, even endured some who's who small talk.

On our way back I realized we were very near one of Phyllis Keene's addresses. I checked the notations I'd made. Lucas noticed me paying close attention to street signs.

"Something bothering you?" he said.

"Not really. It's just I've been searching for this woman. I think we're near one of the addresses I have for her."

"Then let's check it out," he said.

"Sure you don't mind?"

"Are you kidding?" He flashed the smile. "It'd be a kick to help an honest-to-God PI."

We bombed out at the first place, then Lucas insisted we try the second address. Phyllis had already moved from both apartments, the latter one only three days ago. I couldn't hide my disappointment, and Lucas suggested a Starbucks latte to lift my spirits.

The day was overcast and not too humid, so we settled at a table outside.

"What's so important about this woman Phyllis?" Lucas said.

"Long story," I said. "But finding her might break my case wide open—*my* case, not the hairdresser murder case."

"Wish I could find a way to help," he said.

"So do I, believe me." I avoided his serious gaze, pretending interest in the stream of people going in and coming out with their drinks. To change the subject, I said, "Isn't it amazing how many people will drink coffee in this hot—"

I stopped short. Maggie Robbins was exiting the building, coffee in hand. I picked up my cup and tried to hide behind it. Too late. She'd spotted me.

"What is it?" Lucas turned to see what had caught my attention.

"Corie, hi." Maggie waved and headed straight at me, though her eyes were trained on Lucas. "Don't think we've had the pleasure." She shook his hand. "Maggie Robbins."

"Perhaps not, but I'm a fan." He gave her the smile.

"Are you? How nice." Maggie beamed and took a seat at our table, not bothering to apologize for interrupting.

I had wanted to avoid a serious turn in my conversation with Lucas, but not like this.

Maggie looked at me. "How did you two hook up? Corie, I thought you were tight with–"

"Lucas is working on one of Mother's committees," I said, simply to avoid my name turning up with his in the society columns.

"Oh, which one?" Maggie's complexion brightened.

"For the Denim & Diamonds Gala," Lucas said.

"What fun." Maggie bubbled with excitement. "I'm planning to be there."

"It promises to be a great time," Lucas said.

"Have you seen the guest list?" she said. "I asked Corie for one, but she hasn't come through yet. I could do a little name dropping on my spot tonight. Drum up more interest in the auction."

Lucas listed names without hesitation.

Big deal. I couldn't believe anyone would care who was going to the gala and who wasn't. I regretted taking this little jaunt with Lucas when I had important business to tend to.

"I hear the auction is expected to bring in more than any in history," Maggie said.

Lucas was eating up the attention. "That's right. Olivia has outdone herself. And I hear she has a big surprise planned."

"What kind of surprise?" Maggie said.

I'd had enough. I picked up my cup and stood. "Unlike me, Mother enjoys these things. I really need to get back to the office."

"Guess we're out of here," Lucas told Maggie. "Look forward to seeing you tomorrow."

We climbed into his Porsche, and he grinned at me. "I take it you don't care for Ms. Robbins."

My smile felt stiff. "You're very observant."

"What's not to like?"

"She's pushy," I said. "But hey, that's just me. I realize she has an adoring public out there."

"You're jealous."

I gave him a look. "Don't flatter yourself."

The more time I spent with Mr. Turner, the more his egotistical side irked me. I should have known better than to accept a lunch invitation from a man Mother liked.

We drove back to my office in silence, and he pulled in near the elevator bank.

"Thanks for lunch." My tone sounded frigid, but I couldn't help myself. I'd had two lunches with Lucas Turner today–my first and last. I only wished I hadn't already committed to the gala 'cause now I'd have to see him again tomorrow.

In a totally unexpected move, Lucas leaned across the console. I turned away in time to avoid a kiss full on the mouth. His lips brushed my cheek.

"We'll have to do this again sometime," he said.

I ignored that comment, climbing out in a rush and walking quickly toward the building. Maggie Robbins could have the guy.

I yanked open the glass door, stunned to find Wade standing on the other side, briefcase in hand.

*Mind your own business,*
*Keep your nose out of mine.*
*Gave you one chance,*
*Now you're flat out of time.*

# CHAPTER 18

I blew right past Wade, making a beeline for the stairs. He hurried after me.

"Who the hell was that?" he said.

"None of your business," I shot back, jerking the stairwell door open. I took the stairs two at a time, Wade on my heels.

"Not my business? What the hell?"

"That's right. My personal life is my business, not yours." My face was burning and pounding up the stairs wasn't helping. I reached the first landing and stretched for the next stair, but Wade grabbed my arm.

"Hold on a minute." He turned me to face him and let his briefcase drop to the floor. We stood there for a few seconds, staring at each other, breathing hard.

"Last I knew, our personal lives were one and the same," he said, his tone softer. "What's going on?"

"You have some nerve." I tried to pull my arm from his grasp. "Let go of me."

"No way." He moved in close enough for me to feel his breath on my face. His blue eyes seemed darker, almost black. "What's wrong, Corie?"

"The fact that you even have to ask is a very bad sign."

He reached up with his free hand, pulling at his tie as if the knot choked him. "I think you owe me an explanation."

"I owe *you*?" My voice echoed in the stairwell. "Excuse me if I see things a bit differently."

"Fine." He dropped my arm. "You women make me crazy."

I could have bolted, but his statement steamed me.

"Oh, you have too many women to deal with? Whose fault is that?"

"Your imagination must be on overdrive. I don't know what *you're* talking about, but I'm referring to Nora Litchfield. I just came from meeting with that crazy woman, now you're going off the deep end, too."

My blood pressure shot up. "How dare you compare me to Nora."

"I'm not *comparing* you," he said. "I'm telling you I've been through a lot already this afternoon."

"I'm *so* sorry," I said. "I've had a hell of a time myself, and if you weren't so all-fired busy elsewhere, you'd know that."

"Nora is my client, Corie, like it or not, and you can't blame her for being upset about this latest development."

The idiot had no idea I was talking about Laura. I took some deep breaths to calm myself.

"Bank claims they didn't receive any wire instructions," he continued, "and they can't explain what happened to the money."

I crossed my arms. "Jack's probably sitting in some other country, counting that money."

"He's not." Wade shook his head. "Nora's neighbor saw him at the house this morning while Nora was at work."

"Guess that's good news." I resisted an urge to reach out and touch Wade's wavy hair. "But we need to talk about something far more important than Nora and Jack."

His cell phone rang, with seriously bad timing. He answered, cocked his head, and held his other ear closed to hear better.

"Sorry, I was on my way out. Tell the Judge I'll be there in fifteen minutes. No, make that ten."

I turned to climb the stairs, feeling incredibly heavy. I heard him click off.

"Sorry, Corie. I'm late for a meeting."

"No problem." I kept walking. "The ball's in your court. Let me know when you decide if I'm still in the game."

"You're not making any sense," he said. "We'll talk later."

"Sure."

I went to my office, locked the door, and plopped into my chair. Punched the radio on. Toby Keith was singing "You

Shouldn't Kiss Me Like This." *They think we're falling in love. They'd never believe we're just friends.* I stared out the window. Wade and I had been good friends for a long time. Maybe it was a mistake to believe we could be more. Had we ruined everything now?

Trying to shake off the depressing thought, I grabbed a notepad. I jotted down a to-do list to keep from thinking about Wade.

Find Jack Litchfield.

Figure out where Jack's put the money.

Find Phyllis Keene–maybe she knows what he did.

Figure out why Mark Gentry is following me.

Learn more about Nicholas Brandt.

Follow up on the gala arrangements.

Since I didn't know where to begin to find Jack or the money or Phyllis, I logged onto the internet to learn more about the creep who'd been following me. Finding Gentry's current and previous addresses, driving record, and the fact that he'd been married and divorced twice didn't do much for me, so I dialed the phone number for the guy, not knowing what I'd say if he answered. After three rings, I heard the click signaling that a voice mail message would kick in.

"Need a discreet, experienced, and affordable private eye? Then I'm your guy. This is Mark Gentry of In-Depth Investigations. Leave a message. I'll call you pronto." A beep sounded, and I hung up.

Someone had hired a private eye to tail me? Brandt? Jack? Damn. Maybe I should call back and leave a message. Get him to level with me as a fellow P.I.

Right.

My gut told me this all came back to Jack Litchfield, so I had no choice but to dig in and find the jerk. Since the Litchfields were members of Briar Hill Country Club, maybe I could combine tracking Jack down with following up on the gala arrangements. I turned the radio off, grabbed my purse, and read the gala agenda on my way to the truck.

***

It had been many years since my last visit to The Briar Hill Club, but when I walked through the entry doors memories flooded back. Not exactly my fondest memories.

Mother had hosted a tea here for my thirteenth birthday, despite the fact that I wanted a Six Flags amusement park party more than anything. Some friends had roped me into coming here for dinner before the Junior Prom, and I'd cut out and gone to Otto's with a group of less popular kids, leaving my self-absorbed date behind. My last visit was the time Mother dragged me to one of her Garden Club socials where it seemed I was the only person interested in talking about gardening.

I walked down the entry hall, with its ornate chandeliers, highly polished mahogany furniture, and plush carpets. Nothing had changed. The two-story country club had four wings and could accommodate twice as many lavish events simultaneously in their ballrooms. Smaller rooms opened off the main hallways.

Rounding the first corner, I ran into the club's security guard. His hair had gone snow white since I'd last seen him.

"Look who's here," he said with a big smile. "Miss Corinne."

"Hi, Ralph," I said. "It's been a long time."

"Yes, it surely has. What's the occasion?"

"Checking out the set-up for the gala," I said. "They're bringing in some expensive stuff for the silent auction, and Dad is concerned about Mother's safety. He's out of town this week."

"No need to worry. They're adding extra security. You know, in case I need backup." Ralph's eyes twinkled. "We're opening up the Pecos room to the Sabine Ballroom so we'll have enough space to display the auction things and for dinner and dancing."

"I'm sure everything will be lovely," I said. "But I have another reason for coming to see you. I need a favor."

"Name it."

"I hear Jack Litchfield hasn't been around like he used to be."

Ralph looked down, scratched the back of his head, thinking. "Can't say that he has. Haven't noticed the man lately, and used to be if he was around you'd hear him."

"But you still see some of his friends?"

"Oh, sure, every day."

"You mind asking around whether anybody knows how to get in touch with Jack? Quiet like."

"No problem. I'll put my ear to the ground. Keep you posted."

"I'd appreciate that." I handed him one of my cards. "You happen to know a man named Nicholas Brandt?"

Ralph continued the scratching, but shook his head. "Can't say that I do."

"Oh well, worth a try. Now, mind if I take a look at that ballroom?"

"Lord no. Make yourself at home, Miss Corinne. I got to check on a delivery right quick."

"No problem. I remember my way around."

I went upstairs and walked toward the east wing. The club was busy, and I passed lots of people in the hallway, most of them chatting and minding their own business, but a couple of snotty women who frowned as they inspected my casual clothes and scuffed sandals.

I made note of the building exits and decided there should be no problem keeping security tight during the auction. According to the agenda, the extra security staff would arrive an hour before the auction items were unloaded and stay until each item was reloaded for delivery to the winning bidder.

With this relatively painless item crossed off my list, I'd have to move on to one of the more difficult tasks. I took the elevator down, and as I headed for the exit passed a dining room where I heard a familiar voice. I backed up a step and peeked inside. Haley Winter was handing out pamphlets to a table of female diners.

"Serenity in the City will embrace you with tranquility," she said, "and set your elegance apart. Our special treatments for June are microdermabrasion and silk straightening. Come see us." Haley looked stunning in a simple peacock tank dress, her silky hair and sculpted smooth arms an advertisement in themselves. She sounded two hundred percent friendlier than any time I'd spoken with her.

She looked up, noticed me in the doorway, and walked my way. She lowered her voice. "One can never tell where you might turn up, can one?"

"The pleasure is mutual," I said.

Haley scrutinized my clothes. "I would have thought the Club had a dress code."

"And I thought they had strict rules against soliciting. Oh, I'm sorry. I meant solicitors." I gave her a derisive smile.

"Women are always delighted to hear what Serenity

Spa can do for them. You might take advantage of our services yourself."

What a bitch. I lifted a handful of my hair, though the style bore little resemblance to the way it had looked when Zachary finished with me. "I already have."

A man in an austere black suit and immaculate white shirt charged around the corner, approaching us. He wore a gold name badge on his lapel, and when he got closer I recognized him. His badge now held the title "Director" under his name though he had worked in the kitchen back when I knew him.

"Shane Patterson." I clasped his hand. "Good to see you."

"Corie?" He squinted at me. "Man, it's been years."

"Many," I agreed. "I had no idea you were still here."

"You don't exactly come around much." He smiled.

Haley cleared her throat. "Think I'll skip this little reunion." Holding the pamphlets tightly against her side, she turned to walk away. Shane stepped into her path.

"Excuse me, miss, but I came to see you." He looked at me. "Is she a friend of yours?"

"Hardly," I said.

He turned back to Haley. "Are you here as someone's guest today?"

She lifted her chin. "How do you know I'm not a member?"

"I know all the members," Shane said, his tone hardened. "Why don't we step into the hall where we can have a few words in private?"

"I really need to be going," Haley said.

"Yes, you do," he said, his expression all serious.

"I don't appreciate being harassed by the help," Haley said.

Shane took her elbow, gently nudging her out of the dining room. I followed.

"What's this about?" Haley said.

"We don't allow soliciting at Briar Hill," he said, peering at the pamphlets. "I don't know how you got in, and I don't care to see you here again."

Haley turned in a huff and flounced toward the exit.

I enjoyed the performance. This was the most fun I'd had all week.

*Trouble is surrounding me,*
*Seems we're all in jeopardy.*
*Don't understand what's going on,*
*But we can't let them bring us down.*

# CHAPTER 19

I climbed into my truck, planning to call Mother and report that security for her gala was under control. I touched my belt, then checked the truck console before remembering that I'd thrown my new phone into the fountain.

I weighed the aggravation of another trip to the phone store against that of reporting to Mother in person. The sun had gone into hiding. Black clouds loomed in the distance. Late Friday afternoon wasn't the best traffic time, even without the brewing thunderstorm. Going to Mother's won out, only because she lived close.

As I crossed the mile or so to my parents' neighborhood, rain clouds zoomed in and a white fog descended. Fat raindrops spotted the windshield. When I turned onto their street, a police car's flashing lights cut through the haze. My stomach knotted before I realized the car wasn't at Mother's, but parked at the next-door neighbor's. I skidded to a stop and spotted Ruby in the side yard under one of Dad's huge golf umbrellas.

I hurried through the rain and joined her. "What's going on?"

"Just got home from cleaning up your place," she said, "to find out somebody's robbed the Richardsons."

"Oh, no! When did it happen?"

"Less than an hour ago. In broad daylight. Guy in a ski mask held a gun to Barbara's head."

"One guy?"

"That's what I heard."

"Where's Mother? Is she okay?"

"She's with Barbara. You know your mama—she puts

on a good face, but I can tell this hit her hard."

Water rained down on me as I pushed through the soaked shrubbery separating the properties. I ran across the squishy lawn and up to the Richardson house. One officer was in the cruiser. Mother stood under the portico, carefully holding her dripping umbrella away from her clothes and talking with a second officer. She started to greet me with a hug, but took in my sopping outfit and kissed my cheek instead.

"Dear, I'm so glad to see you're okay," she said.

"Why wouldn't I be?"

She didn't answer, introducing me to the officer instead. "Corinne's house was broken into last night," she told him.

I closed my eyes for a split second, hating that she'd found out what had happened. Ruby had promised to keep quiet.

"And where do you live, ma'am?" he asked me.

"West U. But it was nothing."

"That's not true, dear," Mother said. "Ruby told me your house was a total disaster."

I waved a hand impatiently. "That's irrelevant to what's going on here. How's Barbara?"

"Mrs. Richardson is fine," the officer assured me.

"I wouldn't say fine," Mother said. "She's traumatized. Who wouldn't be? Her Cartier diamond-and-ruby choker was stolen. She wore it last night and hadn't returned it to her safe deposit box yet. What dreadful timing."

Dreadful for Barbara, lucky for the burglar.

"At least she wasn't hurt," I said. "Physically, I mean." To Mother having the jewelry stolen was probably equivalent to ending up in the emergency room. "I'm very concerned about you, though."

"Nonsense," she said. "I'm fine."

"For the moment," I said. "Odds aren't looking so good."

"Seems they're no better in your neighborhood. I think you should stay here with us."

Moving in with her until Dad got back would be the daughterly thing to do, but I could go insane in a couple of days.

"Barbara's burglar had nothing to do with what

happened to me," I said. "No valuables were taken from my house. And what makes you think I'd be safer here?"

"We have a state-of-the-art security system," she said.

"And the Richardson's didn't? I don't think any system is secure enough to keep out the River Oaks Banditos." I looked at the officer. "What do you think?"

"The real pros can get past any system if they want in bad enough," he said. "This guy was already inside when Mrs. Richardson came home. Surprised him in the act, I guess. He had a gun on her but she did the right thing. Handed over what he wanted, and he left." He closed his notebook and stuffed it into his pocket.

"The burglar specified what he wanted?" I asked.

The officer pursed his lips and checked his notebook. "Way she remembered, perp said 'I want the jewels.' This was after he'd emptied her jewelry box into a pillowcase."

"Wonder if he figured everybody living in River Oaks *has* jewels worth stealing or if he knew about *her* specific jewels?"

"No way to know," the cop said.

"You think this guy is one of the River Oaks Banditos?" I said.

The cop shrugged. "Mrs. Richardson's the first eye witness. Newspaper came up with this banditos theory. There could be one guy, two of 'em, or twelve. We don't know."

I turned to Mother. "This is exactly why I wish you would stay put for the next couple of days. Until Dad gets back or the police catch the burglars, whichever comes first. We can hire someone to watch the house."

She glared at me. "I refuse to be a prisoner in my own home. And I am not changing my schedule because of some criminal."

"You have more valuables in your house than usual," I said, referring to the auction items. "This danger is too close for comfort."

"I'll keep my jewels in the vault until it's time to get ready for the gala," she said. "Besides, you're the one who always pooh-poohs me when I talk about danger."

"You are so stubborn."

"And the nut didn't fall far from the tree, did it?" she said.

The officer cleared his throat. "Ladies, I believe we've

gathered enough information. Keep your doors locked and your security systems turned on. We'll send extra patrols through the area."

After the cop had climbed into his car, Mother said, "Did you have to make a scene in front of him?"

"You started it when you talked about my burglary," I said. "I'm sure our little discussion didn't faze the man, but I wish you would listen to me and take precautions."

She huffed and turned toward the Richardson house. "I'm going to check on Barbara."

"Fine." I stomped back across the soggy lawn, mulling over this latest in a chain of disturbing events. Ordinarily, I heard of burglaries only on the news. All of a sudden, there were break-ins every time I turned around. This couldn't be coincidence.

I found Ruby in the kitchen, standing over a pan on the stove, stirring rhythmically. The room was fragrant with a cinnamony sweetness.

"Please don't ever say I take after my mother," I said.

Ruby gave me a sideways glance and kept stirring.

"Heaven help me." I peered into her pot. "Smells good."

"Rice pudding," she said curtly.

"What's wrong?"

She tapped her large spoon on the pot and placed it on a spoon rest before turning to me, deep worry lines etching her forehead.

"How do you expect me to sleep tonight?"

"The police officer said he'd send extra patrols through the neighborhood," I said.

"That's not what I'm talking about."

"Then what?"

"Whoever broke into your house meant serious business. You think by having me tidy everything up you can forget what happened?"

"Of course not."

"And if that wasn't enough," she continued, raising her voice, "then Reba tells me about your run-in with Mr. Brandt's bodyguards."

Couldn't anybody keep a secret anymore? "You weren't supposed to tell Mother what happened at my house, and Reba should know enough to keep her mouth shut about my personal business. I'm trying to do a job and–" I stopped. What had she said about Brandt?

"Do you know Nicholas Brandt?"

She put her hands on her hips. "Not personally, but I hear enough about him from Felicia."

"Who's Felicia?"

"My friend who works for Ms. Peabody. You remember Ms. Peabody?"

My impatience flared. "Yes, yes. But how do you know anything about bodyguards?"

"'Cause that Brandt fella moved in next door to Ms. Peabody, that's how. And Felicia doesn't miss a trick."

"So she saw men with Nicholas Brandt. Why would she say they're bodyguards?"

"Probably 'cause every time this fella and his daughter come and go there they are. Like the Secret Service or something. And probably 'cause of their guns."

I was going to strangle Reba and her big mouth.

"What else does Felicia know about Brandt?"

"You shouldn't be fooling with anybody needs bodyguards," she said, not answering my question.

As if Mother's nagging wasn't enough, now Ruby was joining the club.

"I don't even know if Brandt has a thing to do with my job," I said. "I didn't plan to go looking for him. Some guy was following me."

"That's when you should've called the police."

"They wouldn't care."

"You didn't try."

"Maybe you've been around Mother too long," I said. "We used to be able to talk. You used to understand."

"I understand your mama's worried about you, and I'm worried, too. We didn't raise you to go out and get yourself killed over some fool case."

"It's not a fool case, and nothing's going to happen to me." I turned and stormed from the room, almost getting hit in the butt by the swinging kitchen door. I was out of here, rice pudding or no rice pudding.

"Stupid case," I muttered on my way to the front door. Not that I could connect the break-ins or my being tailed to my current case, but I sure wanted rid of Nora Litchfield. Which reminded me of Zachary's call.

Damn.

He was the only friendly person I'd dealt with lately, and he'd expected to see or hear from me today. I fished in my pocket for the piece of paper I'd jotted notes on earlier. There. Zachary's cell number.

I stopped at the hallway phone and punched in the number.

The call was answered on the fourth ring, and I recognized Zachary's somewhat feminine hello.

"Glad I caught you," I said.

"I'm so glad you called."

"Is something wrong? I don't need any more bad news today."

"Bad? Oh, no biggie. But I found something here that's kind of interesting. You might want to come see. Has to do with Carmen."

"Where are you?"

"At the spa."

I checked my watch. After seven. "You always work this late?"

"It was one hellish day." Zachary sighed. "With all the customers buzzing around I couldn't finish my project, so I went out to grab a bite, then came back."

"What project?" I said.

"Cleaning out my new station and getting everything organized. Saturdays are frantic so I wanted it all done today. That's how I found the notes."

"Notes?"

"Yeah. Some are in Carmen's handwriting. Pages of them. And a calendar. She had this stuff under the liner in her perm rod drawer. Seemed weird. I'm trying to figure out what it all means."

"I can be there in ten minutes."

"Sounds good. Front door's locked, so come around to the side window near the Italian restaurant. Knock and I'll let you in."

"Okay."

When I hung up I noticed Ruby standing in the hallway watching me, hands on hips.

"You don't want some of my rice pudding?" she said.

"I'll have to take a rain check. I'm going over to Serenity Spa. One of the hairdressers needs to talk to me."

Ruby clucked her disapproval, but said, "What should I tell your mama when she notices you're gone?"

"Tell her I'll be back. Guess I'll stay here tonight. Maybe until Dad gets home."

Ruby smiled. "Good girl. But you be careful."

"I will." Embarrassed about my little temper tantrum, I was glad she'd approached me. There was enough turmoil in my life at the moment–I didn't need to get crossways with Ruby.

On my way to the spa, I wondered about the notes Zachary had found. Why was he having trouble figuring out what they meant? Turning the corner from Shepherd onto West Gray, I narrowly missed a speeding car that swerved around the corner. The rain had stopped, but the road was still slick and full of puddles. Crazy Houston drivers.

I lost a few minutes weaving up and down the filled parking lot rows before finally snagging a space a few yards away from the spa. I shoved my purse under the seat and got out to the sound of operatic music spilling from Mama Mia's. The scent of garlic hung in the air. People crowded around the restaurant's entry doors waiting for their names to be called. Bad weather hadn't deterred the Friday night crowd.

I rounded the corner to the spa's window nearest the restaurant and knocked several times, with no response. A few lights burned inside, but I couldn't see much of anything through the tinted window so I went to the front and pulled on one of the big double doors. It opened. Zachary must have changed his mind and unlocked it.

I walked through the lobby. The door thudded shut behind me and closed off the outdoors, leaving me with only the sound of water running in the fountain. With the drab weather, the place seemed extra dark. Giant dracena plants and palms cast jungle-like shadows on the wall. Creepy. A chill ran up my spine. I crossed the lobby quickly and entered the spa's interior.

"Zachary?" I called out. "Where are you?"

No answer.

At least I could see better in here. I slowed down, walked to each partitioned area, and peeked around corners. My heart raced, and I felt jittery. Was the potent scent of permanent wave lotions causing a physical reaction? Maybe I was allergic.

"Zachary?" My voice echoed in the stillness.

By the time I reached the fifth divider, I noticed a stench overpowering the chemical smell. I felt like a wild animal sensing danger ahead. Instead of running away, my fear propelled me forward, around the last partition.

I jumped back with a yelp.

Zachary's body lay draped over the beautician's chair, his arms splayed across the chair arms. His head lolled to the left. Blood dripped onto the floor from the bullet hole in his forehead.

*Life is only this brief moment,*
*No one can foresee the end.*
*Now I'm living with the torment,*
*That I couldn't help my friend.*

# CHAPTER 20

I clamped my mouth shut to keep from screaming. How long had it been since I'd talked to Zachary? Ten minutes? Fifteen? The killer might still be here. I froze, heart hammering, afraid to move.

My gaze darted to the doorway, back to Zachary, to the bullet wound, the shocked expression in his wide hazel eyes.

"Oh, my God," I whispered. The last thing Zachary had done was to call me and now he was dead. I stepped toward him, thinking I had to do something, check his pulse maybe. Try CPR. Anything.

*Too late to help him. Get out.*

Unable to move, I replayed our conversation. Did the notes he'd described have something to do with his murder? An unusual thought, but not impossible. Knowing I should run, call for help, I stooped to check the floor, averting my eyes from the blood. No papers there.

My gaze riveted on the breast pocket of his purple shirt. He might have stuffed the notes into a pocket after talking to me. I knew the importance of not contaminating a crime scene, but if the police took custody of the papers I'd never see them. I spotted a box of disposable gloves meant to protect a stylist's hands from chemicals and dyes. I hesitated for two seconds, then went over and put on a pair.

I turned back to Zachary and steeled myself. My pulse drummed in my ears as I pulled on his shirt pocket to peek inside.

Empty.

I blinked back tears and slid a hand into his pants pocket. His warm body reminded me that he'd been alive only minutes ago. Might still be alive if he hadn't called me, if I'd never come into his life. I bit on my lower lip to keep from sobbing.

The right-hand pocket held a ring of keys, the left a money clip with a wad of bills. Tip money, if I had to guess. I shoved the cash back. Slipping a hand between the chair and the body, I confirmed the black rayon pants didn't have rear pockets.

I looked around the room for hiding places. Multi-sized brushes and rods were separated in piles on the counter top. The under-counter trays were empty, and I figured Zachary had found the notes in one of them. Could I assume the killer now had those notes? No. They might still be here somewhere.

And so might the killer.

I automatically reached to my empty phone clip. Damn. I needed to call for help. I scanned the area again. So where was Zachary's cell phone?

Something thumped and I must have jumped a foot.

*Get out now.*

I sucked in a deep breath and ran. I burst through the front door onto the sidewalk, looking around frantically, then headed toward the hordes of restaurant-goers waiting to be called for a table.

"Help," I screamed. "Somebody. I need a cell phone."

Two thirty-something couples stood on the periphery of the crowd. The women looked at me and seemed to back away. I was breathing heavy, shaking so hard it was difficult to speak. I pointed at the spa.

"Over there," I said. "A man's been murdered."

The women gasped.

"Here." One of the men took a phone from his shirt pocket. "I'll dial for you."

He pushed nine-one-one and handed the phone to me. The woman with him put her hand on his arm, and they exchanged a worried look. I realized they were staring at my hands and that I still wore the disposable gloves. Holding the phone between my shoulder and my ear, I peeled off the gloves and stuffed them into my pocket.

I spoke with the dispatcher, answering her questions as best I could, and she told me help was on the way. A waitress arrived with a tray of drinks. The man whose phone I was holding offered me his glass.

"Scotch on the rocks. You look like you need it more than I do."

He was right. I accepted his offer. Even the first whiff had a calming effect on my nerves. I asked him how long they'd been standing out here, thinking someone might have seen the killer, but they had just arrived. I downed the drink and welcomed the burning in my throat. Then I dialed Nora Litchfield's home number. She freaked out when I told her about Zachary and said she'd come over right away.

The important calls made, I waited in the midst of a boisterous crowd celebrating the end of another work week. I watched the spa, wishing I'd have contacted Zachary earlier in the day. Maybe I could have changed the course of his fate.

Under ordinary circumstances, I'd be in touch with Wade by now, but after our last conversation I didn't feel like talking to him. Mourning the state of our relationship and Zachary's death, I sat on a bench and let the tears come.

\*\*\*

The concept that the police might see me as a suspect never entered my mind. Our conversation began calmly enough with me identifying myself and filling them in about my conversation with Zachary, about the notes he'd found, and my discovery of the body. But then one of the officers spotted blood on my sandals. Before I could gather my wits they'd bagged the sandals as evidence, leaving me barefooted and spread-eagled against a squad car.

What were they thinking?

"But I'm the one who called you," I said as a black female officer frisked me, her hands traveling up and down my legs. "You think I'd've called you if I murdered someone?"

"You wouldn't be the first," she said.

"Well, I didn't do it," I said. "Someone came in and killed him in the time it took me to drive over here."

"Whatever you say."

I looked under my right arm and saw her partner standing near their car. He held his head tipped toward his shoulder, and I heard the squawk of his walkie-talkie. I tried to pull my arms down, but the woman smacked them back against the car. "Don't move 'til I say you can move."

This couldn't be happening.

I rested my forehead against the car and glanced down

at my ratty jeans, smudged with dirt from my escape at the wedding planner's office, my baggy red T-shirt. Damn. I shut my eyes, enduring the humiliation of the officer searching me, none too gently.

"And what do we have here?" she said, pulling her hand from my pocket.

Without looking, I knew she had the disposable gloves.

"I put them on to check for a pulse," I said, thinking quickly.

"Uh-huh," she said.

"There was a whole box, sitting out in plain sight. You'd have done the same thing." I squeezed my eyes tight, battling tears.

With a final pat around my ankles, she straightened and pulled me away from the car. "Turn around, please."

I faced her. "I came here on business. I don't have a weapon. And you can't possibly think I killed that man."

I expected a wisecrack, but the male officer came over, stopping a couple yards short of us. He beckoned to her and she joined him, holding her hand up to me with the "stay" signal usually reserved for dogs.

They had a whispered conversation, their eyes never leaving me. From their expressions, you'd think I'd slithered out from under a rock. I remembered Mother's constant lecturing about the importance of looking your best every time you go out in public, and this was one time I wished I'd taken her advice.

Usually, I avoid name dropping, but these were not usual circumstances.

"Listen," I said, "I'm Frank Poole's daughter. Corie *Poole* McKenna, that's what the "P" is for on my license."

"Is that right?" the male officer said.

"It's true. Frank Poole is my dad. You know who he is? He owns the Globe."

"I know," he said.

"Well, he's my father. Honest."

"So maybe we should give him a call."

"Okay," I said. "He's in New York right now. We can try his cell phone."

"Maybe later," said the woman, "after we get downtown."

Panic rose in my chest. "I realize I must look like a bag

lady at the moment, but you have no idea what kind of day this has been."

"Seems you've had a rough week." The man walked over to me. "I put your name in the system and came up with several hits. So how many crime scenes you usually make in a week?"

I chewed my lower lip and studied the officer. He looked too young to be a cop. Fine blond hair curled around his ears. His cheeks were dimpled, even though he wasn't smiling. I decided to ignore his question and asked one of my own.

"Aren't you going to look for those notes?" If the cops found evidence, they'd know I wasn't making the whole story up. "The papers could help us figure out what's going on."

Dimples' forehead wrinkled. "What'd these alleged notes say?"

"If I already knew what they said, I wouldn't be so concerned about finding them, would I?"

As soon as the words flew out, I regretted my sarcastic tone. This might be a good time to mention that I wanted to call my lawyer.

The officer scowled at me and leaned closer. He sniffed the air. "How much have you had to drink tonight, Ms. McKenna?"

The Scotch. Damn.

My shoulders sagged. Before I could explain, Nora's Navigator screeched into the lot and captured the cops' attention. She jumped out, wearing an elegant silk lounging outfit, but with tousled hair and a wild look in her eyes.

"Good heavens, this can't be happening." She looked from the spa, to me, then to the cops. "Zachary can't be dead. He can't. Tell me it's not true."

"Take it easy, ma'am." Dimples pulled out a notebook. "Why don't you give us your name?"

"Tell me what happened!" she shouted.

I gave the officer Nora's name and explained that she was the spa owner and my client. At the moment, she looked more like an escapee from a psychiatric hospital.

"Nora," I said. "Please calm down."

She swung toward me. "I've had enough of you telling me to stay calm. Not one single goddamn calming thing has happened in my life since I've known you. You're supposed to be solving problems, damn you, and all you're doing is creating more."

She looked at the building again, and her eyes widened. "What are they doing? Wait! You can't do that!" Nora took off at a trot toward the spa's entrance.

I turned around. Two more officers had come outside to string crime scene tape along the front sidewalk. I started after Nora, but Dimples caught my arm.

"Come with me," he said. "I'd like you to wait in the car."

Unfortunately, he wasn't talking about my vehicle. He led me to a squad car and opened a door with one hand, the other pushing down on top of my head as he guided me into the back seat.

The last thing I heard before the door closed was Nora yelling, "You can't close down my spa. Tomorrow is a Saturday, for Heaven's sake."

*Sittin' here behind these bars,*
*I'm feeling sad and lonely.*
*But I can't always lean on you,*
*You're never gonna own me.*

# CHAPTER 21

Thanks to Nora's lack of support, I ended up at the police station where a couple of homicide detectives questioned me about the evening's events. No one seemed to care about my prominent family background. I couldn't blame them given the host of rich and famous who made the news after committing crimes. After talking with the detectives for a few minutes, I decided they were dead serious about me as a suspect. Even though I hadn't officially been arrested, I exercised my rights to remain silent and to contact an attorney.

I stubbornly placed a call to Joe Garrett instead of Wade. Garrett was a criminal attorney whom I did some work for, and I hoped the fact that I called such a top-dog in the field didn't make the detectives think I needed the very best. I got Garrett's voicemail, left him a message, and settled into the hard interrogation room chair to wait.

My thoughts were on Zachary, how happy he'd been, how alive. I couldn't envision the man having an enemy, so why was he dead? The same reason Carmen had been killed? No way could this be coincidental. Two hair stylists killed in the same week. Co-workers at Serenity Spa. Was it possible that some cryptic notes jotted down by Carmen were behind both murders?

I stared at the two-way mirror and wondered if detectives were standing on the other side and watching me right now. I resisted an urge to stick out my tongue, and propped my elbows on the table. Cold emanated up from the hard tile floor like it does on the Galleria's skating rink. Probably an investigative tactic–freeze the truth out.

At least they'd had the decency to retrieve my tennis

shoes from my truck before hauling me down here. They could keep my sandals–I'd never wear those things again. I tapped my feet, rubber soles playing out a distressed rhythm on the floor. I couldn't seem to hold still, which probably made me appear guilty–if anyone was in fact watching through the glass.

I clasped my icy hands and concentrated on remaining calm. I had enough sense to rein in my agitation, which was tough, but I did a lot better than Nora. From what I'd seen of the annoying woman, she couldn't control her emotions any more than a dog could keep from howling at sirens.

Not that Nora didn't have a right to be upset tonight. No telling what I would think in her place. That a psycho hairdresser serial killer was out there stalking my employees? That my spa had been jinxed? Maybe that my husband was out to ruin my business by killing off my most popular employees?

I frowned, dwelling on that possibility. Jack Litchfield wouldn't ruin a business that he stood to get a portion of in the divorce settlement. Unless he figured the two million he already had was as much as he'd ever see. Somehow, I had to find Jack and prove to Nora that I *could* solve a problem. But first I had to get through this interrogation. I rested my forehead on my fists and wondered how long it would be before Joe Garrett got my message. I nibbled my lower lip, stifling a yawn.

The next thing I heard was the click of the door opening.

"Corie. C'mon, get up."

A hand touched my shoulder and rocked me gently. My arms were crossed on the table, my head resting on them. I felt woozy.

"Let's go."

Wade?

"Don't often see anyone fall asleep in this place." Another man's voice.

Had I been asleep? I managed to open my eyes and saw two sets of legs–one in jeans, one in gray dress slacks.

"Guilt usually keeps 'em wide-eyed and bushy-tailed. This one must be innocent."

Laughter.

I lifted my head up far enough to see my watch. God,

it was almost midnight.

I pushed myself into an upright position and glared at Wade and his cop friend, Charlie. "Of course I'm innocent. What'd you think?"

"She's all yours." Charlie swept his arm like I was first prize on some game show.

"Thanks, pal," Wade said. "Once again, I owe you."

"Don't worry. I'm keeping track." Charlie grinned as he backed out, leaving us alone.

I pushed my chair away from the table. I noticed how good Wade looked in stonewashed jeans and a white shirt even though I wasn't necessarily happy to see him. "What does he mean, she's all yours?"

"I'm getting you out of here," he said. "C'mon."

"Where's Joe?"

"Dallas. Called me the minute he got your message. Sorry it took this long." He crossed the room and came around to my side of the table. "You okay?"

"Sure. Fine."

"Jesus, Corie. Charlie told me what happened. Why didn't you call me?" He placed his palms on the table and leaned over, turning his head to study my face.

This wasn't the place to answer that question. "I can't leave," I said. "The detectives are coming back." I hugged myself tightly, my facade of control slipping. "Guess they think I've done something."

"No, they don't." He stepped closer. "I've cleared everything up. You're going home."

"But Zachary was murdered. First Carmen, now Zachary. I've discovered two bodies within days of each other. I can't just leave."

Wade glanced nervously at the two-way mirror, then back to me. "The cops are going to prepare a statement based on what you've already told them. You can sign it later. For tonight, they're all finished with you."

"But I'm not finished. I have too many questions."

He put a hand on my arm. "Stop talking. This is a police matter. Let it go."

I stood, my voice rising. "I need to know if they found those papers Zachary told me about. I need to see those papers."

"Corie. You're not gonna talk cops into sharing their

evidence with you."

"I have to try." I got up and walked to the door, looked out into the hallway. "Where are those detectives?"

"They left. You're not talking to anyone."

I gritted my teeth. He was right. I ought to be running for the door, but how could I drop everything with the vision of Zachary's body so clear in my mind? He might be dead because of me, and I had to know what had happened.

"I called Joe so he could be here when I talked," I said, "*not* to get me out of talking."

"I'm glad you called," Wade said, "but I can't allow you to–"

"You can't allow me?" I felt my face go hot. "You know what? I've changed my mind. I'll talk to the cops without an attorney."

"No, you won't." He came up from behind and put a hand on each of my shoulders. "Dammit Corie, you were smart enough to ask for a lawyer, so now wise up and take my advice before somebody decides they ought to keep you overnight."

My body stiffened in frustration. "Nobody asked you to come here. I didn't need rescuing."

He turned me around and looked into my eyes. "Funny. Looked to me like you did."

His voice was soft, low-key, but it rankled. Our faces were only inches apart. We stared at each other for what felt like ten minutes before his expression softened and he said, "I love you, you know."

My knees went slightly weak, but if he thought three little words would fix everything he was wrong. I wouldn't allow myself to lean on Wade, not if he was going to end up back with Laura.

"Do you?" I said, finally.

Hurt, or was it resignation, flickered across his face. "Why won't you trust me?"

"This isn't about trust. I'm the one tripping over dead bodies lately. You come in here like some hotshot, thinking you can fix everything and the problem will disappear. Well, it's not going to disappear."

"Okay, fine." He twisted away. "You're going to be that way, be that way. I don't know what your goddamn problem is, but I'm tired of waiting around for you to talk about it."

"Then don't," I snapped. "I can take care of myself."

Wade stood still for two seconds with his back to me. Then he pounded his fist on the door jamb and left without a backward glance.

***

When the cab dropped me back at my truck, Mama Mia's restaurant was still crowded, restaurant goers not deterred by the crime scene tape strung around the spa next door. I paid the driver and climbed out, feeling the weight of Zachary's death and a terrible sadness. I'd never claim to be the bravest investigator in the world, but I did okay. Inside, I was an emotional coward. I knew it and Wade knew it. Maybe he'd stick around waiting for me to change and maybe he wouldn't. I got into my truck, exhausted and fighting tears.

I turned the ignition, my eyes trained on Serenity Spa, and forced my thoughts away from Wade. A killer had walked in and out of that building tonight and was on the loose. That really ticked me off. I might have passed the killer on the street, might have seen the bastard.

Statistics show people are often killed by someone they know, and I wondered if that was the case with Carmen and Zachary. My hands tightened on the steering wheel as I checked off a list of acquaintances they would have in common. Spa clients, co-workers, Trey, Phyllis, Nora, Jack. Damn. Even if Jack wasn't the killer he could be involved somehow. I had no choice but to throw all my resources into finding that jerk.

It was one-thirty in the morning by the time I got home to an enthusiastic greeting from Midnite. I sat with her, stroking her fur and letting her nuzzle my arms and legs with her wet nose. Nothing like a happy dog to make you feel loved and accepted. After a while, I got up and checked the answering machine. The digital read-out told me I had six messages. Maybe Wade had called.

Even though I didn't want to talk to him, I punched the play button. The first message, left at ten-ten was from Ruby, asking if I was still planning to spend the night at Mother's. She'd fixed the guest room for me. I closed my eyes. God, I'd forgotten my promise to spend the night over there. Next was Kit, letting me know she'd fed and played with Midnite, our standing arrangements for whenever I wasn't home.

Then Reba, her voice excited. "Hey, girl, I called that guy, Aaron, and we met for a drink. Ooh–he is hot with a capital H. And get this. He invited me to a shindig tomorrow afternoon at, you'll never guess, the home of Nicholas Brandt himself. I'm going undercover. Call me."

I stared at the machine. Oh, this was <u>not</u> good.

The last three messages were from Ruby at thirty minute intervals, each one sounding more concerned about where I was. She'd been my ally ever since my teenage years, and I still wanted her approval. Not only that, I'd never forgive myself if something happened to Mother because I was too self-absorbed to stay with her and keep an eye out for trouble.

I <u>had</u> to spend the night at Mother's, at least what was left of the night. With all those valuables in the house, she was a sitting burglary target. I glanced down at my wrinkled, dirty clothes, knowing my face and hair looked even worse. Taking a deep breath, I headed for the shower.

*The whole world's going crazy,*
*But that's not fazing you.*
*You only care about yourself,*
*There's nothing I can do.*

# CHAPTER 22

I woke in Mother's guest room to the muted sound of voices and laughter. I groaned and rolled over, not wanting to open my eyes and admit that it was time to get up. The events of the night before flooded back, and I massaged my temples to ward off a headache.

The conversational sounds seemed to be coming from outside. I could pick out Mother's throaty tone. I squinted at the clock and saw it was almost nine. According to the printed gala agenda, the movers weren't expected until much later to take the donated items to the country club. So why was Mother cavorting around outside, especially after what had happened next door yesterday?

I crawled from the bed and looked out the window, but only her flower gardens were visible from this room. I pulled on my jeans and T-shirt and gathered my hair into a barrette as I padded downstairs barefoot. The smell of coffee lured me to the kitchen. Ruby wasn't around, and I figured she was out for her early Saturday morning trip to Central Market. I fixed myself a mug of coffee with plenty of cream before heading through the study and out the French doors to the terrace.

I spotted Lucas Turner's Porsche parked next to my truck and did a quick backstep. Too late. Mother was waving to me from a temporary bar set up between the swimming pool and the tennis courts.

"Darling, over here."

She was too far away to see me roll my eyes or hear me mutter, "Oh, great."

Reluctantly, I headed toward the foursome dressed in fashionable tennis gear and sipping drinks. Muriel, her husband, Mother, and Mr. Movie Star. It was *way* too early in the day to deal with Lucas no matter how good he looked in tennis duds. I said good morning and steered my gaze away from him.

Mother and Muriel bombarded me with their usual gushy hellos. Muriel's husband waved from the bar where he was mixing a Mimosa. I tried to avoid Lucas but he came over and kissed my cheek, a move Mother and her friend observed with great interest.

"Dear, how nice you stayed over," Mother said. "I'm surprised. What's the occasion?"

I frowned at her. "I thought the occasion was to make sure all your expensive doo-dads stayed safe and secure until we move them to the country club. But here you all are playing tennis like you don't have a care in the world."

Mother looked at me like I'd spoken a foreign language. "The police are patrolling the neighborhood regularly, dear."

"It's a big neighborhood," I said. "What's to keep some burglar from pouncing on you in between patrols?"

"There's no need to be paranoid." Mother made a face. "You care to join us? Lucas is an excellent teacher. He could help you with your backhand."

"No, thanks. I'm not here to play." Nor was I in a playing mood. "So has the plan changed?"

"Plan?" Mother said.

"No change," Lucas said. "We're sticking to the agenda I gave you yesterday. Movers due to arrive in a couple of hours, along with some off-duty cops. Everything gets carefully packaged, then loaded up and taken to the country club. No sweat."

"Okay," I said. "I'll grab some breakfast then, before it's time to go." I turned toward the house.

"Leave the work to the movers, Corinne," Mother said. "You should join me and Muriel at the spa. We're scheduled for manicures and hair appointments before the gala, but I'm sure they could fit you in."

"Scheduled?" God, they hadn't heard.

"Yes. You know I have a standing Saturday appointment, but today I'm also having a hot oil treatment. You really should try that, dear." She reached out to stroke my hair. "Your hair looks awfully dry."

I closed my eyes for a second. "Mother, there's been another incident."

Her hand stopped moving, her fingers heavy on my scalp.

"Incident?" Muriel said.

I nodded. "At Serenity Spa. A murder."

"Oh, my Lord," Mother said. "Who?"

"Zachary."

With a cry, Muriel sank into a patio chair, hands clutched to her chest.

I filled them in on the details, leaving out my visit to the police station.

"This is insane," Mother said when I finished. "Poor Nora. How will she handle the schedule after losing two employees?"

"There is no schedule for now," I said. "The police closed down the spa."

"Why?" Mother's eyes widened. "They can't do that, can they? What about my appointment?"

"They can, and they did." I didn't try to hide my annoyance any more than Mother was hiding the fact that she cared more about her precious appointment than the deaths.

Lucas filled the awkward moment. "They have to close down the area, Olivia," he said, "to search for evidence. That's standard operating procedure. Nothing anyone can do about that."

"But–" Mother said.

"Don't panic," Lucas said. "I'll bet Nora has had the phone forwarded and is making other arrangements for those with appointments today."

Oh brother. The guy probably was a spa regular himself. I could see him having his nails buffed, his beard waxed.

Mother smiled, her relief apparent. "Yes, of course."

"Why don't we make a call?" Lucas turned to me and winked. Like he was helping me out by calming her.

I watched them go inside, thinking I might be sick. Did self-centered wealthy women grow more obnoxious as they aged? If that was the case, I might have to move out of state soon.

Muriel had joined her husband at the bar and got busy knocking back straight champagne, not paying a bit of attention to me. If these women were more concerned about missing their manicures than the possibility of being victimized, there was no point in me hanging around. I went into the kitchen, scribbled Ruby a note, and left.

By the time I arrived at my house, I'd decided that the only reason I would attend the gala tonight was to fish for leads about Jack Litchfield. Not because I expected one second of enjoyment from the evening, and not to act as Mother's private security guard. Dad would have to understand.

Kit and Midnite were out front, playing catch. I couldn't help but smile. The only way I'd ever move away from here was if I could take Kit with me.

"Sorry I seem to be gone more than I'm home." I gave the girl a hug. "Hope Midnite is behaving herself."

"She is." Kit threw the tennis ball for Midnite to fetch. "She did get upset, though, when that lady came by a while ago."

"Lady?" My heart rate jumped. "What lady? Not the one who was here the other night."

"No, no, no." Kit laughed. "Not her. This was a regular lady, came up and knocked on your door. Midnite and I were playing with my friend Hannah and her new puppy."

Midnite ran to me and dropped the ball at my feet. I picked it up and threw, then wiped a slimy hand on my jeans. "A regular lady, huh? What was she driving?"

"Some white car."

"Was she selling something?"

Kit shook her head. "I don't think so. She didn't say."

"Did she leave a card or anything?"

"Nope. Said she'd see you some other time."

"What'd she look like?"

Kit shrugged. "Snooty."

Now it was my turn to laugh.

Kit intercepted Midnite, took the ball and ran around me, giggling and dodging Midnite like a running back dodging a defensive end.

"Describe snooty." I grabbed the girl's arm so she'd hold still.

"Dressed up in this outfit probably costs like a thousand dollars. Fake blonde hair, and with these perfect red toenails." Kit made a face.

"Kind of like my Mother?"

"Not quite that bad," she said.

We enjoyed the joke, and I was about to invite Kit to join me for a late breakfast when the front door at her house banged open, and her mother yelled that it was time to get ready for a birthday party. Kit gave Midnite a hug, told us goodbye, and headed across the lawn.

I hurried inside, her party reminding me that I needed to talk Reba out of whatever scheme she'd come up with for the shindig at Brandt's this afternoon. The phone rang before I made it that far. It was George Doyle.

"I can't take this any more," he said.

Here we go again. "What's the matter, George?"

"Somebody's got to do something about that disrespectful little jackass."

Trey. I blew out a breath. "Why? What's he doing?"

"Carting Carmen's things to the curb. Throwing them on a heap like they're garbage."

"What kind of things?"

"Clothes, linens, books, you name it. Punk's got no respect."

"Maybe he's tossing items ruined during the break-in," I said.

"No. There's a mountain out there. You should see. He's throwing away everything."

I wasn't sure what he expected me to do.

"Where's his father?" I said.

"Went to the funeral home." The words choked out like he was holding back tears. "To make arrangements."

I knew how George had felt about Carmen, and I could imagine that watching Trey throw away her belongings was working him into a frenzy.

"Maybe they called Goodwill to come pick up the stuff," I suggested.

"They didn't. Punk told me as much. I tried talking to him, but he went ballistic. Told me all of Carmen's stuff was crap. Came at me like a hoodlum."

"Are you okay?" After the episode with Ruben, I was surprised George had approached Trey. "I think you'd better stay in the house."

"I *am* in the house," he said. "But not for long. Saturday trash pickup is usually before noon. And if that's not bad enough, now he's messing with her car. He's out there with tools and a roll of wire doing God knows what. Already put a decal on the back window. Says H-O-T. I'll show that worthless little punk hot."

"For God's sake, George, stay in the house."

"I'm telling you, I won't stand by and watch."

I rolled my eyes. "Please. Stay inside until I get there."

I hung up the phone, wondering how and why I had become George Doyle's personal crisis hotline.

*Boys will be boys,*
*They'll fight over toys.*
*And when they can't agree,*
*They always run to me.*

# CHAPTER 23

I spent the drive over to Carmen's house asking myself why I didn't simply tell George Doyle to handle his own problems. The situation was a private matter, one that shouldn't concern me. But the old man had grown on me, and I didn't want to hear later that he'd been beaten to a pulp by Trey Salinas. Or worse.

The first thing I noticed when I turned onto Carmen's street was that George hadn't exaggerated. A huge mound of clothes, shoes, pillows, wicker baskets, and general household bric-a-brac sat by the curb. Any minute, the Saturday morning garage-salers would sniff out the stash and start picking through the pile.

I pulled into the driveway behind a black BMW. All four doors and the trunk stood open, and long, jean-clad legs I assumed belonged to Trey stuck out the right rear door. On the other side of the car, a couple of open cardboard boxes labeled Sony were stacked next to a black plastic garbage can. I wondered if someone had told the kid he could commandeer the car or if he'd made the decision on his own.

At the sound of my truck door slamming, Trey climbed out of the car holding a pair of pliers. He scowled and wiped his free hand on his faded Smashing Pumpkins T-shirt. Before he could say anything, a loud thump drew our attention, and we turned in unison.

George emerged from his garage, barreling down the driveway with a large green wheelbarrow. He veered off the concrete and bumped across the grass, coming to a stop near the car. I saw that he'd lined the wheelbarrow with a pale blue bed sheet, and a Louisville Slugger baseball bat rested on top.

"What the hell?" Trey said.

"I told you." George directed his words to me. "See what I told you?"

"Stay away from me, old man." Trey came around the car. "I warned you."

"When you start acting like a human being, maybe I'll start paying attention to what you say," George said. "Until then, trash is free for the taking." He grabbed the wheelbarrow handles.

Trey rounded the car and lunged at George, shouting, "Mind your own business."

Moving at a speed I wouldn't have thought possible, George snatched up the Slugger. He gripped the bat like he was itching to hit one out of the park.

"George, don't." I jumped between the two and held my arms out like a traffic cop. "Calm down right now. Both of you."

"Go ahead, you old fart," Trey yelled. "Hit me. Just try it."

"Don't tempt me." George raised the bat.

Trey stepped closer, daring him. "You don't get it, do you? The old lady didn't give a crap about you or anybody else."

"That's not true." George's eyes blazed.

"This is insane." In one quick motion, I reached out and grabbed the bat.

George tried to wrench it away, but I held firm. "Let it go, George."

Our eyes met. He reluctantly loosened his grip, and I took the weapon from him. "I know everyone's upset about Carmen, but this isn't helping."

"He's not upset," George said. "Anyone who cared about Carmen wouldn't throw away her things." He walked over to the garbage can. "I saw you tossing CDs in here." He bent over the can and came up with a handful of loose papers and CD cases, glaring at Trey with wet eyes. "She loved this music."

"Well she's dead now," Trey said, "and who wants to listen to that shit?"

I expected George to react, and he did, but not like I thought he would. Tears ran down the creases in his cheeks like rainwater flowing down mountain crevices. After a moment, he turned and placed the things he'd been holding into his wheelbarrow. Then he continued rifling through the garbage can, finding more items to rescue.

I turned to Trey. "I think you should apologize to Mr. Doyle. Just because you don't care about your aunt doesn't give you an excuse to stomp on other people's feelings."

"I don't give a damn about the old lady, you're right about that. She didn't give a damn about me either. Serves her right, getting killed." His lower lip jutted the way a little boy's would when he didn't get his way.

George wasn't paying attention to Trey now, more concerned with retrieving his Carmen memorabilia, but I felt like slugging the kid with his bat. Instead I said, "You have one huge chip on your shoulder."

"So would you." He turned away and went around the car. He bent over to pick up the wire he'd been working with.

I followed him. "Why is that?"

"There's a lot you don't know."

"So tell me."

Dark bangs fell over one eye as he looked down at the ground and chewed on his lower lip.

"Trey, did you kill Carmen?"

His head jerked up. "No way."

"Then I wish you'd explain what the problem is. You're acting guilty."

"I'm not," he said, raising his voice. "She hated me, but I would never do something like that."

"Doesn't look like there was any love lost on your part either," I said. "So what was up between you two. She do something to provoke you to murder?"

"I didn't kill her," he said, his voice cracking. "I would never have hurt her. She was my mother."

I stood there, dumbstruck. "What did you say?"

"Duh," he said. "She wasn't my aunt, she was my goddamn mother and she didn't want me. Left me with her brother week after I was born and never came back."

"I'm sorry," I said after a second.

"Who cares? She didn't give me a thing while she was alive, not even the truth. At least I got the car." He pulled on the wire and knelt on the back floorboard. "Now you know, so leave me alone. I got work to do."

I turned around and almost bumped into George who'd come up behind me, his eyes wide.

I guided the man away from Trey, over to his wheelbarrow. "Did you have any idea?"

"None."

"So at least we know where the hostility is coming from. Not that it's any excuse."

"Why should we believe him?" George said. "Carmen never said a word about having a child. He could have made the whole story up."

"He could have, but it makes sense." I glanced back at the car. "Maybe he came here hoping she'd acknowledge him but she didn't. That would be rough."

"I guess so." George looked skeptical, like he didn't want to believe his friend Carmen would keep such a secret.

"I don't think he'll stop you now if you want to keep some of her things. You need some help?" I picked up a B. B. King CD. "Carmen liked blues?"

George nodded with a wan smile. "B. B. was her favorite."

I looked at the crumpled papers in the wheelbarrow and retrieved a yellow lined tablet page, studying a list written in blue ink. The first few lines read "Evans Virgin Islands second weekend; Cook opera 13th; Strickland D.C. til 20th." The list filled the whole page and half of the back. Some of the lines were marked with an asterisk. I picked up more of the papers and found copies of a March and April calendar stuck between advertising circulars and unopened junk mail. Several dates were circled. Notations had been made on many of the days, but I had no idea what things like JS-V or GC-O meant.

George peered over my shoulder. "What's that?"

"I don't know." I held up the page. "Have any idea what these initials mean?"

He swiped at his damp eyes and reached for the yellow page. "This is Carmen's handwriting, but not on the calendar."

My mind flashed back to the call from Zachary. What exactly had he said? I squeezed my eyes shut, remembering. Some in Carmen's handwriting, he'd told me. Pages of them. And a calendar.

I opened my eyes and went to the garbage can. There was more yellow near the bottom. Without a second thought, I turned the can upside down and dumped the contents on the driveway. I fell to my knees to pick through tin cans, wadded-up fast food sacks, and junk mail. I snatched up more pages that smelled like leftover French fries.

"What's the matter?" George hovered over me.

"I can't be sure, but these papers might have something to do with why Carmen was killed." I sat back and scanned the pages. Nothing made any more sense than the first page had. I looked up to see Trey watching.

"Now what the hell?" he said.

I waved the sheets at him. "Where did you find these?"

"I don't know," he said in a who-the-hell-cares tone.

I jumped to my feet. "Lose the attitude, Trey. This is extremely important. Where did they come from?"

"In there." He pointed at the trunk. "I took out the carpet to wire my speakers."

"Where? Show me exactly where they were."

He rolled his eyes but walked over to the trunk, lifted the fitted carpet, and pointed. "They were stuffed in here, next to the spare. Figured it had to be trash. I mean, who keeps important papers in their trunk?"

Someone who doesn't want them discovered, I thought. Someone who knows the pages are important enough to kill for.

*Goin' to a party,*
*Though they didn't invite me.*
*They'll never know I'm there,*
*If they did, I wouldn't care.*

# CHAPTER 24

I scanned Carmen's notes hurriedly, but nothing made sense and Trey's scowling didn't help.

"Mind if I keep these?" I said.

"What do I care? Take all her crap if you want."

I turned away from the kid, folded the pages, and put them in my pocket. I tossed garbage back into the can, uncrumpling pages and inspecting everything to make sure there were no more puzzle pieces. The documents would have to be turned over to the police, no doubt about that, but not before I had a chance to make copies. Maybe by some miracle I could figure out what they meant.

George had walked to the curb where he retrieved articles of Carmen's clothes, holding them with reverence like they were garments worn by some star in a famous movie. I hated to see the poor man grieving all by himself, but with everything else going on sitting with him was out of the question. I forced myself to look away, threw the remaining trash into the can, and went back to the wheelbarrow.

I thumbed through the papers in there and tossed pieces one at a time before coming to an envelope with the return address "Store-'N-Stuff." On first glance, it appeared to be junk mail advertising with the storage facility logo in the corner. The envelope bore a regular postage stamp and a four-day-old postmark. Everyone in Houston might have received a similar envelope from Nicholas Brandt's company, but maybe not.

I looked over my shoulder to be sure Trey and George weren't watching, then ripped the envelope open. A sheet of Store-'N-Stuff letterhead was folded around a company check made payable to Carmen Messina in the amount of five hundred dollars. There was no typed letter, only a brief handwritten note scrawled across the page.

"Ms. Messina–I like opportunists. Help me and there's more where this came from. Nick."

My arms dropped to my sides. What in God's name did that mean? George was approaching me with a pile of clothing draped over one arm, so I stuffed the check and envelope into my other pocket.

"I'm going to contact the woman's shelter," he said. "They'll make sure the clothes go to someone who needs them. Carmen would want that."

From what I'd heard about Carmen in the past few days, I couldn't imagine her giving a flip where her clothes ended up, but I hadn't really known the woman.

"Great idea, George." I smiled, trying to make him feel appreciated. "I'd like to help you clean up, but I need to get going. Mind if I use your phone?"

He didn't and I dashed into the kitchen to call Reba. I dialed her home number and drummed my fingers on the counter until her machine picked up. I disconnected and stabbed in her cell number.

"Girl, you drop off the face of the earth or what?" she said when she heard my voice.

"Wish I could sometimes," I said. "Listen, what's the deal with Brandt today?"

"Barbeque starts in a half hour," she said. "I'm with Aaron now."

"Damn, Reba. Is Aaron right there with you?"

"No. We're at the Shell station. He stopped for cigarettes and to fill up his Corvette. You oughta see this ride. It's the finest–"

"Reba, hush. I don't think you should go nosing around over there. It might be dangerous." I told her quickly about Brandt's check to Carmen.

"Don't worry about me."

"I'm already worried. Why is Brandt having this barbeque anyway?"

"It's like a company picnic." She lowered her voice. "Hey, he's on his way back to the car. What's with the questions?"

"I'm coming over there," I said.

"I don't think you oughta do that. What if somebody

recognizes you?"

"They won't."

George had entered the kitchen with a handful of floral-patterned clothes. I watched as he lovingly placed them on his kitchen table, then set down a pair of hot pink strappy sandals that he'd hooked over a finger.

"But they might," Reba said. "What about Brandt's girlfriend, that bridal consultant? She'll recognize you for sure even if the bodyguards don't."

"Trust me." I eyeballed the sandals, trying to decide how close Carmen's shoe size was to my own.

***

Thirty minutes later, I sat in my truck near the end of Del Monte Drive in River Oaks and watched as guests arrived for Nicholas Brandt's barbeque. Judging by the number of cars already lining the street this was no small affair, so I could probably blend in without being spotted instantly. The host hadn't sprung for valet service, to my advantage. I could park on the street and, if things didn't work out, make a quick getaway.

I was nervous about going inside, but I couldn't ask for a better opportunity to learn more about Brandt's connection with Carmen, Jack Litchfield, and Mark Gentry, the private eye. I checked my rearview mirror one more time, grateful for the bright sun that allowed me the benefit of sunglasses. With my naturally big hair contained in a tight braid and uncharacteristic rosy red lipstick, I could barely recognize myself. I topped off the look with a narrow brimmed straw hat and climbed out of my truck, feeling ridiculous in Carmen's hot-pink sandals and orange-and-pink flowery tunic. My jeans didn't exactly complete the ensemble, but Carmen had been a head shorter than me and I couldn't fit into any of the woman's slacks.

As I neared the two-story Colonial home, the air was heavy with the scent of beef brisket cooking over mesquite. I walked up the drive toward a gray Carrera parked nose out with a vanity plate that read BOSS 01. Ahead of me, two nicely-muscled construction worker types in jeans and T-shirts struggled with a monstrous cooler. Instead of heading for the front door, they veered onto a stone path to the left of the house. I hurried after them.

A black wrought iron fence surrounded the back yard.

I jogged as best I could in the high-heeled sandals to get ahead of the men before they reached the gate.

"Let me help." I reached for the latch and flashed my best smile. "You've got quite a load there."

The heftier of the two gave me a once-over and grinned. "Shiner Bock. Bartles & James for the ladies." He wiggled his eyebrows.

"Sounds great. I'll stick with y'all." I wanted to keep up the conversation for an I'm-with-them appearance. As we passed through the gate, music and the buzz of voices up ahead grew louder.

"This is such a nice idea, getting everyone together," I said.

"You must be new," said the second guy. "Nick throws a party couple times a year."

"Yeah." I hoped he wouldn't question me further.

"I'm Josh," said the first guy, as we rounded the house and the backyard came into view. "Josh Wessels. This is Ted Gentry."

Gentry.

I smiled at Ted. "Nice to meet you. Any relation to Mark?"

"Yeah. Brother."

A man of few words.

They passed me, no doubt eager to park their cooler, and I scanned the back yard. Dozens of people milled around a rectangular swimming pool–drinking, eating, chatting. No sign of the other Gentry. No bodyguards. No Madge, but then wedding planners probably worked Saturdays. No one appeared to pay the least bit of attention to us as we approached a flagstone patio.

A gigantic black barbeque pit stood under a live oak tree, smoke billowing from it like a three-alarm fire. Nearby, men sat around a table, enjoying cigars over a poker game. A Ricky Martin number blared from speakers affixed under the patio eaves. The guests–many in blue jeans and boots, a few cowboy hats–looked more like Robert Earl Keen fans, but what did I know?

The guys parked their cooler under a banquet-sized table laden with picnic foods and opened the lid. I accepted a wine cooler from Josh, twisted off the cap, and turned to Ted, trying to appear casual. "So, is your brother here?"

"He don't work for the company." Ted popped the top on a beer, giving me the eye. "How d'ya know Mark?"

"Friend of a friend." I turned to Josh and changed the subject. "Wonder where Nick is. You see him?" I had no idea what Brandt looked like.

"Never far from the pit," Josh said. "Man loves to cook. Me, I prefer eating." He patted his stomach.

"Me, too. I'm starved." I edged down the buffet table, picking at potato chips, putting distance between myself and the two men. A lively Gloria Estafan number was next and three of the female guests hooked arms over each other's shoulders and screeched along.

Yeesh. They sounded bad.

I worked my way down the table for a better view of the barbeque pit which was across the pool from me. I picked up a deviled egg. A fifty-ish man with an unmistakable air of authority stood next to the pit, industrial-sized tongs in hand. He wore his dark hair combed straight back exposing a high forehead creased with worry lines.

"That's him."

I jumped at the sound of Reba's voice behind me and dropped my egg.

"Jeez, you trying to give me a heart attack?" I glanced around to make sure nobody was paying attention to us. They weren't. The singers had begun flashing some skin, so all male eyes were trained in their direction. I grabbed a napkin and knelt to clean up the mess. Reba stooped beside me.

She eyed my clothes, which for once were more flamboyant than hers. "Quite the get-up."

"Surprised you recognized me."

"What are those? Peonies?"

I looked down at the flowered print of Carmen's blouse. "How would I know? Anything interesting here?"

"Not yet," she whispered. "Aaron introduced me to Brandt. Guy's not very talkative. Never smiles. Haven't found anybody who knows Litchfield, Carmen, or that PI."

I stared at her. "I hope you're not going around blurting out names."

"Of course not. I only talked to a couple of women. Just casual conversation."

"I'm sure." I scooped up the egg remains and stood.

Reba straightened, pouting. "Give me some credit."

"I'll try. Been in the house?"

"Far as the powder room." She picked up a carrot stick and crunched off a bite. "It's quiet inside."

"Sounds nice. Peaceful. Compared to them." I rolled my eyes toward the women who had upped their volume.

"You could teach them a thing or two about singing."

"Not today." I made a face. "I'm going in. Please try to be discreet."

"That's my middle name."

"Uh-huh."

I entered the house and dropped my sunglasses into the pocket of my blouse, unsure of my next move. A man's office was always a good place to start snooping. Surely someone of Brandt's stature, business owner and all, had a home office. I checked out the kitchen first, where remains of food preparation littered the counter top. Nobody in there. I moved through the dining room and across the wide entry hall.

The formal living room was decorated in dark purples and blacks with tall, spiky, potted plants near each window. A harsh abstract painting hanging behind the purple tweed sofa contrasted with soft-looking photographs of an attractive young woman lining the mantel. No magazines or books in this room to tell me more about the homeowner. I peered into the foyer and waited, listening, for any sign that I was not alone in the house. Silence.

I removed my sandals and looped the straps over my wrist, then took the carpet-covered stairs two at a time. The upstairs landing was an eight-by-twenty gallery featuring pictures of the same young woman I'd seen in the photos downstairs–everything from her as a young child on a pony to a teenage photo taken at some sort of pageant. My parents had some photos of me around their house, but this was extreme.

About ten feet to either side, a hallway branched off toward the back of the property like the house had his-and-her wings. I turned right and stopped when I heard voices. Carefully, I peered around the corner. Yikes. I pulled back. It was them–the bodyguards–posed like sentries on either side of a door near the end of the hall. I couldn't see any weapons from where I stood, but they were definitely the same two guys. If that was Brandt's office they were guarding, I'd probably made this trip for nothing.

I backed up a few steps and tried to calm my breathing.

I should go back downstairs and get while the getting was good. But I wasn't ready to assume those guys were watching the office. I crossed the landing and peered down the opposite corridor. Deserted.

Three doors opened off of this wing. I tiptoed past the first, a nondescript bedroom, and the second, a work-out room. The last room, nearest the rear of the house, was an office.

So what *were* those men guarding? That's what I wanted to know, yet I wasn't about to approach them. Since I'd found an office, may as well check it out.

Looking over my shoulder to make sure I was still alone, I stepped into the room and silently closed the door behind me. Sunshine streamed through French doors that opened onto a balcony, so I wouldn't need to turn on lights. Framed movie posters decorated the walls–The Deer Hunter, Born on the Fourth of July, Leaving Las Vegas. Depressing choices if you ask me. A tall black leather couch faced a large-screen TV surrounded by built-in shelves holding hundreds of videotapes and DVDs.

Papers were strewn haphazardly across the desk top. Newspapers, blueprints, invoices, phone messages. A framed photograph of the same young woman stood next to the telephone. A laptop computer sat on a separate table, but it was turned off, the top snapped shut. Probably didn't have much time to use the computer if he watched tons of movies. I picked up a pencil and used the eraser end to move papers around, looking for something of interest.

No familiar names on the pink phone message slips. No convenient jotted notes explaining why Nicholas Brandt would have paid money to Carmen Messina.

Disappointed, I stuck the pencil through the center drawer pull and yanked it open. Yeesh. The drawer was stuffed with junk–a catch-all for everything from matchbooks to extra shoelaces. I tried the top side drawer. This one was full, too, but with a checkbook on top. One of those large styles, three checks per page.

I flipped open the cover and turned the stubs back to the record of the most recent checks written. There was the one to Carmen dated last Monday. One to Mark Gentry for two thousand dollars ten days ago. So Brandt had hired Gentry. But why?

A rattling noise sounded behind me. I jerked upright

and pushed the desk drawer in. One of the French doors opened, and a young woman darted inside, a navy blue duffel bag slung over a shoulder. She spun around, eyes wide, mouth open in surprise.

"Who are you?" she said in a low voice.

I ran my tongue over dry lips, realizing this was the young woman from the photographs, probably Brandt's daughter. She wore a loose-fitting pink knit sundress with bulky tennis shoes. Odd combination, but the girl was so stunning nobody would care what she wore. She had brilliant blue eyes and an alabaster complexion framed by silky black hair.

"I was at the party," I said. "Needed to borrow a phone."

She stared at my sandals, then her gaze shifted to my bare feet.

"These things are killers." I lifted a leg and rubbed my foot.

"Help yourself to the phone," she said in a see-if-I-care tone. "Just don't let Hitler find you in his inner sanctum." She tiptoed over to the shelves next to the TV, slid out a stack of DVDs, and reached into the opening.

"You live here?" I said.

"Yeah. Lucky me." She pulled out a cigar box and flipped up the lid. She peered into the box like she was trying to decide between smoking a Churchill or a Corona. Then she reached inside and came up with a key.

She put everything back the way she'd found it and moved toward the door I'd come in through. She didn't seem surprised that the door was closed, but she did turn around as she reached for the doorknob. "Hey, you didn't see me."

"See who?" I said.

She smiled and left the room.

What was that all about? I went to the French doors and looked out. The balcony ran the length of the house, the door to this room one of two opening onto it. Oak tree foliage partially shielded the partiers from my view and vice versa. There were no stairs from the balcony to the ground, so the girl must have come from that other room. I hurried to the door and opened it.

A bedroom–this one decorated with a distinctly feminine hand in shades of lavender and green. Clothes were thrown across the bed, so many that no one would be able to sleep there until they were cleared away. A television set was turned on, playing a DVD movie–the shopping spree scene from *Pretty Woman*–at a volume louder than I would choose.

I glanced at the other door into the room and noticed the lock button was depressed. I envisioned the house's layout, betting those bodyguards were standing right outside that door. My heart rate sped up at the thought, but I told myself they'd never hear me over the TV and I wouldn't stay long.

A computer desk was built into the corner, the computer's monitor displaying a screen saver of the Eiffel Tower. I crossed the room. When I touched the mouse, the Microsoft Word screen appeared with a message displayed in extra-large font: "I CAN'T TAKE ANY MORE–REGINA."

What did that mean exactly?

I switched to another open program and photographs filled the screen. Some of the young woman I'd just met in passing, Regina I supposed, with other women her age, a few pictures of children, one of a kid holding a gray cat. I hit the down arrow a few times, scanning pictures. I froze when a familiar face stared out at me. I right-clicked on the picture to enlarge it.

Why would this young woman have a picture of Jack Litchfield on her computer? He could be a friend's dad, I supposed. Jack and Nora didn't have children, but maybe he had a kid from a previous marriage. Or maybe he was related to the Brandts somehow. Nora had never discussed the family tree with me. I went to the next page, then the next, and found a photo of the two of them together. Regina and Jack sitting at a table in some restaurant. He had his arm around her, not in a fatherly way, and a big smile on his smarmy face.

*Well, well, Jack. You do show up at the strangest places.*

I went back to Word and checked her documents list. Nothing except what appeared to be school assignments and a couple of letters to colleges. I switched to the internet screen, but Regina wasn't logged on. I checked the desk drawers, empty except for some jewelry boxes, makeup, and a ream of printer paper.

I pulled the wastebasket out from under the desk's knee hole and rifled through trash for the second time this afternoon, smoothing out some crumpled pages. Nothing exciting. Then I noticed a piece of paper that had fallen behind the wastebasket and crawled under the desk to reach it. The page was empty except for "Continental Airlines–Flight Search Results" and "Page 7 of 7" across the top, www.continental.com and today's date at the bottom.

Damn. I pictured the duffel bag slung over Regina's shoulder, then the message on the computer screen.

*I can't take any more.*

So she turns up the movie volume, packs a bag, and takes off.

I left the bedroom the way I'd come, then dashed across the balcony, through the office, and down the front stairs. I practically flew out the front door. Nicholas Brandt was busy entertaining guests. If Regina wanted to leave unnoticed, today might be a good day to do so. I ran across the front lawn and looked up and down the street.

All quiet out here. So where did she go?

A car engine started up. Revved.

I turned around in time to see Regina behind the wheel of the Carrera. The car zoomed out from under the porte cachere. She steered onto the lawn to go around cars parked in the driveway and bumped through a flower bed before turning back onto the drive. After the barest hesitation, she hung a right on the street, and peeled out.

Damn. Now what?

Let her go. Turn around.

Forget what you saw. Act like nothing happened.

Run to the back yard screaming "she's getting away."

Follow her.

The decision wasn't even close. I ran toward my truck, asphalt biting into my bare feet.

*She was on the road that day*
*Just a little past two.*
*She was runnin' away,*
*What's a girl to do?*

# CHAPTER 25

I caught up with the Carrera on San Felipe, headed toward the 610 Loop. Common sense told me that a young woman like Regina could have a dozen places to go on a Saturday afternoon–to work out at the local health club, shopping at Uptown Park, or to meet a friend for a late lunch. But why all the secrecy?

When we reached the Loop, she took a right onto the feeder and then immediately entered the freeway. I stayed several car lengths behind, not that she would have noticed me even if I were glued to her bumper. The girl changed lanes constantly, speeding whenever traffic allowed, then slamming on her brakes when it slowed. The moment she turned north on I-45, I knew we were headed for the airport.

When Dierks Bentley's peppy tune "What Was I Thinkin'?" came on the radio I turned up the volume. He had a point. What *was* I thinking? This trip wasn't on today's agenda. The drive-time to the airport alone, round trip, would eat up more than two hours. I had to deal with the Denim & Diamonds Gala tonight, much as I dreaded attending. But more than anything I wanted to prove to bitchy Nora that I *could* find her slimy husband, that I did *not* create more problems than answers. Not to mention proving to Wade that I could get to the bottom of his client's predicament without any help from him.

Regina had some connection to Jack Litchfield, and it wasn't like I had a ton of other leads. It bugged me how she was the second woman associated with Jack who seemed to be running away. Since I couldn't find Phyllis Keene, I wasn't about to let Regina out of my sight. The fact that I was witness

to this clandestine trip of hers might give me the upper hand
if I confronted her. Not to mention we'd left the bodyguards
behind, a definite plus for me.

Once I convinced myself that following her was
worthwhile, I began to think ahead. Sticking close to Regina
wasn't a big problem on the road, but things might get dicey
once we reached the airport. So while I endured the freeway
crawl, I threw Carmen's sandals in the back and pulled on my
running shoes. Shed her blouse in favor of my gray v-neck
underneath. I fished my tri-fold wallet out of my bulky purse
and stuffed it into a pocket.

Much better. Ready to roll.

When we finally reached JFK Boulevard, Regina
bypassed the park-and-ride lots and I breathed a sigh of relief.
I'd have had a hard time escaping notice seated across from
her on one of those shuttles. She opted for the terminal garage,
and I slowed down to leave some ground between us before
turning in after her.

Regina found a spot in the first row we came to on the
second level, but I wasn't so lucky. She was already out of the
Carrera when I drove by, and I cruised down several rows
before catching a break. I climbed out of my truck and hoisted
myself up on the running board to scan the garage, catching a
glimpse of pink inside the elevator before the doors closed.

No way was I going to lose her now.

I dashed across the garage and took the stairs. At street
level, Regina was in the flow of pedestrians moving briskly
through the terminal entrance. I made a death-defying run
across the road and burst through the doors. Then I stopped
short, huffing like a geriatric marathon runner.

Jeez. Spotting Regina in this mass of humanity was
about as likely as finding a lost contact lens on the beach. My
gaze skimmed the crowd, searching for her pink dress. To my
left, people lined up to use the e-ticket computers. To the
right, passengers inched along in lines, waiting to check their
luggage.

No Regina.

I skirted a group of chattering teenage girls and
sidestepped suitcases to check out those passengers who'd
finally rid themselves of their luggage to move on to the
security checkpoint. The zigzagging line reminded me of
lengthy amusement park waits, except at the end of this one

you only earned the right to have your bags and shoes x-rayed. Which is what Regina was doing right now.

I spotted her placing her duffel bag and tennis shoes on the conveyor belt. A stern-faced guard keeping watch on the area looked me over, and I realized I wasn't going any further without producing my own ticket.

Damn.

I hurried to the ticket counter and pulled out my credit card. I waited impatiently, standing on tiptoes to keep an eye on Regina. She retrieved her bag, bent to put her shoes back on, then moved purposefully ahead and turned toward the gates to her left.

Double damn.

It took me a good ten minutes to buy a ticket to Dallas and make it through the security line. Then I raced down the concourse to find Regina, slowing at gift shops and eateries to scan the customers inside.

Every gate was filled to capacity with people, either lounging in the chairs or tripping over each other in their race to line up for boarding. I made a dozen false starts toward young women in pink, which I decided must be the hot color this season.

As I moved from gate to gate, my mind raced. Where the hell was she? Had she already boarded? No. Not enough time. Ladies' room up ahead. She could be in there. Rest room or gates? Gates first.

A few yards past the restroom, a man in a yellow T-shirt stood in a gift shop doorway talking on a cell phone. His back was to me, but something about the guy seemed familiar–the build, the tanned arms. I slowed down. He turned slightly, and I caught his profile.

Mark Gentry.

My pulse, already racing, picked up a notch. I backstepped and ducked into the ladies' room alcove, then edged forward to take another look. Gentry snapped his phone shut but didn't make any move to leave the shop. He picked up a Houston Rockets mug, but I didn't think he was interested in souvenirs. I followed his gaze to a gate located diagonally across the concourse.

From where I stood, I couldn't read the destination sign, but Regina paced next to the row of seats, checking her watch, scanning the crowd.

I looked from her to Gentry. What the heck was going on here?

I watched them, shifting position to allow a mother with a baby carrier and a toddler in tow to enter the restroom. I mulled over the possibility that Gentry's being here was a huge coincidence. Not a chance. And he wasn't after me this time, since I hadn't even known I'd be coming to the airport today. He was watching Regina, same as me.

I kept one eye on him, one on the girl, though at this point Gentry's reason for being here interested me almost as much as Regina's. I considered a direct approach. Tap him on the shoulder and ask him what he was up to. There'd be no danger in asking. The man didn't have a weapon or he wouldn't have gotten this far. Not that he could have concealed one in those snug jeans.

Regina stopped pacing abruptly, and I could tell she'd picked out Gentry. He grabbed a book off a shelf and turned his back, but too late. He'd been made. The girl marched toward him, her mouth set and her cheeks reddening.

I flattened myself against the tiled wall and had no trouble hearing Regina from where I stood.

"What are you doing here?" she yelled. "I told you to leave me alone."

"I don't work for you," Gentry said.

"Don't you dare tell my father I'm here. This is _my_ life."

"I can't let you leave with him," Gentry said.

Was he talking about Jack?

While a boarding announcement drowned out their conversation, I theorized that Regina and Jack had planned a trip, despite her father's disapproval. So where the heck was Jack?

When the loudspeaker clicked off all I could hear was a baby crying inside the ladies' room. I leaned forward to peer around the corner and saw Regina stomping in my direction, Gentry on her heels.

I jumped back, heart thumping. She was coming in here. I retreated to the first sink and stuck my hands under the automatic faucet. The woman with the baby was finishing up a diaper change as her little boy darted around the legs of an older woman a few sinks down from me.

I watched the door. No Regina yet.

"Caleb, come over here right now," the mother said, but her son wasn't listening. He had stopped running and stood staring up at the other woman.

I couldn't blame the kid. She was a sight with godawful thick makeup, garish shoulder-length red hair, and a prominent Adam's apple that made me reach up to feel the size of mine. The woman looked at her ticket, then stuffed it in the pocket of her paisley jacket.

Seemingly uncomfortable under the kid's scrutiny, she snatched her carry-on and stepped around him to head for the door. I was right behind her, determined to try the direct approach with Gentry and Regina. My gaze drifted past the woman's knee-length skirt to her bird legs and black lace-up flats.

I stared as she hurried to the exit. Wait a minute. I knew those legs.

"Jack," I yelled.

He glanced over his shoulder and made a face. "Aw, Jesus, not you again. I'm not talking to you."

I grabbed for his arm but he bolted, taking a left out of the restroom. Gentry and Regina seemed momentarily dumbstruck as they watched Jack run away from the gates. I charged after him.

Jack hiked up the skirt so he could run faster. We raced down the passageway, dodging passengers who stared after us. For all the claims of beefed-up airport security, I didn't see any officials around.

Jack moved surprisingly fast, like all the jogging he'd done over the years had been training for this day. He disappeared down the escalator to baggage claim. I hadn't noticed Gentry pounding up behind me, but we hit the escalator in tandem. I barged ahead and grasped the rails tightly to keep him behind me as I ran down the moving steps.

"Hands off, Gentry," I yelled over my shoulder. "He's mine."

"No way." He didn't sound surprised that I knew his name.

"Whatever your stake is," I said, "mine's bigger."

"Don't count on it."

We reached the bottom of the escalator, and Gentry hung a left. I frantically scanned the baggage carousel area. The crowd was even thicker down here. No redheads in sight.

A woman screamed, and I saw her mountain of luggage toppling from a wheeled cart. A hefty security guard barreling through the crowd was waylaid by falling luggage, but I spotted the guard's target–a man pushing people aside as he raced toward the ground transportation exit.

Jack.

He had lost the wig, and if he got out that door I would lose him. I took off. Jack seemed to put on an extra burst of speed as I chased him, and he was closing in on the exit. Then Gentry rounded the corner, and Jack put on the brakes.

He pivoted and ran toward me. I braced myself, ready to make a tackle. Jack spotted me and veered off, skirting people who surrounded a rotating baggage carousel. I looked for the security guard, hoping for some help, but he had stopped running. I craned to see why and saw another guard had joined him. The second guy had Mark Gentry by the arm.

No time to gloat. Jack was darting along the back wall where unclaimed luggage stood behind a chain-link enclosure. I guessed he was making for the opposite exit this time, so I circled an empty carousel to cut him off.

Jack cast worried glances over his shoulder and seemed to have lost track of me. I came up on a row of unclaimed suitcases sitting outside the enclosure. On impulse, I grabbed one and flung it into his path. His foot smacked into the luggage, but he caught his balance and leapt onto the carousel, running on the unmoving conveyor belt like a racehorse around a track.

I blocked out the cries of alarmed passengers and focused on Jack. I ran around the carousel's perimeter and finally came within an arm's length of him. I stretched and grabbed a handful of his skirt, then with one final umph yanked him off balance. We both went down and my ribs slammed painfully into the carousel's rim. Jack hit the conveyor belt butt first and fell back, one leg twisted awkwardly beneath him.

Groaning, I crawled up beside him and placed a hand on his shoulder.

"Going somewhere, Jack?" I said, panting.

His complexion had turned one shade pinker than the blusher he wore. "Get off. Let me go."

"No way."

He put on his best pitiful expression. I spotted the security guys, with Gentry in tow, heading for us. Jack probably couldn't see past the people who had gathered around, drawn to the scuffle like flies to road kill.

"You have to let me go," Jack moaned. "He's gonna kill me."

"I doubt Nora could be so lucky."

"What are you talking about?"

I leaned closer. No need for everyone to hear the Litchfields' private business. "Save her the trouble of divorcing your sorry butt."

"She can have her damn divorce." Jack grimaced and struggled to straighten his leg. "I'll sign papers. Whatever. Just let me go."

"I'll be sure to tell her. But you're not leaving with all the money."

"All what money?" He stopped moving.

"Can it, Jack. Don't pretend you didn't steal the money."

"She says I'm stealing? That's classic." Jack snorted. "What a bitch."

"Did Carmen know you took the money?" I said.

"What?"

I lowered my voice. "Did you kill Carmen so she wouldn't tell Nora what you're up to?"

"You're out of your mind. I didn't do anything to Carmen. And if Nora has a problem with the little bit of money in my possession she can kiss my–"

"Two million is a pretty good hunk of change," I interrupted.

"Two million?" With a burst of adrenaline, Jack sat up. "Nora would never let me get my hands on that kind of money."

The security guards pushed through the crowd. "Break it up," the hefty guard said to the onlookers.

Jack saw Gentry and raised his hands defensively to his face. "Don't let him hurt me."

"Nobody's hurtin' anybody," the guard said.

"He'll kill me," Jack whined.

"Who's going to kill you?" I pointed to Gentry. "This guy?"

"Not him," Jack said. "Nicholas Brandt."

"Why would Brandt want to kill you?" I said, but the second guard stepped between us.

"Somebody better explain what this is all about and make it good," he said.

Gentry and I showed our licenses and told the guards we had each been hired to find Jack.

The hefty guard gave Jack a hand to help him off the conveyor. "Christ, you going to one of those drag queen conventions or what?"

Jack scowled and crossed his arms over his fake boobs.

"He was hoping to slip out of town without anyone noticing," I said.

"Yeah," Gentry said, "and for the record, Nicholas Brandt is a respected member of the River Oaks community. He's not going to kill anyone."

"Is that right?" I turned to him. "Since when are money launderers respected?"

"Money launderers?" Gentry burst out laughing. "Where'd you hear that b.s.?"

I frowned, thinking how gossip was one of Mother's greatest talents. The guards had watched our exchange with interest, looking like spectators at a tennis match. Now the hefty one said, "Let's move this to the office."

Remembering my stint at the jail, I cringed at the thought of being restrained in any way, shape, or form. "That's not necessary."

"If we got money laundering going on here, it is," said the partner, taking Jack by the arm. "You, too, miss. Let's go." As they led the three of us away, the crowd parted like the Red Sea.

"Give us a break, guys," Gentry said as the guards pointed us toward the elevator. "There is no money laundering. If I know Mr. Brandt, he started that rumor about the money laundering himself."

"Why would he do that?" I said.

"So nobody'd invite him to all those hoop-de-doo River Oaks parties."

I could relate, but I wasn't admitting anything to Gentry. "So why does Brandt need bodyguards?"

"What bodyguards?" Gentry said.

"You know." I eyed the security guards. "Those men in black with the-" I made some vague hand motions, hoping that Gentry would get my gist without my mentioning the Uzis. "Ah," Gentry said. "Those men would be for his daughter's benefit."

"Regina?" I said.

"You got it," Gentry said. "Would you want your only daughter running away with this jackass?"

I looked Jack up and down. "Hardly."

We reached the elevator and one of the guards pushed the up button. We waited, Jack in front near the doors, then me and Gentry, the guards bringing up the rear. Like they expected we'd try to make a run for it.

"Regina is not going anywhere with me," Jack said. "I haven't talked to her in weeks. I swear."

I said, "Then why is she here?"

"Where?" Jack swung around and got in my face. "Goddamn it, that's exactly what I was trying to avoid. All I want is for that little bitch to leave me alone."

"Oh, Jack."

The voice came from my left, and we all turned in unison.

Regina came up beside Jack, looking stricken. For a couple of seconds time seemed to freeze. Then her expression hardened and she reached out and slapped his face, a hearty smack. "You bastard."

Jack reached up and rubbed his cheek, smearing his makeup. "Look, babe." He gave her a palms up, "I told you this wasn't meant to be."

"You were running out on us," she said.

Us?

"No, I–"

"Don't bother lying. I'm not letting you go."

"Yes, you are."

She shook her head. "I grew up without a mother, Jack, and I'll be damned if our baby is going to grow up without a father."

My eyes widened and my jaw went slack. I looked at her belly and noticed for the first time the soft roundness beneath her knit dress.

I looked at Gentry. "Father? Did you know about this?"

"Yup." Gentry smiled. "Got the court order for paternity testing in my hip pocket."

*Boy, I think you made your bed,*
*Remember all you did and said,*
*Since the day that you were wed,*
*Now things are comin' to a head.*

# CHAPTER 26

With Gentry's legs extended, his boots reached to the center of the small waiting area outside the airport security office. He sat next to me, hands clasped behind his head, and leaning back in his chair. I couldn't help but notice well-defined biceps beneath his yellow shirt. How did he look so cool and relaxed after what we'd been through? My shirt felt plastered to my skin with sweat. I smoothed back my hair and strained without success to hear what the guards were saying to Jack and Regina behind closed doors.

Gentry's presence put a big kink in my plans. "Where do we go from here?" I said.

"I'll take him with me in the Jeep," Gentry said, like there was no question he'd take custody of Jack once we left the airport. True, his client had a big emotional claim on the man, but mine had a two-million-dollar beef.

"Unacceptable," I said. "I'm not letting Jack out of my sight."

Gentry looked around the sparsely furnished room and gave me a sarcastic grin. "You already did."

"Not funny."

"Chill. We've got the man now, or at least we will once they finish with him." He looked at the closed office door. "They've been in there forever."

The security guys had spent a few minutes grilling us, but Jack and Regina had been in that office so long my butt felt like it had molded into the hard plastic chair.

"Maybe they showed Jack the secret exit tunnel," I suggested.

Gentry scowled. "If they have a death wish. I want this

problem off my desk today."

"So do I, but I didn't hear Jack agreeing to cooperate with you."

"He will," Gentry said. "Guy's a wuss. And his flight left. What else is he gonna do?"

"You heard him agree to go with me to the law office. He wants to put the divorce case behind him." During the elevator ride up to security, Jack had practically begged me to take him there so he wouldn't have to deal with Regina. "He doesn't want to face Brandt or those thugs."

"All he has to do is give up the DNA." Gentry glanced at the wall clock, pulled in his legs, and straightened. "Testing center's only open for a couple more hours. You can follow me over there, then he's all yours."

"No." I crossed my arms. "Jack said he'd sign divorce papers, and by God he's going to sign them before he changes his mind." Assuming I could get in touch with Wade. He'd need some time to draft documents. Once Jack and Nora signed a final decree, Wade would have to hold it until the required sixty days had elapsed after filing the petition, but then he could take Nora to court and she'd have her divorce. I sighed. God, I wanted this case over.

My gaze dropped to Gentry's cell phone, clipped to his belt. I needed to let Wade and Nora know what was going on, but I couldn't leave Gentry while I searched for a phone. He'd snatch Jack and disappear.

"The DNA test will only take two minutes," Gentry said. "Be reasonable."

"Are you calling me unreasonable?"

"You're hard-headed."

"I'm logical. That baby won't be born for what? Five or six months? You can't confirm Jack is the daddy until then."

"I won't be able to confirm anything then if Jack is gone," he said calmly. "My client wants the DNA collected now."

I decided to ignore the comment and glanced around the room again. Why the hell didn't they have a phone? I'd rather give up Oreos for life than ask Gentry for a favor, but that seemed like the only option.

He must have sensed me watching him because he fixed me with a hard, brown-eyed stare. "What?"

"I need to use your phone."

"Where's yours?"

It seemed like weeks since the day I'd run into him at the cell phone store. "Long story. C'mon, let me borrow it."

"Why should I?"

"'Cause I did you a favor by tackling Jack. If I hadn't, he might have gotten away."

"But *I* found him."

"We both found him, but you'd never have recognized him in that getup."

"*I'm* the one who learned his travel plans," he said.

"From Carmen Messina?"

"No, straight from a business associate–a guy you didn't even have on your list."

I jumped up, hands on hips, and glared down at him. "What list?"

He shuffled his feet and stared at the floor.

My brain took a second to catch up. I had kept tons of notes and a lengthy list of people who might lead me to Jack. "Oh, my God. You're the one who broke into my office."

Gentry held up a hand. "Actually, the door was unlocked."

"I don't believe this. You burglarized me, and now you're trying to order me around?"

Gentry rolled his eyes. "I didn't take anything. Read some notes on a tablet, that's all. Don't try to make this into a big deal."

This guy was a piece of work. "You assaulted my friend."

"Look. Sorry about your boyfriend, but he kept coming at me."

"You jackass."

He stood and met my gaze. "Tone it down. We don't want security on us again."

"There is no *us*," I said. "And maybe I *do* want security on you. In fact, I ought to call the cops right now."

"And tell them what?"

"To arrest you. For breaking and entering. Assault and battery. You're a damned criminal."

"You wouldn't," he said.

"Wanna try me?"

"You have no proof."

"Don't I?" I gave him a smug smile. "Your fingerprints

are all over my office." The cops hadn't bothered dusting for prints, but Gentry didn't know that.

His arrogance deflated like a leaky balloon. He let go of my arm. "Look, I apologize for the whole mess."

"You could lose your license."

"I was desperate," he said.

"That's no excuse."

"You know Jack. He kept slithering away every time I got close. I ran out of leads. My client lost patience."

"And I should care about this because. . .?"

He softened his gaze, and I wondered how many women he'd conned with that expression. "You saw how Jack treated Regina. She deserves better. Our clients each deserve their piece of the guy."

I couldn't argue that point. "You could have talked to me."

He shook his head. "Not really. Mr. B gave strict instructions. He didn't want anybody connecting him or Regina to Jack."

"Well, that cat's out of the bag." I paused, thinking of Regina and her father. "Why does Jack say Brandt's out to kill him?"

"I told you, he's a wuss." Gentry shrugged.

"No. Seriously."

"That's privileged information."

I waited.

"Okay, Mr. B made threats. 'You're a dead man,' like that. He only meant to scare the s.o.b."

I remembered how wary Jack had acted the day I'd served him with the divorce papers. So he'd been hiding from Brandt, not from me and the threat of divorce.

"And now you're planning to hand him off to Brandt?" I said.

"No. I told you. Brandt hired me to find Jack and get him tested. End of story."

I didn't buy it. Maybe Jack deserved whatever they planned to dish out, but Gentry wasn't putting in any calls to Brandt or the thugs with the Uzis. At least not until Wade and Nora had what they needed from Jack.

"Give me that phone," I said.

He unclipped his cell phone. "What are you gonna do?"

I grabbed the phone and savored the discomfort in his eyes. "Not only am I taking Jack, but you're staying with us until the deal is done so I can keep an eye on you."

"What about the DNA testing?"

"Your problem, not mine." I flipped the phone open and started dialing.

"You calling the cops?" he said.

"Not if you cooperate."

***

Two hours later, we reached the law office. I'd called Reba and she'd arranged a settlement meeting with Jack, Nora and Wade. A red-faced and puffy-eyed Regina had separated from us at the airport, wanting no part of the face-off with Nora. We made such good time traveling back into Houston, and I felt so sorry for the girl that I decided to swing by the diagnostic testing center after all. Jack acquiesced after reading the court order. Not that we gave him a choice. Gentry was sappy with gratitude, but I'd done it for Regina's sake, not for him or his client.

I pulled my truck into a spot near the elevators, relieved that this nightmare of a case was about to end. I checked out the cars in the parking lot, then turned to look at Gentry and Jack in the back seat. "Looks like everybody's present and accounted for."

Jack seemed edgier than usual, staring out the window. I followed his gaze to Nora's vehicle, parked near Wade's Lexus.

"What's that bitch doing here?" Jack said.

"Couldn't very well talk settlement without her," I said, climbing out of the truck.

Gentry got out, too, but Jack wasn't moving. I bent over and looked at him. He appeared comical and fearful at the same time, with raccoon eyes and a lipstick-stained mouth.

"You said you wanted to get this over with," I said. "Let's go."

"Not if I have to see *her*."

Gentry reached past me, grabbed Jack's arm, and hauled him out of the truck. "Face the music, Jack. This won't hurt a bit."

"You never met my wife," Jack whined.

We walked toward the elevator, Gentry dragging Jack along.

"Nora's mood will improve after you tell her where you put the money," I said.

"How many times do I have to say this?" he snapped. "I don't have the goddamn money."

"Save your b.s. for the meeting," I said.

Inside, Wade was standing at Reba's desk, waiting for a document to finish printing. We hadn't talked since he'd abandoned me at the jail the night before, and I wasn't eager to face him.

"Good timing," he said when he saw us. All business. "I just finished the draft settlement agreement."

He gave Jack and Gentry a once-over and, despite Jack's appearance, didn't miss a beat. "Mr. Litchfield, have a seat in the conference room. I'll be right there."

Wade pointed to the room adjoining his office. Jack tried to veer the other way but Gentry grasped his shoulders and urged him in the right direction. They went into the room and Gentry closed the door behind them. Wade turned to me.

"Who is that?"

"Somebody I ran into." Obviously, he didn't recognize Gentry as the man who'd thrown him across my office. And I wasn't about to bring that up now.

Wade looked at the closed door, then back to me, but didn't pursue the subject. "Reba tells me you followed Litchfield to the airport."

"I *found* him at the airport, I didn't follow him."

"Don't get all technical." He moved in closer and lowered his voice. "I thought I told you to hold off."

My back stiffened. "I don't remember agreeing to take orders from you."

He reached out to me, but I backed away. "I see you're still in a mood," he said.

"I don't need you to point out my moods. I've had a hellacious day, and I thought you would be glad to see Jack." Heat traveled up my neck. "He's in a mood to sign whatever you want him to sign."

"I *am* glad to see him. I just don't like the way you run off half cocked. It's dangerous."

"And I don't like you telling me how to do my work. Not today, not ever."

We stared at each other for a moment, neither of us willing to back down. Wade moved first, putting a hand on my cheek.

"I'm sorry," he said. "I shouldn't have left you last night. You just make me so damned angry sometimes."

"Oh, so it's my fault." His anger was nothing compared to what I felt remembering the sight of him with Laura.

"Don't put words into my mouth." He tipped my chin up and waited for me to look at him. "I know you've had a rough day. And thank you for getting Jack over here. Now, will you forgive me?" He smiled.

I wanted out of here. "Okay, forgiven. Now, shouldn't you get to your meeting?"

A door banged open, and Nora's voice echoed through the otherwise quiet office. "You son of a bitch. Tell me right now. Where in hell is my money?"

"Damn, she wasn't supposed to go in yet." Wade grabbed his papers off the printer and hurried into the conference room.

Gentry came out, wide-eyed. "And you were worried about me handing him over to Brandt?"

"She's all bark." For Wade's sake, I hoped that was true. Before he closed the door, I caught a glimpse of Nora pacing and waving her arms in time with her yelling.

"Whew," Gentry said. "I say Jack gives up the dough in thirty seconds."

"Whatever happens, it's out of my hands." I brushed my palms together. We headed for the exit. Despite all he'd done, the guy was starting to grow on me.

"Looks like everything worked out for both of us," I said. "Guess I could drive you back to the airport for your Jeep."

"No need. I called a cab from the conference room. I'll wait downstairs."

Damn. I'd taken my eye off him for two minutes, and he'd used the phone. "You call your client, too?"

"Not yet." Gentry glanced at me. "Don't worry. Nobody's going to storm the building to break up your precious meeting."

I believed him. "In that case, here's your phone back." I handed over his cell phone.

"Thanks for going to the lab." He looked at me. "You're beat. Go home. Put your feet up."

"I wish. I'd rather spend all night shuttling people to

the airport than go where I have to go tonight." We reached the elevator and I stopped. "Think I'll kill a little time in my office first."

He punched the down button, then turned to me. "You got something going with the lawyer, huh?"

I raised my eyebrows. "How'd you know?"

He grinned. "I'm an investigator."

"So why do you ask?"

He shrugged. "'Cause you're a good-looking, intelligent, competent woman. Oh, and a damned fine investigator. Thought we might get together sometime."

"You can stop kissing up now," I said. "I'm not going to turn you in."

"And I was going to write you from my jail cell," he said.

I smiled. "Darn. I've always wanted an inmate penpal."

"Better luck next time."

"Yeah."

The elevator dinged. "Enjoyed working with you," he said. "We make a good team."

"That's a matter of opinion." I shook his hand quickly as the doors slid open.

He handed me a business card before stepping into the elevator. He turned around. "Call me if you ever need help on a case."

I glanced at his card as the doors began to close.

He put out a hand to stop them. "By the way, you didn't have anything on me."

"What?" I looked up.

"No proof I was ever in your office," he said, grinning. "I wore gloves."

I stared at him. "You jerk. You led me on."

He wiggled his eyebrows, grinning, and pulled his hand back. The doors slid shut.

Men! Their sole purpose in life must be to drive women crazy. I stomped down the hall to my office.

Listening to my messages, I tried to put Gentry out of my mind, thinking instead about Jack and whether he would admit where he'd stashed the money.

After hearing the work-related messages, I called my home voice mail, knowing Mother would have made some calls by now. Sure enough, she'd phoned twice, once to ask why I'd left in such a hurry this morning and again to ask what I planned on wearing to the gala.

After the next beep came a hesitation before a female voice said, "This is Phyllis Keene." The connection was so full of static, I could barely make out her next words.

"We need to talk."

I perked up, listening hard to hear the number, then disconnected voice mail and dialed. After three rings a mechanical voice told me to leave a message, and I did.

I paced the office, waiting to see if she'd call me back. Phyllis was the last person I expected to hear from, especially after she'd run away from me the other day. But if Jack didn't give up the money, Phyllis might be able to point us in the right direction. Within two minutes, the phone rang and I snatched up the receiver.

"Phyllis?" I shouted over the loud music on her end. Sounded like The Rolling Stones.

"Yes," the woman said. "Remember me?"

"Sure." I pressed a finger against my free ear.

"We need to talk," she said, repeating her message.

"Yes, we do. Matter of fact, I have a question for you right now."

"Not on the phone," she said.

"Why not?"

"We need to meet."

"Give me a break," I said. "You have something to say, why can't you tell me now?"

"Not on the phone," she said again.

Why did everything have to be such an ordeal? I sighed. "Okay, we'll meet. The sooner the better. Tell me when and where, and could you please speak up?" Her voice was drowned out by Mick Jagger hollering, "I can't get no satisfaction," but the noise didn't seem to bother Phyllis.

"Litchfield Enterprises. You know the place?"

Dumb question. "Of course."

"Twenty minutes," she said.

Mick sang, "'Cause I try and I try and I try," but before he could finish, a dial tone buzzed in my ear.

*Put an end to my confusion,*
*Tell me, girl, I have to know.*
*Why you feel the need to run,*
*Tell me now, before you go.*

# CHAPTER 27

I ran all the way to my truck and cranked the ignition before the door was shut. I checked the dashboard clock, knowing I should be headed home now to get ready for the gala, but this couldn't wait. As I peeled out of the lot, I wondered why Phyllis was suddenly eager to talk. This whole scenario reminded me of last night–when I'd rushed over to talk with Zachary only to find him dead. That wasn't going to happen again.

I made it to Greenway Plaza in eight minutes flat. The sun had gone into hiding and afternoon was quickly becoming dusk as I turned into the driveway running between the building and the parking garage. A van was parked near the building's side entrance, carpeting protruding from its rear doors. A rolling garbage bin full of lumpy discarded carpet sat on the sidewalk, and a couple of Hispanic men apparently on a cigarette break checked me out as I maneuvered past the van. I followed the drive that curved around to the garage's entrance.

A couple of cars dotted the parking area, but I didn't see Phyllis's Mercedes. I took a front-row space, figuring that at this off-peak time she had probably parked in one of the reserved executive slots right behind the building rather than over here. I jumped out of my truck, eager to hear what the woman had to say. Tejano music drifted through the garage, probably coming from the work crew's van or maybe a boom box.

Before closing the door, I grabbed the subpoena for Phyllis. Wade might still need her at the hearing if he didn't settle the case before then. I stuffed my keys into a pocket and hurried toward the breeze-way connecting the garage to the building. The keys met with some resistance and the sound of paper crumpling. Oops. I'd forgotten about Carmen's notes. I smoothed the pages and slid them along with the subpoena into a rear pocket. I still had no idea what the notes meant, if anything, but that problem would have to wait.

When I reached the tiled walkway, I immediately spotted a black wallet on the ground near the stairwell.

Hmm. Someone's going to be looking for that.

Feeling like a good Samaritan, I bent to pick up the wallet. A violent blow hit my lower back and flattened me. My face smashed against the tile and my breath came out in a whoosh. I placed my palms down, trying to get leverage. The attacker jumped on my back, straddled me, and pinned me to the floor. He wrapped a hand around my braid and yanked my head back. When I opened my mouth to scream, a lump of wadded-up cloth was shoved inside. I tried to roll, but his knees were pressed tight and held my arms against my body. I couldn't budge.

I heard a ripping sound. A roll of duct tape came around in front of my face. He pressed the tape against my mouth to secure the gag, then wrapped it around my head several times. His hands, encased in black gloves, moved deftly, efficiently. Something pulled over my head. Everything went black.

Blind now, I fought an overwhelming panic. My face throbbed where it had hit the floor. I was moaning, the sound echoing in my head.

What did he want? The wallet? My truck?

His weight slid down, over my buttocks, to rest on my legs. God, he was going to rape me.

I jerked my head and shoulders up, but he mashed on my shoulder blades. My nose hit the tile and pain coursed through my head. I stiffened, expecting my clothes to be ripped away. He grabbed one of my hands, then the other, and brought them behind my back. In seconds, my wrists were taped together. My heart pounded harder than ever. Blood roared in my ears.

I had to do something. The guy didn't seem all that heavy. If I made one fast twisting move, I might be able to throw him off. My body tensed, but before I could try anything  hard metal jabbed against my neck.

"Don't make me use it."

I froze. The voice sounded rough, but definitely female. Despite the threat, a measure of relief washed over me. This wasn't about rape. Then what? Was this Phyllis? I didn't think so. The wimpy Phyllis I knew could never overpower me this way. And if she had a gun, why had she waited to use it?

The woman lifted off me and pulled me by my shirt. "Get up."

The cold metal didn't stray from my skin. I was envisioning something smaller than a gun. The object felt pointy. I didn't want to be shot *or* stabbed. Somehow, I had to make her drop the weapon. I stood, and she pushed me forward. What was this about? Kidnapping? But we moved only a few feet before she stopped and told me to get back down on the floor.

Whoever this woman was, she was seriously pissing me off. I moaned again, hoping to distract her as I lifted my right leg and kicked backwards as hard as I could. I connected with something, but it wasn't a solid hit. I was off balance without the use of my arms, and when she shoved me I toppled. My right shoulder slammed into the floor.

She ripped more tape. Then a phone rang. Weight came down on my side and pinned me at the waist. Her foot.

"Jesus–" she said. "Everything *is* under control."

I lay there like a roped calf, wishing someone would hear us and come to investigate. We couldn't be far from the elevator. The work crew was practically right around the corner.

Without sight, my other senses seemed to intensify. The floor beneath me felt cold, rough. An odd mixture of scents came through the mask–cologne, mildew, ammonia.

"Don't worry," she said. "I'll *be* there." Her voice had a nasal, unnatural quality. "I took care of it. She's not going anywhere."

I heard the phone snap shut and her weight lifted off my waist. She secured my ankles with the tape, making short work of it. I sensed when she had moved away from me, then heard creaking hinges, and a latch clicked. After that, a different noise. A drill? What the hell? Footsteps, growing faint.

After a few minutes, my breathing slowed enough for

me to realize I was alone. I could still hear the music, though it seemed far away now. The whole ordeal had felt like three hours, but I guessed she'd done her dirty deed in less than three minutes. Could be she was still out there, but no way was I going to lay here and do nothing. If the woman came back, I wanted my hands free.

I rolled forward and my knees thudded into something. Damn. I tried again, but the space was too cramped to get any momentum. Rolling backwards only pinned my hands beneath me. Not good. I stayed on my side and tried to separate my hands, writhing and twisting until I couldn't ignore the pain in my right arm any longer. May as well be handcuffed.

My face was sweaty and itchy under the head covering. The material felt wooly, like a ski mask. I'd suffocate if I didn't get this thing off soon. Keeping my head against the floor, I lifted my hips to scoot down, hoping to work the mask up and off but before I could make any progress my feet rammed into a wall.

I lay there for a second, trying to overcome a major mood swing. I wanted more than anything to get ahold of that bitch, but anger wasn't going to help the situation. Only a calm, cool head would get me out of this mess.

Maybe I wasn't strong enough to rip the tape, but I was pretty flexible. I bent my knees and pressed my calves to the back of my thighs, stretching to bring my feet closer to my hands. My fingertips reached the tape around my ankles. Thank God for long legs.

I picked at the tape for what seemed like an hour. My face sweated from the hot breath trapped in the mask. Finally, I found an end and managed to get an edge of the tape under my fingernail. Bit by bit, I peeled the tape back, shifting my legs as I unwound it, forcing myself to keep going despite cramps biting into my thighs and fingers.

My ankles free at last, I maneuvered into a kneeling position. Okay. But what I really needed was to undo my hands. I positioned myself next to the wall and inched to a standing position. I hobbled around the space, frantic, moving backwards, fingertips first. I stumbled over something that caused an avalanche. From the sound of it, I was guessing broomsticks, mops. This had to be the janitor's closet.

I located the door, but with my hands restrained I couldn't reach the doorknob. The music played on, which meant the work crew hadn't left. I slapped and kicked the door as hard as I could in my awkward position. Somebody had to hear me. I kept that up for a while, with no results. When my last ounce of energy was expended, I slumped against the door and took a few deep breaths to calm my heartbeat. The mask felt more itchy now, damp with my sweat.

Who was that woman? Was she in cahoots with Phyllis? Why did she leave me here? Was she coming back? My thoughts drifted to Carmen's lifeless body in the pool. Zachary sprawled across the chair. Dead. Did this have anything to do with them?

I mentally listed what I knew about my attacker. She was strong. She wasn't working alone. She had a plan. She didn't take anything. She stuck me where I'd be out of commission for a while. Obviously, someone wanted me out of the way. But why? Think harder.

The attack was well orchestrated. She seemed to be in a hurry. I didn't know what was on her agenda for tonight, but for me it was the Denim & Diamonds Gala. Mother would flip out if I didn't show up for the big event.

So was there some reason to keep me away from the gala? Was I going to see someone or something there they didn't want me to see? Everyone would be decked out for the big event. A gathering of Houston's rich and famous, each trying to out-do the other. Gaining attention with their big donations and impressive diamonds. My thoughts crystallized.

Oh, God. The diamonds. *Mother*.

Adrenaline spurted through me. If the door wouldn't open, I had to find another way out. Locking me up had something to do with the burglaries. I was sure of it.

I shuffled across the floor, worried about tripping over something, and rammed into metal shelving nose-first. I turned around and stretched my fingers to feel along the shelves. Toilet tissue. Packages of paper towels. No help there. The shelf edge was smooth, rounded metal. Damn.

As I moved around the shelf, my arm scraped something rough. The piece ran diagonally on the unit's side. A brace. I ran a finger along the metal and found a jagged section. I began working the tape around my wrists across the rough edge. I sawed like a madwoman, oblivious to metal cutting into my skin. Sweat ran down my arms, burning the cuts, but I tore through the tape and yanked my wrists free.

With shaking hands, I pulled the mask off. I undid the duct tape, cringing as I ripped the tape from my hair, and spit out the gag. Hunched over, with hands on knees, I took in big gulps of air and fought the urge to throw up. When the feeling subsided, I felt my way back to the door, guided by the sliver of light coming in underneath. The knob turned but the door wouldn't open. I found a light switch next to the door trim and turned it on. Nothing.

Damn that bitch.

I ran my hand along the door and found a latch, flipped it. The door still didn't budge. I yanked on the knob with all my strength. No good. I pounded some more, doing a better job of it this time, and started hollering.

"Help! Somebody! I'm trapped in here!"

I stopped, put an ear to the door, heard the music. Where were those yoyos?

I felt around the floor until I found a broom. Holding the bristle end, I extended the handle up and started poking toward the ceiling. God, this must be a tall room. I kept trying, jumping as I poked, and finally the handle hit the ceiling with a hollow thud.

I dropped the broom and made my way back to the shelves, shaking them to test their strength. The unit appeared to be bolted to the wall. I grabbed the highest shelf I could reach and climbed, pulling myself onto the top. Pressing close to the wall to avoid tumbling off, I rose, stopping when my head hit the ceiling. I pressed my palms against the ceiling and a panel lifted out of the suspended grid. Dim light shone through the opening.

Yes! I pulled myself out into an open crawl space between the closet and the parking garage roof. It was nearly dark now, garage lights casting an eerie glow.

I looked around, saw no movement. The music had stopped. After a minute, I crept to the edge of the crawl space, swung my legs over the side, and dropped to the garage floor.

I pulled out my truck keys, took a second to catch my breath, then froze when I heard running footsteps.

Oh, God. She was back.

I flattened myself against the cement block wall. Now what? Run for my truck? No, she'd spot me. Find a weapon. Attack her from behind?

Voices broke through my ruminations. A stream of

Spanish I couldn't understand. Then English. Men. I'd attracted the workers' attention after all.

"In here? Is she in here?"

How did I know that voice? I held back, listening to more Spanish, then pounding, fists on metal.

"Corie, are you in there? Corie! Dammit, somebody screwed this door shut. Give me that."

I crept to the wall's edge to peer around the corner and saw Mark Gentry grabbing a sledge hammer from one of the workers. Why was he here? He hefted the tool like a fireman intent on breaking into a burning building.

"Corie!" he yelled again. "If you can hear me, stay away from the door. Just stay back. I'm gonna get you out."

I stepped from behind the wall. "What do you think you're doing?"

He put the hammer down and ran over to me. "Trying to rescue you, dammit. What does it look like?" He grabbed my arms, searched my face. "Are you okay? I've been all over this office building looking for you. What happened?"

I blinked hard and shook myself from his grasp. "I have to go. There's no time."

I ran toward my truck, but he followed. "Tell me what's going on."

"You tell me what the hell you're doing here," I said, not slowing down.

"I had the cab follow you," he said.

"Why?"

"'Cause you didn't sound all that excited about your plans for the evening–then all of a sudden you burst out of there like the place was on fire. I figured you might need help."

I stopped running for a second, appraising his earnest expression. He'd tried to rescue me.

"I do need help. C'mon."

*I know that this is it,*
*The night they plan to make the hit.*
*But they're not gonna score,*
*We won't let them out the door.*

# CHAPTER 28

As we raced to the truck, I yanked out my keys, nearly ripping my pocket apart in the process. What if I'm too late? What if the thieves already struck? What if–

*Don't finish that thought. You're not too late.*

I juggled the keys and tried to focus my thumb on the unlock button. Damn. Triple damn. I reached the truck and grabbed the door handle to steady myself.

"Here. Let me." Gentry loomed over my shoulder.

"I can do it." Anger obliterated my fear. I punched unlock and pulled the door open.

"I'm driving," he said.

"No." I got in and jabbed the key at the ignition switch.

"I'm driving," he repeated. "Look at yourself. You're in no condition."

He grabbed my left wrist and lifted my hand from the steering wheel. I was trembling like a junkie going through withdrawal.

"Move over."

I hated admitting he was right, but this was no time to risk a car wreck. I tossed him the keys and slid across the bench seat to the passenger side.

Gentry jumped in and cranked the ignition, shifted into drive. "Where are we going?"

"Briar Hill Country Club."

He nodded. "I know the place."

We took off and I slumped against the seat, attempting to organize my jumbled thoughts.

"Tell me what's happening." Gentry made a c'mon motion with his hand like a traffic cop.

At the speed he was driving, it wouldn't take us long to reach the club, so I spilled the story quickly.

When I had finished, he said, "You think Jack Litchfield sent his secretary to attack you?"

"She could be in cahoots with the burglars, but she wasn't the woman who jumped me."

"Sure about that?"

"You've seen Phyllis," I said. "She's a twig. You think I couldn't take her?"

"My money's on you. But if it wasn't Phyllis, then who?"

"Someone who wanted me out of the way."

"Obviously," he said, "but I don't see these burglars storming a country club to hold up a ballroom full of people. That's not their M.O."

"I know that," I snapped. "But they're into jewels. They hear about this gala and have visions of one humongous haul."

"So these two-bit burglars are reading the society page to choose their next hit?"

"They wouldn't have to. Mother and her friends don't keep a low profile, believe me. They're constantly blabbing about their social calendars, as if anyone cares."

"Thieves might hit the residences tonight, knowing the owners are out," he said.

I'd already discarded that notion. "Mother is at the gala wearing enough jewelry to drape the chandeliers at Buckingham Palace. Rest of her stuff is locked up tight in a bank vault." I folded my arms over my chest and looked at him.

Gentry was shaking his head. "It's an awful big risk. Roomful of people. Cell phones. No doubt a couple of handgun-toting good ol' boys. How do they control that? Pipe in gas through the A-C ducts?"

Dread settled like a cantaloupe in the pit of my stomach. "I'd rather not think about that right now. Let's get over there and see. Okay?"

We drove about a mile in silence. Gentry tried to make a light, but the car in front of us stopped on yellow. We screeched to a halt inches from its bumper. He drummed his fingers on the steering wheel.

I tapped my feet on the floorboard and wondered how burglars went about plotting each heist. First target a person or a place, I guessed, then determine the perfect date to hit that target. For an event like tonight's gala, the date was a given.

I leaned forward and pulled papers from my back pocket. I threw Phyllis's subpoena on the floor and smoothed Carmen's notes on my lap.

Gentry reached up and turned on the interior light. "What's that?"

The calendar sat on top, initials jotted in various calendar squares. Today's square said BHCC. I stared at the page for a second before the light in my brain flicked on. I pointed at the square. "Briar Hill Country Club."

Gentry leaned closer to read the page. "Where'd you get that?"

"From Carmen Messina," I said. "The first murder victim I found this week."

He jerked upright. "What?"

I stared at him, surprised by his reaction. "I pulled her out of a swimming pool and tried to save her, but she'd already drowned."

"Carmen's dead?"

The light had changed and a horn honked behind us. Gentry seemed oblivious.

"You knew Carmen?" I said, my attention drawn away from the pages.

"Yeah. She was feeding me lines on where to find Jack. Knew a lot about him."

"Why would she tell you?" I rubbed my throbbing temples. "I thought they were friends."

"Apparently they are, or were. Used to be more than friends, from what I heard." The horn behind us sounded again. Gentry straightened and mashed the accelerator.

"Did you tell Carmen *why* you wanted to find Jack?"

He shook his head. "She didn't ask. Said she'd tell us anything we wanted to know if the price was right. Mr. B paid her five hundred bucks."

Little did Gentry know Brandt's check was now in my pocket. I wondered what else Carmen Messina would do if the price was right. I'd known there was something screwy about that woman. Nobody except George Doyle had anything good to say about her.

Gentry glanced at the papers again. "What else you got there?"

I scanned the other curlicued notations on the calendar and found B Rich written on Thursday.

"Mother's neighbor, Barbara Richardson, was robbed at home." I stabbed the page with my index finger.

"Looks like you're onto something," Gentry said.

I hurriedly flipped through the other pages, running a shaky finger down the notes scribbled in the bold handwriting George had identified as Carmen's. They'd meant nothing to me the first time I studied them. Now they did. Especially the last entry. D&D Gala. A chill ran up my spine.

"Talk to me," Gentry said.

"Carmen knew what was going on with the burglaries," I said. "She was hiding these papers. What if she was killed because of them?"

"That's a leap."

"I know, but what if I'm right?" I flipped back to the calendar page. "Dammit Gentry, this is the burglar's hit list, and tonight's the last entry. They won't care who gets hurt. Floor it."

***

The gala was in full swing when we arrived at Briar Hill. Gentry and I stood in the hallway outside the kitchen and peered into the ballroom every time one of the wait staff breezed through the set of double doors. We'd come in through the service entrance, and though we'd earned some curious stares no one in the kitchen had tried to stop us or ask what we were up to.

"See how easy this is?" I said. "Anyone could waltz in here."

"Maybe so, but it looks like the party is running smoothly," he said.

"For now."

I started for the ballroom, but Gentry stopped me. "Wait. What are you gonna do?"

"Make sure Mother's all right," I said. "Then alert security and find that woman."

"If that woman dressed for the event, you won't recognize her." He gave me a meaningful once-over. "She sure as hell won't have any trouble picking you out of the crowd."

I looked down. My scratched arms had bloody streaks

and bits of duct tape stuck to the hair.

"Good," I said. "Save me some time."

Gentry's head shake said he thought I was nuts, but he stood aside for me to pass. "Well, I'll hang back. Keep an eye on things in general. You might need somebody to cover your butt."

"Whatever."

I left Gentry and entered the ballroom, scanning for Mother. Sterling silver clinked against dessert dishes and coffee cups. In the dimly lit room candles glowed from table centerpieces. Gentry was right. With all the designer ball gowns and upswept hair, how could I expect one woman to stand out?

Several people turned to stare as I navigated between tables, but I ignored them. I tuned out the orchestra's stodgy version of "Don't Rock the Jukebox" and heard Mother before I saw her. She was seated at a stageside table. I'd been holding my breath without realizing it, and now I exhaled in a huff. She was okay.

I hurried in her direction, noticing that she was the center of attention as usual. She'd dressed the part in a striking strapless purple gown. And then there was the necklace. A dozen or so sparkling strands fell in front and down her back. Must be a zillion diamonds. Jeez.

I came up behind her as she pushed her chair back and stood. "Time for the big surprise," she said before she turned around and saw me.

"Mother," I said. "Surprise."

She took me in with one swift glance, looking like she wanted to whip the crisp white cloth from the table to cover my head, pretend I wasn't there. Instead, she said, "Corinne. How nice you could make it."

Without a backward glance to her friends, she strode toward the stage, fixing me with the follow-me-young-lady glare I'd known since childhood. I trailed in her Obsession-scented wake. A man in a cowboy-cut tuxedo fit for the Country Music Awards climbed the side stage steps as she swished by.

"Five minutes, Olivia," he said.

She nodded to him before veering into an area set off behind the steps. As soon as we were secluded from the guests, she turned on me.

"Good Lord," she whispered. "What are you doing here looking like, like–

"Mother, listen. There's trouble."

"I should say so. Look at your clothes, your hair. I can't believe this."

"Stop." I held up a hand. "The River Oaks burglars are here. I'm not sure what they're planning but–"

"What happened to your arms?" She took my left hand and turned my arm to better see the scratches.

"I'll explain later. Right now we need extra security."

"Don't be ridiculous. We have half a dozen off-duty policemen here. Maybe you didn't recognize them in black tie, but we've taken every precaution."

The music ended and the announcer began. "Ladies and gentlemen, I trust you've enjoyed the fabulous dinner and you're ready to pull out those wallets as we continue to announce the lucky winners in our second annual Denim & Diamonds Silent Auction."

"I have to go," Mother said.

"But you're not safe," I said, raising my voice. "Look at you, dripping in diamonds. You're a perfect target."

She touched her necklace and gave me a sympathetic smile one might give an agitated Alzheimer's patient. "Don't worry, dear. Everything is fine." Her gaze lifted over my shoulder. "Isn't that right, Lucas?"

I swivelled. Lucas Turner had entered from a side door, holding a clipboard. He'd perfected the Mr. Movie Star persona tonight in a jet black tuxedo, but the scowl he gave me ruined the image. Guess he didn't approve of my appearance either, but I didn't give a hoot.

"I expected you earlier." Lucas gave me a fake smile. "What's the problem?"

"Corinne's overactive imagination is all," Mother said. "No problem."

"Good," he said. "You're up in ten seconds, Olivia. Chop chop."

Chop chop? Please.

Mother scurried toward the stage, Lucas on her heels. For a second I felt like walking out the door and ignoring the whole situation. "Here's a quarter, call someone who cares" ran through my head. But I'd made that promise to Dad. And I knew something very bad was going down here.

I went back into the ballroom where Mother was now on stage. She approached the microphone and began her thank-you-everyone-who-made-this-night-possible speech. The remaining auction items sat on a banquet table stage left. Two beefy men stood nearby looking uncomfortable in their monkey suits. Probably rent-a-cops. Lucas Turner stood behind the table, ready to slap the hands of anyone who came too close. The guy was on a power trip.

Except for a trail of women I guessed were coming and going from the ladies room, the audience seemed fixated on Mother's speech. I noticed Gentry leaning against the back wall, his head in continuous scan-the-crowd mode.

I gazed across the ballroom. Maybe I was wrong. No one looked suspicious, yet something seemed out of sync. The hairs on my neck stood at attention. I backed up to a wall so nobody could jump me from behind.

Mother was still prattling on. ". . . thank our esteemed charter member, Mrs. Lorna Wilson, a dear friend to us all, for her priceless donation. You may remember her days as an accomplished horsewoman, and we have something special to show you tonight." She swept an arm to the screen behind her. The lights dimmed further, and the screen filled with a woman on horseback surrounded by a cheering crowd.

I was in no mood for home movies. I eased along the room's perimeter, checking out the women at each table, bypassing those over fifty and those who didn't look athletic enough to paint their own toenails. Things were under control in here. Maybe it was time I checked the corridors around the ballroom.

When I pushed on the swinging exit door, someone pulled it open at the same time. I tripped, falling into a black-gowned woman. I gasped, expecting to be hauled up by my collar, and lifted my head slowly.

Maggie Robbins, holding a wine glass, grinned down at me. "Hello, Corie. How nice to see you yet again."

I climbed to my feet. "Hello, Maggie."

Her brow creased as she inspected me. "I smell a story here. What's going on?"

"Nothing at all," I said through gritted teeth. Yet.

"Come on," she said. "You can trust me. By the way, who's that hunk you came in with?"

"How'd you see me come in?"

"I was out in the gardens having a smoke. Bad habit, I know." Maggie sipped her wine and watched me intently.

I looked up and down the deserted corridor. All quiet out here, too.

"Looking for Lucas Turner?" she said cattily.

I scowled at her. "No. Why would I?"

"I saw you with him at Starbucks, remember?" She raised her eyebrows.

"Of course I remember. So what?"

"Well, I thought you and Wade Alexander were tight. But then there you were all over Lucas." She swirled her wine.

"I was not," I said, "and what business is it of yours anyway?"

"Wade, Lucas, now yet another man. You know, Corie, you shouldn't be greedy."

"What are you talking about?"

Maggie pouted. "I'm still alone, in case you haven't noticed. That first day I saw Lucas at Serentity in the City, I felt a connection. He–"

"When did you see him there?" The hairs on my neck were inexplicably standing up again.

Maggie drained her glass. "Couple weeks ago, I guess."

"What was he doing? Getting his hair cut?"

"I don't know." Maggie shrugged. "*I* had an appointment for a haircut. With Carmen. She was late. She's *never* late." Maggie's gaze drifted like she was off down memory lane. "Poor Carmen. I can't believe she's gone."

"So where was Lucas?" I said.

"I couldn't wait for Carmen forever," she said. "Finally, I just had to leave without the haircut. And there they were. Lucas and Carmen. In the parking lot. Talking."

Lucas Turner and Carmen Messina? Strange how everyone seemed to have a connection with Carmen.

"Anyway, I must get back in there. Did they announce the big donation yet?"

I frowned. "What big donation?"

"You didn't hear about your Mom's surprise?" Maggie said. "Mrs. Wilson is donating her famous diamond-and-ruby studded bridle and reins for the cause. They say the set appraises at over eight hundred thou."

Oh, my God.

I turned and yanked open the ballroom door, just as a woman let out a blood-curdling scream.

"Fire!"

*Why is it they all run away?*
*Guess it just ain't been my day.*
*I swear this one won't disappear,*
*Not as long as I am here.*

# CHAPTER 29

Thick smoke billowed across the ballroom. I froze in the doorway as the crowd erupted into full-fledged panic mode. Guests surged toward the exits like passengers headed for the last *Titanic* lifeboat, stumbling over each other as they raced from the smoke. I wanted to run out ahead of them to safety, but my instinct told me not to. I'd been on the lookout for the thieves' big move all night and this could be it. Besides, I wasn't going anywhere without Mother. Knowing her, she'd try to pack the auction valuables and get them to safety before she thought about herself.

I hunched my shoulders and plowed into the crowd, bucking the stampede. The fire alarm went off, its whoop-whoop-whoop clashing with the screams of frantic women. Smoke kept pouring into the room from somewhere near the stage. A man's voice came over the P.A. system, telling everyone to remain calm and move to the nearest exit.

Calm. Right.

The message repeated as I pushed between people and sidestepped overturned chairs to make my way to where I'd last seen Mother. I crawled under a table to make some headway, smooshing over gooey dessert spilled during the uproar, and emerged wiping my hands on my jeans. I climbed onto a chair and craned to find her.

There she stood, next to the table displaying the auction stuff, having a pow-wow with the security officers and Lucas Turner. Why weren't they getting the hell out?

From this vantage point I could clearly pinpoint the source of the smoke–the corner stairwell. To Mother's credit, she was casting nervous glances in that direction, yet she showed no sign of leaving.

"Olivia," I yelled, waving my arms wildly, hoping to attract her attention. "Olivia!"

No luck.

I looked at the stairwell again. Something wasn't right. The exit door must be propped open for all that smoke to stream into the ballroom. That was probably a fire code violation. And stairwells were concrete, constructed as a place of refuge in case of fire or worse. So how did a fire start in the stairwell anyway?

Or maybe there was no fire. The smoke made a damn fine diversion. Any second now, someone could grab Mother.

*Get her out.*

I jumped off the chair and shoved my way around people, my heart thudding in time with the alarm. I was so intent on reaching Mother that I yelped in surprise when someone grabbed my elbow.

I whipped around, ready to scream obscenities and saw Gentry. I blew out a breath.

"Going the wrong way," he yelled in my ear.

"I'm not leaving without my crazy-ass mother," I shouted, dragging Gentry until he let go. "Look at her. Like she hasn't a care in the world."

He followed my gaze. "The woman in a gazillion diamonds? That's *your* mother?"

I glared at him. "Yes, and I'm gonna need help getting her butt out of here. Something's going down. I don't think there's any fire."

He understood instantly. "Shit." He grabbed my hand and took the lead, doing a better job of paving the way.

I peered around him. Mother and the officers nodded as Lucas talked animatedly with his hands. Then the little group split up, the officers coming into the crowd, Turner crossing to the room where Mother and I had spoken earlier. She waited by the table, wringing her hands.

Gentry and I squeezed through the mob and ran over to her.

"What are you doing?" I yelled, taking her arm. "You need to move it right now."

"In just a minute," she said. "Lucas is bringing the jewels."

"The jewels, of course." I slapped my forehead with

the heel of my palm, wanting to slap her.

"Don't be snide, Corinne. I am saving the jewels and we'll be out in two seconds."

Gentry stepped in. "She's right, ma'am. There's no time to spare."

She appraised him, then looked at me. "Are you going to introduce me to your friend?"

I threw my hands up. "This isn't a cocktail party, Mother. It's an evacuation. Let's go."

"But–" she began.

"Mark Gentry, ma'am," he said. "Trust me, we can't risk smoke inhalation. We'll meet up with your friend outside." He offered his elbow, escort style, and she linked her arm in his. Amazing.

"Right behind you," I said, pushing them toward the exit but constantly sweeping the area with eyes squinted against the smoke.

I spotted Lucas as he emerged from the room behind the stage like an apparition in the smoky corner, a black duffel bag slung over his shoulder. I froze. He wasn't headed our way, didn't even look around for Mother. Maybe it was something about his posture, but in that instant I knew he had been one of the burglars at Carmen's house the night of her murder. Even without that realization, I'd have known something was up when he disappeared into the stairwell without a backward glance.

Right into the supposed fire.

Mother and Gentry were a couple yards ahead of me. Gentry would keep her safe. I had to go after Lucas and the jewels. I opened my mouth to report where I was going, but they would stop me or try to follow me. No time.

I snatched a napkin from a nearby table, dunked it in a water glass, then held the wet cloth over my nose and mouth and followed Lucas into the stairwell.

The walls shrank in on me as smoke clogged the space. The shrill fire alarm was unbearably loud, clanging inside my head. My eyeballs felt like they'd been wrapped in hot burlap. I groped until I found a handhold. Grasping the railing with my free hand, I began a tentative descent.

Lucas Turner. That bastard had been right under Mother's nose the whole time. Kissing up to her, making sure he was in on the gala every step of the way. And who knew what else. My blood boiled just thinking about him being in her house. God, I wanted to get my hands on him.

I took the steps faster, choking back the urge to cough so I wouldn't alert the bastard I was coming after him. How big a lead did he have? What was his next move? Where would he go? Probably somewhere far away, now that his cover was blown.

I couldn't let him escape. Not only because of what he'd done to Mother or to save the jewels. He was a murderer. I was certain he'd killed Carmen Messina because of what she knew.

By the time I reached the first landing, the smoke had thinned. The air was still hazy, but at least I could see. Whatever the source of the smoke, I had passed it without even realizing. I picked up speed, ignoring a door that went back into the club. Turner ran less risk of being seen and stopped in the parking garage—that's where he was headed. He could be in his car and gone before anyone figured out what had happened.

Not if I could help it.

I raced down the steps and pushed through the door into the garage. No smoke here. I threw down the soggy napkin and gulped air as I scanned the area. Deserted. The place was cavernous and ominously still. Guests wouldn't be retrieving their valet-parked cars until after the threat of fire was cleared up. Plenty of time for Lucas to make his getaway.

So where was he?

From somewhere behind me, I heard the whine of an engine trying to turn over. I rounded the stairwell and edged along the cement block wall. My eyes watered, refusing to adjust to the dim garage lighting, but I heard the noise clearly. Was it Turner's car? Had his lucky streak come to an end?

I moved away from the stairwell, toward the whiny engine and a well-lit square that must be the exit ramp. Soon I pinpointed the noisy vehicle—not Turner's Porsche, but a black van parked at the end of a row near the exit, nose out. Was that him in the van? The windows were tinted too dark for me to see anyone inside.

I snaked down the center of a row, squeezing between bumpers, and came up behind the van. My heart threatened to beat itself right out of my chest as I crouched behind the vehicle. Now what? I had no weapon. No cell phone. I swore that when this was all over I'd go out and buy ten of the damn things.

For whatever it was worth, I memorized the license number. Then I rose to peer around the driver's side and did a double take when I got a clear view of a face in the side mirror.

Haley Winter.

I fell back to my crouched position. Haley.

Was Turner in there with her? He had come down ahead of me. Two against one. Not good odds.

I poked my head around the passenger side. No one visible in that mirror. I inched up to peek through the van's darkened back windows. Haley's silhouette in the driver's seat. None on the passenger side. Unless Turner was lying flat in the back, she was alone. For now.

I whirled to scan the garage. Nothing.

My mind raced. Haley and Turner. Together. Tracking social schedules. Robbing Houston's rich and famous. I could see it now. Carmen found them out, so they killed her. I'd bet my last dollar Haley was the bitch who'd tied me up and left me in that closet.

I wanted her bad.

I stood, planning to creep up to the driver's door, but then the door swung open. The garage went quiet as she quit cranking the ignition.

"Goddamn Lucas," Haley muttered. "Where are you?"

I flattened myself behind the van. Something popped. The hood release. Haley got out, leaving the driver's door standing open, and went around to the front. She lifted the hood.

Perfect.

I moved quickly, poking my hand in to yank the key from the ignition. I rounded the van, coming up behind her, closing a fist around her keys to keep them quiet. She wore black knit pants and a black turtleneck, standard burglar attire. She leaned over the engine, still muttering, her ponytail obscuring her face.

As I moved in close, I caught a whiff of her cologne. Not that I needed the extra piece of evidence. Anger coursed through me as I remembered my chin hitting the tile floor when she'd attacked me. I lunged at her and grabbed her ponytail with my left hand, jabbed keys into her back with the other. I twisted her hair around my knuckles for a firm grip and yanked her head back the way she'd done me.

She howled and tried to wrench away.

I yanked harder on the hair, pushed the pointy keys firmly into her back. "Shut up. Where's your partner?" I prayed he wasn't creeping up behind me.

Haley gripped the front of the van for balance. "I don't know what you're talking about."

"Yeah, you do. Where's Lucas?"

"Fuck you, bitch."

I gave her head a good shake. "It's too late to cover things up. I know all about you two."

"Oh, right."

"Carmen Messina had you figured out, and now so do I."

Haley hesitated, then said "So you gonna try bleeding us dry like that bitch did?"

"No, I'll see you both rot in jail. Where's Lucas?"

She cocked her head to look at me. Hatred burned in her dark eyes. "In your dreams, bitch. I should've killed you like he told me to."

The words hit me like a slap in the face. If she'd listened to him I'd be dead in that closet right now. I shivered and must have involuntarily loosened my grip. With a gut-wrenching scream, Haley shoved backwards into me and twisted out of my grasp. As my knees buckled, she plowed into me and knocked me onto my back. The keys fell. My head thunked on the concrete.

Then she was on me, straddling me, her knees pressed into my sides. A horrible déjà vu. She wrapped her hands around my neck, squeezing hard. I wouldn't get another reprieve.

I writhed from side to side and kicked my feet, doing my best to throw her off. She held fast. She was more powerful, but my will to live was damn strong. I kept squirming and stretched my arm, feeling around for the keys, gasping for air. Things were getting fuzzy.

I stretched harder. There. Metal. I grasped the ring, lifted my arm and stabbed a key into her side.

She hollered and released my neck. She grabbed for my hand, but I jerked out of her reach and jammed the key into her neck this time. She karate-chopped my arm and the keys flew. Somehow I managed to throw her over and take the upper position.

I had never been in a struggle like this in my life–nothing but tooth and nail to fight her with. We rolled on the concrete like female wrestlers with no rule book, clawing and biting, tearing at each other's hair.

I managed to come up on top a second time, but I couldn't hold out much longer. Haley ripped at my shirt, trying to throw me. Then a noise rose above our howling and grunting. I turned my head toward the sound. Headlights hit the garage wall. A car.

*Thank God.*

We weren't directly in its path, but the driver would surely notice us and stop to help. Haley took advantage of the distraction to topple me. I butted my knees against her legs to keep her from climbing on top. I looked toward the car. Saw a flash of red as it turned and came toward us.

Haley placed her palms on my torso and leaned on me as she pushed to her knees. She glanced toward the car and smiled.

Oh, God. The red Porsche. Lucas.

I gritted my teeth, curled my fingers into a tight fist and punched her in the face. I sat up, trying to roll her, but she slammed me down again. My skull hit the concrete like a thunderbolt. I couldn't move. Everything went fuzzy and black.

I heard the car screech to a halt. Weight lifted off me.

Through a fringe of lashes, I saw Haley looming over me.

Then a noise, pop-pop-pop, before the car raced away.

Something sticky and wet rained down before I felt her hit the ground beside me.

*I heard what you said,*
*Words spin round in my head.*
*But it's her that you wed,*
*And now I'm seein' red.*

# CHAPTER 30

I opened my eyes and squinted around the hospital room. Everything was so antiseptic, so white, so painfully bright. The blinds were down but open enough to let the sun peek through the slats.

Morning. Finally.

I felt like I'd survived sky diving without a parachute. A cast weighed down my left arm. Fractured wrist, they said. Even my eyeballs ached. Instead of moving them, I turned my head and saw Wade dozing in the visitor's chair. I'd told him he didn't need to stay, but I was glad he had.

The horror of last night flooded back, as it had every time the nurse woke me. Much as I wanted to block the memory, I flashed on the icy execution that Lucas had carried out inches from me. Tears stung my eyes. I had fought for my life, but I never meant for Haley to end up dead.

I blinked away the tears, and then Wade was standing over me, holding my hand.

"Hey, sweetheart. How're you feeling?" He leaned in close to kiss my check.

"Super, considering that damn nurse woke me up a million times during the night."

"If your mother'd had her way, the nurse would have slept at your feet. Thirsty?" He offered me the cup from the bed table, and I thankfully sipped water through the straw.

When I'd had enough, I said, "Where is Mother anyway?"

"Convinced her to go home, believe it or not. That woman is tougher than the toughest judge or jury I've ever faced, but she was worn out. Finally listened to reason."

"I'm surprised *you* stayed."

"Why?" His brow furrowed.

Wade never went out in public looking the way he looked now–wrinkled shirt, tousled hair, bloodshot eyes. Knowing he'd spent the night made me feel all warm inside, but in my mind's eye I saw him with Laura as they laughed over glasses of wine.

"You've been kinda distant," I said.

"I've been busy," he said. "There's no place I'd rather be, Corie, than right here. You know that."

He sounded sincere, but I *didn't* know.

He leaned over again, this time kissing me lightly on the lips. "I love you and I'll prove it, as soon as those bruises heal."

He winked, but I wasn't in a playful mood. And I didn't want to think about the bruises. They reminded me of Haley, and Haley reminded me of Lucas Turner–that vile, vicious, conscience-deprived bastard.

"Did they find Turner yet?" Using my good arm, I pushed to a sitting position. Razor blades sliced into my skull.

"Haven't heard."

I moved my legs toward the edge of the bed, every muscle screaming. "Well then, let's go find out."

"You're not going anywhere." Wade had an arm across my chest, one hand on my shoulder, and was pushing me back toward the mattress when a brief knock sounded and the door opened.

"Time to rise, sunshine." Mark Gentry poked his head out from behind a huge bouquet of spring flowers and grinned at me before he noticed Wade.

"Hey bud, they frown on manhandling the patients around here." Gentry grinned and crossed the room to place the flowers on a counter.

Wade straightened, glaring as Gentry walked around to the opposite side of the bed. In contrast to Wade, Gentry looked clean and crisp in a white dress shirt, starched jeans, and his ostrich boots. I laid back, self-conscious in my hospital gown and wondering why I even cared. I hurt too much to care.

"You're looking chipper," Gentry said to me.

"Only hurts when I blink."

Gentry laughed, but the men were eyeing each other like two prize fighters. I introduced them and briefly explained Gentry's interest in Jack Litchfield to Wade. They shook hands across the bed.

"Flowers are gorgeous," I said to break the tension. "Thanks."

"My pleasure," Gentry said. "You get the full report on last night?"

Wade said, "Could you wait? She's supposed to rest."

"No," I said. "Fill me in."

"First off, your Mom's fine. Kind of freaked when you disappeared, but I handled her."

"She already *knows* Olivia is fine," Wade said.

Gentry ignored him. "Helped load up all her stuff once everybody realized someone set off a smoke bomb, no fire."

"I know that meant a lot to her," I said.

"Man of the hour," Wade said.

Gentry again pretended Wade didn't exist. He perched on the bed near my feet. "Cops got fingerprints on Turner and Winter, aliases by the way, and found out they're wanted in five states. Been operating under this M.O. for a while, different names in each city."

I slapped the mattress. "Damn. I should have known something was up with those two. Did the cops catch Turner?"

"Not yet," Gentry said. "But they found his car in long-term parking at Intercontinental."

Wade said, "Probably out of the country by now."

"Maybe," Gentry said.

Wade paced to the window, then turned around. "But if they were partners, then why'd he kill her?"

"Looks like he planned all along to ditch the chick," Gentry said. "The van's fuel pump relay was gone. She was stuck right where he knew she'd be. Definitely premeditated."

I closed my eyes. Damn Lucas.

Wade said. "Are you done? Corie needs some sleep."

My eyes popped open. "Not here. I want to go home. Now."

"You look good to go," Gentry said, then turned to Wade. "Hey, what happened with the Litchfields? You settle their case?"

Nora. I'd forgotten all about her. Hard to believe it was just yesterday when I'd taken Jack to Wade's office for the meeting.

Wade shook his head. "No such luck. Jack stuck with his denial–says he never took any money."

"You expected him to admit it?" Gentry said.

"I'm not stupid," Wade said. "He's not off the hook. We'll be tracking down that two mill, believe me."

I said, "You mean *I'll* be tracking it."

"No way," Wade walked back to the bed, his expression stern. "You're taking a couple of weeks off."

That's what he thought. Before I could respond, my favorite nurse came in, looking disappointed 'cause she didn't have to wake me. Did she work twenty-four seven or what? The chubby black woman's pants legs swished together as she crossed the room.

"Time for your meds," she said. "Monitor your vitals."

"You should know them by heart," I said. "I'm checking out anyway. Where are my clothes?"

The nurse chuckled. "This ain't a hotel, hon. We're keepin' you till at least one, when the doctor makes his rounds." She stuck a probe under my tongue, and I reluctantly pressed my lips together.

She held her fingers to my wrist. "Best settle back now and get your rest."

She frowned at the men. "Shoo. She needs quiet time." Then she turned back to me and said, "Your mama took your clothes, hon. Said you couldn't be seen in those dirty ol' rags."

Gentry was already through the door, Wade close behind him.

"Wade," I muttered around the thermometer, "do something."

He shrugged. "You want clothes, you got 'em. I'll stop by your place."

If the meds had been pills, I'd have hidden them under my tongue, but the nurse from hell injected me in the butt and knocked me out.

A few hours later, I was wide awake and starving. Lunch arrived–if you could call a bowl of clear soup, saltines, and green Jell-O lunch. Where's a big juicy What-A-Burger when you need one?

And where the heck was Wade with my clothes?

I swung my legs over the side of the bed, stood, and caught sight of my black-and-blue face in the mirror. I stuffed my frizzy hair behind my ears. Jeez. Too bad Barnum & Bailey wasn't in town.

My left arm felt heavy in the cast, and I was clutching

the back of my open hospital gown and searching the floor for some slippers when the door opened. I hoped it was Wade and not Mother. God only knew what she'd bring me to wear.

The visitor was neither. Wade's ex, of all people, peered around the door at me.

"Laura. What a surprise." I backed up to the bed and sat down, resisting the urge to smooth my hair and straighten my gown.

Laura wore a patterned silk dress and heels. Her blonde hair was swept into a perfect French twist and silver earrings with turquoise tips dangled from her lobes. She held a burgundy tote bag that didn't match the outfit and looked oddly familiar.

"Corie," she said. "How are you?"

Stupid question, but I answered her as if we were still the best of friends we'd been before she cheated on Wade and left him to marry her lover.

She crossed the room and placed the tote on the visitor's chair. The air between us was frigid, but I asked about Wade's kids and Laura filled me in.

When the small talk petered out, I said, "Why are you here?"

She smiled sweetly and pointed to the tote. "Brought you some clothes. Wade meant to come back, but he got held up at the children's school."

I wondered what, or who, had conveniently sent him to the school when he was on a mission to fetch my clothes.

"And that's the real reason you're here?" I said.

She gave me a brittle smile. "I've been meaning to come see you ever since I've been back in town."

"Really?"

"I've missed you," she said, oozing fake sincerity. "And I see you haven't changed a bit. You never were one to stand still, and you haven't stayed in one spot long enough lately for me to catch up with you."

I figured Laura was the woman who'd come by my house when Kit was there. "Guess it's lucky for you I ended up in the hospital."

She made a face. "I didn't say that."

My eyes stayed on hers. "Let's not waste time. I'm a busy woman, and from what I gather so are you."

"What's that supposed to mean?"

"I think you know."

Laura put a hand on her hip. "I know you've been seeing Wade," she said. "And I intend to put a stop to that."

I felt my back go rigid. "Is that right?"

"We belong with him," she continued. "The children and I."

"Who says?"

"They miss him."

"I'm sure they do. And Wade misses them. With you living closer, they'll be able to spend more time together."

"We all will." She went to the door. "I want Wade back, Corie, and I'm here to put you on notice."

She threw me a smug look and left. Her heels tapped down the hallway.

"Duh," I said to myself. "Your hiring Wade for your divorce put me on notice."

\*\*\*

Two hours after they sprung me from the hospital, I was home and preparing to enjoy a huge lunch with Reba and Kit.

"I can't believe the nerve of that bitch," Reba said after I'd told her about Laura's visit.

I shrugged. "She sees what she wants, and she's going after it, I guess."

"She sees what she *used* to have," Reba said. "And the grass looks greener. Too bad."

Reba had picked me up from the hospital after confirming that Wade couldn't–he was busy sitting with his sick daughter. Or so Laura claimed.

"Wonder what Mommy did to make the kid sick?" Reba said.

"Let's not talk about Laura," I said. "Might ruin my appetite."

"Have some chips and dip." Kit placed a bowl of chili con queso dip and a basket of chips in front of me. The girl was helping Reba prepare exactly what I needed most at the moment–serious comfort food.

Thick burgers sizzled on the grill nearby. Reba had cut up potatoes for homemade french fries. My freezer was stocked with half gallons of my favorite Blue Bell ice cream flavors. What more could a girl want?

We ate outside on the deck with Midnite making laps

around the picnic table in search of fallen crumbs. My bulky cast made eating difficult, but I managed to stuff myself. I stirred what was left of my Tin Roof Sundae and wondered exactly where Wade stood in this reconciliation plot.

"I wouldn't even *want* my Mom and Dad to get back together," Kit said as if reading my thoughts.

"Wade's kids are a lot younger than you," I said. "They really miss him." Not to mention he was a much better Dad. Kit's father came around twice a year, if she was lucky.

Midnite pushed her nose against my arm, trying to make up for a couple days' worth of lost attention. I smiled at her and patted her head. "At least you love me, don't you baby?"

She wagged her tail.

"Enough of your poor-me crap," Reba said. "It's not like you, Corie, and you're gonna snap out of it. With my help."

I looked up. "Oh yeah?"

"I want to help." Kit looked at Reba. "What do we do?"

"Two can play Laura's game," Reba said, addressing Kit. "First we'll get some concealer to cover those bruises. I'll fix her hair." She glanced at my clothes–a loose T-shirt and comfy knit shorts. "You have one of those Wonder bras?"

I sat up straighter. "No, and I wouldn't wear one if I did."

Reba ignored me, addressing Kit again as if I weren't even there. "We'll find a nail place that's open Sundays. Those ratty tennies have to go. After a pedicure with deep rosy polish, she'll feel like a new woman. Then we'll hit Macy's. Find a nice girly sundress and get her some cute sandals."

Kit giggled.

"You sound like Mother," I said.

"Don't insult me," Reba said. "I'm the one who saved you from spending the rest of the day with your mother."

"True." I stood and gathered dirty dishes to take inside, balancing plates on my cast. Between the food we'd brought home and the prescription pain pills, I was feeling half decent. "I owe you, but stop scheming. I have plans later."

"With Wade?"

"No."

"Only a crazy woman would dream up excuses to avoid a pedicure," Reba said. "What plans?"

Cradling an armful of dishes, I headed to the screen door. "Wade isn't hiring anybody else to solve this Litchfield problem. *I'm* going to find the money Jack stole. I've already called Nora and set up a meeting at her office. No sense wasting time."

I toed the door open with one of my old rattie tennies and turned to look at Reba. "And don't get any bright ideas. The spa is closed. No pedicurist on duty."

*There's more to life than money,*
*You'd better believe it, honey.*
*But if money's what you want,*
*Then I'll join you in the hunt.*

# CHAPTER 31

I arrived at Serentity in the City around seven. The strip center's parking lot was surprisingly crowded for a Sunday night. As I searched for a free space, I decided it must be all-you-can-eat spaghetti night at Mama Mia's. I noticed restaurant-goers gawking at remnants of crime scene tape around the spa. A couple strolling down the sidewalk paused to peer through the front window. Seemed the news of three spa employees dead within a week drew the morbidly curious.

I squeezed my truck into a spot near the back and struggled to swing my sore legs out without moaning. I'd skipped a scheduled dose of pain meds so I'd keep a clear head. Nora and I planned on compiling a list of every person her slimy husband ever associated with. No way Jack took two million dollars without bragging to *somebody*–a friend, relative, maybe an old college buddy. One way or another, I was going to find out what had happened to the money.

After hearing Reba's critique of my appearance, I'd changed into a striped top that stretched over my cast and looked fine without a Wonder bra and wore slacks that covered my black and blue legs. I'd tied my hair back and was sans makeup except for plum lipstick that complemented my bruises.

I must have cleaned up pretty well because Nora didn't comment on my appearance when she let me in. The dim lobby, lit only by early evening sunshine streaming through the half-closed blinds, didn't keep me from noticing that she wasn't herself. Her complexion was pale, her eyes droopy, and she seemed fidgety. Understandable, I figured, after losing three employees and all that money.

The lobby was quiet except for the fountain. As Nora locked up behind me, I watched the spray hit overhanging palms and run down over smooth stones and into the surrounding basin. An image meant to instill peaceful thoughts, but I'd never feel peaceful here. All I could think about was the night I'd discovered Zachary's body in this place.

I shivered and turned. Nora adjusted the blinds next to the door, shutting out daylight. I wouldn't have thought she owned jeans, but she wore a pair today with a knit leopard-print shirt. Her hair was pulling loose from a matching spotted clip.

"Damned reporters," she muttered. "Better they think nobody's around."

"Reporters have been here?"

"Here, home, everywhere. Asking inane questions. Wanting to know how I *feel* about what's happened. How the hell do they think I feel?"

"Ignore them. They'll go away eventually." I had fended off plenty of reporters in my life.

We crossed the lobby and headed for the beacon of light coming from the interior teak door. I caught our reflection in the mirrored cases displaying the beauty products, Nora's expression determined, mine a pained grimace. We went into the spa and Nora shut the door behind us, further blocking off any light that might be seen from out front. Her steps were short but hurried as we headed down to her office. I fell behind, legs aching as I watched Nora race-walk ahead.

"Not bad enough my husband robs me blind," she said over her shoulder. "Now this horrid news about Haley."

I wasn't sure if she meant Haley's murder or the fact that she'd used the spa as a cover, but I didn't want to go down that road. Not right now.

"I heard the meeting with Jack didn't go well," I said.

"Jack is a lying sack of shit," Nora said. "He *has* my money."

She turned a wall switch that dimmed the hallway lights and entered her office. I stopped short at the doorway. Nora picked her way around dusty cardboard boxes–some stacked, some open with papers scattered nearby on the floor. She stopped in front of a stack and slapped her palms on the top box. Dust flew.

She turned to look at me, and in the harsh fluorescent light I saw eyes so bloodshot I wondered if she'd been drinking. "Do you think he gave my money to that little slut?"

I shook my head. "No. Regina's father hired a PI to find Jack because Jack gave her nothing. He was ducking his responsibility."

"You mean her pregnancy," Nora said.

"Yes." I felt embarrassed for Nora. "Look, I know how difficult the situation is–"

She lifted her chin. "You don't understand. I don't give a *damn* about Jack's women. This business is all I have, all I care about. It is *so* hard to keep things going. I'm missing two stylists, I have no manager, everyone knows what *she* did, and then damn Jack–" She clenched her fists and squeezed her eyes tight. "*Damn* him. I worked so hard. You have no idea. He had no right."

"I understand, Nora, but–"

Her eyes popped open. "I do *not* want to hear *any* buts. I will *not* be ruined, do you understand? Not by Jack. Not by anyone."

I actually felt sorry for the woman. "I'm here to help, remember?"

Nora blinked as if she'd just come out of a bad dream and realized who I was.

I looked at the boxes. "What is all this?"

She pulled off a box lid and threw it on her desk. "Jack's stuff. I hauled these out of our storage room. He kept everything. Maybe there's an old address book in here somewhere."

I pulled a notebook and pen from my purse. "Then let's get to work. What do you say?"

Nora agreed and brought us each a bottle of water before we began. Amazing how her demeanor had changed from emotional reaction to logical determination as if someone had thrown a switch. She worked doggedly, rooting through paperwork like an IRS auditor. Our list of characters from Jack's past grew steadily with stars marking those Nora thought I should check out first.

While we were at it, we compiled a second list–this one of banks and institutions Jack had dealt with. Not that he'd hide the money in plain sight, but Wade might want to subpoena records to be sure. I figured Nora felt better occupying her mind with work and so did I–better than dwelling on the deaths or on my uncertain future with Wade.

After a while, my legs cramped and the water made its way through my system. I stood, rolled my head from side to side, and stretched my aching neck. My arm throbbed like crazy under the cast.

"I need a break."

"Fine." Nora, cross-legged on the floor and paging through papers in her lap, didn't look up.

I headed down the hall in search of a ladies' room. Each step was agony. What the hell was I thinking when I'd suggested doing this tonight? I could be home eating chocolates, petting Midnite, with Kit bringing me icy Cokes when I snapped my fingers. Instead I'm looking through dusty boxes' with a woman who cares about nothing except her money and who even on a good day drives my blood pressure up.

Duh.

I made a wrong turn into an alcove of shampoo basins, lost my bearings, and ended up in the manicure section. No ladies room here. Instead of going deeper into the maze, I backtracked till I reached familiar ground. Probably save some steps if I used that restroom off the lobby. I traipsed down the main hall, went through the teak door, and closed it behind me.

A smidgen of light came through crevices of the blinds, creating twilight and throwing creepy plant shadows on the wall. I had half a mind to flip on some lights, damn the reporters. But no sense getting Nora riled up when we were almost finished with our project.

I was halfway across the lobby when I heard a noise.

I froze. There couldn't be anybody out here. Nora had locked the door.

There, again. A clunking sound. Maybe the fountain motor, or whatever it was that kept the water flowing, was malfunctioning.

I pivoted to go back and check it out and noticed the plants in the fountain were moving. What the hell? I circled the check-out island to get a better view. A man stood balanced on top of the waterfall with one foot on the rocks, one on the fountain's second-tier basin. He groped around in the thick philodendron that draped the top tier.

I ducked behind the check-out counter, waited a second, then eased up to peek over the counter and caught his profile. My breath caught.

Lucas Turner.

He dug deeper into the plants, searching. As he stretched, the stone under his foot rocked against the one beneath. The clunking noise I'd heard.

I looked at the front door which seemed just as Nora and I had left it. Guess locks meant nothing much to a professional burglar. But why was he here? What the hell was he doing up there?

Whatever the reason, I had to call the cops.

My gaze traveled down the counter top to the phone. Six feet may as well have been six hundred. If I went for it, he might spot me. I looked across the room to the door I'd come through, but Lucas was between me and the door.

Damn. I *could* make a run for it. Get Nora and lock ourselves in her office. Call the cops from there. But I wasn't moving fast enough. And even if the cops came, Lucas could be gone by then.

No way in hell. I'd been through too much to lose this bastard now.

So then what?

I looked around frantically. Nothing remotely resembling a weapon in sight.

Except for the stones.

They didn't appear to be cemented together, just stacked in an aesthetic arrangement. Lucas lifted his arm. He pulled something from behind the plants, and held it up with a triumphant stance.

Some kind of package. It was now or never.

I moved in quickly and in one motion grabbed up a rock and whacked it into the back of his knees.

He fell toward me. I yelped and jumped aside. Lucas came down hard, his shoulder slamming into the rocks. The package he'd retrieved bounced to the lobby floor. I stepped into the water, prepared to hit him in the head, but his hand shot out and grabbed my forearm. The rock slipped from my fingers. Splashed.

I tried to twist out of his grasp, but lost my footing because of pebbles and coins lining the basin floor. I fell on top of Lucas, my cast fully immersed.

"Let go of me, you son of a bitch," I yelled.

Lucas pulled me toward him. "You."

I fought to catch my breath.

"You're like a bad penny," he said. "What the fuck are you doing here?"

"I'm the cleaning lady," I said.

He tightened his grip on my arm. "Who else is here?"

"You don't see anybody, do you?" I wanted to scream for Nora, but that might end up getting us both killed.

Lucas pulled me closer, until we were practically nose to nose. His breath hit my face. Water gurgled around us, between us. The wet cast weighed me down like a ball and chain.

"I'd like to take advantage of this provocative pose," he said, "but I'm afraid I can't spare the time." He shoved me off of him. "Get up."

I struggled to my feet, dizzy from the effort. My brain raced to come up with a plan, knowing Lucas could snap my neck in an instant if I tried something. He grabbed my shirt and yanked me along as he climbed from the water. When he turned around, I saw the gun aimed at my chest.

Oh, my God.

I eyed his wet clothes, the water dripping from his hand. Would the gun fire after being wet?

"That the same gun you used to kill Haley?" I said.

He smirked. "Brilliant detective work."

From the corner of my eye, I noticed a sliver of light. The door opening. Nora slipped into the lobby. God, Nora, go back. What was she doing?

"Not so brilliant," I said. "I have no idea why you would kill your own partner." I used my good arm to support the heavy cast. Water from my sopping clothes puddled around me.

"Simple," he said. "She was about to screw me." He indicated the package on the floor, then went to pick it up.

"What's in there?" I said.

"The jewels, what else?"

From last night? My brain felt numb from trying to blot out pain. No way *those* jewels were here. He must be talking about jewels from the house burglaries.

"My sweet, stupid partner," Lucas said. "She slipped

out one night thinking I was down for the count. But I followed her here and watched her stash the gems. Learned a long time ago, never trust a woman."

"You just kept her around long enough to use her," I said.

"Couldn't have pulled off last night alone." He gave me a cold, hard smile and picked up the package, which I saw now was actually a square insulated tote. He unzipped the bag to reach inside.

As his gun hand wavered, I thought again about making a move. Too risky. With this hundred pound cast I didn't have a chance.

"So when you decide women can't be trusted, you simply kill them?" I said.

"*Women*?" Lucas's brow wrinkled. "Oh, you mean that girly guy who worked here? He was just in the wrong place, wrong time."

My blood boiled. "I *meant* Carmen."

"Ah yes. The blackmailer." He continued rooting in the bag and came up with an envelope. "I'm not copping to that one. Might check with her other victims." He held up the envelope like a game show host. "And here we have the grand prize. Care to choose? The bag of jewels or the envelope?"

I didn't respond, but he went on.

"In the bag, stones worth, say, two-fifty on the black market, not counting the take from last night. But in the envelope, ah. Poor Haley had such a gift for hacking bank accounts, you see, and this envelope holds the key to two million smackeroos safe in an off-shore account." He kissed the envelope, then stuffed it into his shirt pocket.

Nora came out of the darkness, charging into Lucas like an angry rhino. The blow caught him off guard and sent the gun sailing toward the display cabinets.

"That's my money, you bastard." She beat his chest furiously with her fists and moving so fast he couldn't seem to get a hand on her. "Give it back."

I was on hands and knees, feeling around for the gun, when the magnitude of his announcement hit me. Haley had stolen Nora's money, not Jack. Nora would do what she could to keep Lucas from getting away with it, but she couldn't hold him back for long.

God, find the gun. Find the gun.

I crawled along the floor, keeping one eye on their struggle. Ignoring the wrenching pain, I balanced on the cast arm and swept the other across the floor in front of me. But Lucas had finally gotten a grip on Nora. He threw her into the shelves and she went down hard.

Bottles, jars, and broken mirror shards rained down around her, but Nora didn't seem to notice. She pushed off the floor and sprang at Lucas as he tried to recover the bag of jewels.

She jumped on his back, screaming, "Give me that envelope."

"Bitch," Lucas yelled. "Get off me."

Nora tore at his hair. "I'll kill you."

I gave up on the gun and grabbed a can of hair spray instead. I yanked off the cap and sprayed Lucas full force in the face.

He threw Nora off his back and brought his hands to his eyes, howling.

Nora reached into his pocket and pulled out the envelope. She stuffed it down her cleavage, then scrambled around on the floor and came up with the gun. She held the weapon on Lucas.

"Corie, get the jewels," she said. "It's over for this son of a bitch." She advanced on Lucas and he backed away, nearing the fountain.

I picked up the tote, watching Nora. I didn't like the look on her face.

"Hold him there, Nora. Don't get too close. I'm calling the police."

Nora took a step toward Lucas. Her face burned red and splotchy with anger. Her hand shook so hard I was afraid she'd either drop the weapon or Lucas would jump her and gain control of it.

"Why don't you give me the gun?" I said.

Nora ignored me.

"Smug son of a bitch," she snarled, advancing another step. "Why is it everybody thinks they can put one over on me?"

Lucas touched his cheek where Nora had raked her nails and held his hand out, looking at the blood. "Guess Haley was right. You are a fucking bitch." He stepped toward her.

"Stay back," she said.

"Can't blame your husband for dumping you."

"Shut up."

Lucas took one step too many.

Nora fired, and he collapsed at the base of the waterfall.

I stared at Lucas, not believing what I'd just seen. He wasn't moving.

Not another body. God.

Nora walked toward him.

"Don't," I said. "He might still be alive."

Nora didn't appear to hear me. She stood over Lucas panting, the adrenaline still charging through her veins. Her eyes darted left and right before settling again on Lucas.

We both stared at him for a second. That bastard. Why had he denied killing Carmen?

"I'll call nine-one-one," I said. "Everything will be okay. You'll see."

She pivoted. "Yes. Everything will be fine. Soon."

What did she mean?  Was she talking about her husband?

Nora stared at me, the gun at her side.

"Guess Jack wasn't lying about the money." I smiled, but Nora didn't. My eyes tracked from her face to the gun and back. She was making me nervous. Was she in shock from shooting Lucas or what was her problem? I looked at his still body. "You can put the gun down now. He isn't going anywhere, but we need to get some help over here."

I made a move toward the phone.

"I already called," Nora said. "Soon as I heard you yelling."

"You did?" I turned around.

Nora raised the gun and pointed it at me.

"What are you doing?" I said.

"Police should be here soon," she said. "I'll have to tell them he killed you first. I had to shoot him defending myself."

"Have you lost your mind?"

Bad choice of words.

Nora's eyes narrowed. "I know *exactly* what I'm doing."

"But why kill *me*?"

"You'd have figured everything out eventually. Better to end things right now."

As she spoke the words, the truth dawned. How often had I heard Nora's mantra? *My* money, *my* money, *my* money.

"Carmen knew about the two million, didn't she?" I said.

"She tried to blackmail me. Said she'd tell Jack."

"You could have reported her to the police. Blackmail is a crime."

Nora shook her head sadly. "If I didn't kill her, I'd have to share the money with Jack. And he'd wasted so much already."

"So he didn't know about your secret account," I said.

"He may figure it out yet," she said, "but you'll take the rest of the secret to your grave." Her arm was shaking so badly I didn't know how she kept a grip on the gun.

"Wait," I pleaded, taking a step toward her, my hand reaching out. "I don't work for Jack. I work for you. I'm not obligated to tell anyone anything."

"But you would," she said, her voice trembling. "I have to do this, you know, because I told you. *Nothing* is going to stand in my way."

Instead of coming closer to me she took one step backwards, then another, as if trying to distance herself from the killing. Her arm went rigid and her finger moved on the trigger. She took one more step back and her foot landed on a hair spray can.

She rolled, yelping as her knees buckled. Her arms went out for balance.

I dove at her. Blinding pain coursed through my body as I hit the floor near Nora's feet, my good hand coming down on broken mirror shards. Nora toppled into the mess of bottles and cans but didn't lose her grip on the gun.

She lifted her arm and the weapon arced toward me. I rolled away and flattened myself amidst the bottles and cans. A shot hit the shelves behind me.

Damn.

I picked up a bottle and threw it at her, then another and another. I stood, grabbing cans from the shelves and throwing as fast as I could throw one-handed. I kept pelting her, but she didn't stay down.

Nora snarled like a wild animal. She rose to her knees and the gun came up again.

No way, you bitch.

Using my last ounce of strength, I lunged at her and smashed my cast into her temple.

Nora fell, out cold.

As I pried her fingers off the gun, sirens sounded in the distance.

*Your sly smile still drives me mad.*
*With all that's happened I'm so glad,*
*Things will work out fine, you'll see,*
*As long as you're still loving me.*

# CHAPTER 32

Despite my doctor's recommendation that I rest for several days, I went back to work Tuesday morning. I was catching up on paperwork, including the billing for Nora's case – even though Nora was sitting in the Harris County jail awaiting arraignment on murder and attempted murder charges. She could never pay for everything she'd done, but she *would* pay my hourly rate, along with a surcharge for trying to kill me.

Lucas Turner was still in the hospital after narrowly surviving the gunshot wound. No telling how many charges he'd face or in how many states.

Typing was a real challenge with my brand new cast on the left, bandaged fingers on the right. A nurse had spent an hour tweezing glass fragments from my hand, leaving my fingers in pretty bad shape. I picked at the keyboard and tried to fill my mind with work. I didn't want to think about the murdered hairdressers or about Trey, who'd come here hoping to find his mother only to lose her forever. Yet that's all I *could* think about, fitting the pieces together in my mind.

No one knew why Carmen had called the meeting with Maggie Robbins, girl reporter. Maybe she realized she'd gotten in over her head and was ready to tell all–about the burglaries, Nora's hidden stash, maybe both. But she'd pushed her luck and got herself into major trouble.

Zachary bothered me most. He was the innocent one in all this. Lucas had shot him to get those notes Zachary had found. Papers he wouldn't have thought twice about if it hadn't been for me.

The phone rang and Mother's cell number popped up.

I answered it anyway.

"How's my favorite daughter?"

"Dad? Are you home?" I couldn't help but smile.

"Almost," he said. "Driving in from the airport. Glad to know you're well enough to be at the office."

"She's where?" Mother's voice in the background came through loud and clear. "She should *not* be working. That doctor told her–"

"Pipe down, Olivia," Dad said, then to me, "Good to hear your voice, honey. Just wanted to say that when I asked for a favor I didn't intend for all this to happen."

"You know Mother," I said. "She can't stay out of trouble."

He laughed. "True."

Mother said, "Frank, let me talk to her for a second."

Then she was on the line. "Corinne, dear, I wanted to ask you about Wade. He was awfully attentive, spending the night by your hospital bed. What's going on between the two of you?"

Good question. I had really wanted to talk with Wade about Laura, but with Mother and the nurses and doctor coming and going I didn't have a chance. And I didn't want to talk with her about Wade now.

"You're breaking up, Mother," I said. "Must be a bad signal. Hello? Hello?" I hung up my end and went back to work, feeling like a guilty child.

When I'd finished writing reports and printing invoices, I checked my e-mail. I went down the list clicking delete-delete-delete, then stopped at a message from "the treyster." It was dated late the night before and the subject line said "Thanks." I clicked it open.

*Dear Ms. McKenna – The cops told me Mrs. Litchfield killed my mom and you caught her. Thanks. They told me what mom did. I know that's wrong, but she was still my mom. Wish I'd told her how I felt while I had the chance. I'm glad I came here even if she didn't want me to. I'm gonna stay. Mr. Doyle said he'd help me get enrolled in college. Sorry I was such a dork. Trey Salinas*
*P.S. Mr. Doyle says thanks, too.*

I was sure it had dawned on the poor kid that Nora sent

him on that wild goose chase to the airport so she could come in and kill his mother–that if he hadn't gone, he might have prevented her death. Sounded like he'd be okay, though, as long as he didn't dwell on his guilt.

I closed my eyes and thought about things left unsaid. If Wade chose to reconcile with Laura, I'd be devastated. But the hurt would run even deeper if I'd never told him how I felt. I jumped up and headed for his office.

Reba wasn't at her desk. Voices came from behind Wade's closed office door, but I barged in anyway. He'd been leaning back in his chair and straightened when he saw me.

"Corie! What is it?"

A woman's voice bleated from the speaker phone, oblivious to my entrance. "-and he said he won't give me a dime, that I need to get a job."

I went over to Wade and leaned close. "Sorry to interrupt, but it's really important."

The client went on, "He can't do that, can he? I mean, just because he wants a divorce he can't simply quit paying the bills."

"You're right, Mrs. Hawthorne," Wade said. "Don't worry about the bills."

"What a relief," she replied. "You know, just the other day. . ."

Wade looked at me and lowered his voice. "You okay?"

I nodded and swallowed around the lump in my throat.

He watched me for a second, then leaned over the blabbing speaker phone.

"Mrs. Hawthorne, excuse me," he said. "I have an emergency, but I *will* call you right back." He raised an eyebrow, and I nodded. "I have your number here, and I'll call you in a few minutes."

The client reluctantly agreed.

He hit the disconnect button and turned to me. "What's this about?"

I inhaled, then dove in. "You need to know how I feel, but how could you when I don't tell you? And I don't tell you because I'm afraid of being hurt, I guess. I mean, well, maybe I have other issues, too–"

"Sweetheart, slow down." He stood and hugged me, then backed off to search my face. "Where's this coming from?"

I looked into his eyes. "If you want to reconcile with Laura, tell me now. Tell me the truth. I want you to be happy, even if it means I can't have you."

"Can't have me?" He shook his head like he was chasing away a mosquito, then smiled. "Corie, sweetheart, you already have me."

"I saw you with Laura," I blurted. "At your place."

His eyebrows crawled together in confusion. "So?"

"It was late. And she was there. With you."

He thought for a second, then said, "That must have been the night she had a flat. She was in the neighborhood and asked me to help. We called triple A."

"You fell for that?" I took a step back.

"She did have a flat. I'd have changed the tire, but her spare was bad, too."

"You were drinking wine," I said.

"Laura was stressed out about the tire."

"I'll bet."

He grinned. "I've never seen your jealous side before."

"I'm glad you're enjoying it 'cause if Laura sticks with her plan you'll see plenty more."

"You lost me. What plan?"

"She wants you back," I said. "She told me that night at the hospital. I wanted to rip her head off."

He quickly covered a deer-in-the-headlights expression with a smile. "You've kept that possessive streak hidden, too. I take it you told Laura to back off."

"She left before I could, but I will. Assuming that's what *you* want. I'll do whatever I have to."

His eyes narrowed. "Does that include telling your Mother about us?"

My shoulders sagged. "You know how she is."

"I do," he said, "but keeping me a secret makes me wonder what you really want."

I looked up decisively. "I want you."

"That's a good start." He threw me a crooked grin and held out his arms. I fell into them like a sap. "Everything will work out," he said into my hair. "Nobody said relationships were easy."

After a few more minutes I went back to my office, leaving Wade to call Mrs. Hawthorne. We had more issues to settle. He hadn't exactly denied interest in Laura's plan and I hadn't committed to telling Mother about us, but at least he knew how I felt.

I was staring at my blank computer screen when I heard a knock. I looked up as Mark Gentry stuck his head in.

"You're a trouper, gotta hand you that." He whipped an arm out from behind his back and produced a pot of daisies. "Something to liven up the place."

"What's with you and the flowers?"

"Sister's a florist," he said. "Gives me a discount."

"I see. Thanks." I positioned the pot on the corner of my desk, then looked at him. "Nice duds. You going undercover?"

He wore a gray business suit today complete with red silk necktie.

"Depends." He dropped into a visitor's chair.

"On what?"

"Guess your case is all wrapped up," he said, ignoring my question.

"I suppose. Nora may be convicted before the divorce is actually final, but my part's done. Jack's not exactly a straight arrow, but he's not guilty of hiding community property money. At least none that we know about."

"Guy spends too much to have any left to hide," Gentry said.

"Right. And if the test proves he's a father, he'll soon be shelling out child support. How's that going?"

"Mr. B has an attorney drafting paternity papers." Gentry leaned forward. "I was thinking, I sure could use some help."

"With Brandt?"

"No, that's over."

I held my hands up, revealing my cast and bandages. "I'm handicapped at the moment. What kind of help?"

"I need backup phone work for this case I'm on."

"I could handle that. If you really need the help."

"Actually, on *this* job it's phone work, but I'm talking about something bigger. I mean, we do work pretty well together. Don't you agree?"

I pretended to think hard, then gave him a noncommittal shrug.

He smiled and his eyes crinkled. "You know we did."

"So?"

"I think we should partner up." He placed a hand on the desk in front of me. "We'd make a great team."

Whatever I had expected, it wasn't this. Was he waiting for me to plop my bandaged hand on top of his to seal the deal?

"You don't have to answer right now." He sat back and ran his hands through his hair, seeming more relaxed now that he'd said his piece.

I was too stunned to speak.

"You could put your name first," he said. "Actually, it'd sound best that way. McKenna & Gentry. Or McKenna Gentry. Like that C&W group."

He sounded so excited I had to smile. "Montgomery Gentry."

"Right."

"I like their music." I wondered how I'd like having a partner. "I'll give it some thought."

"Great." He stood and snapped his fingers, then pointed at me. "I'll get back to you."

"Okay, yeah. Later."

I sat there after he left, grinning like a fool. Wow. I'd never considered working with a partner. Especially not with Mark Gentry.

Might be fun.

Final Decree

Houston PI Corie McKenna spearheads investigations by day and relaxes by writing country music lyrics at night. But when a routine divorce case turns into murder and Corie finds herself tangled in a web of greed and deception, even the most soothing ballad won't slow her down. Struggling to prove her obnoxious client is innocent, Corie follows a trail from a seedy warehouse to the medical center's disinfected hallways, and finally to a men's club, where she makes a disturbing personal discovery. Attorney Wade Alexander urges her to bow out, but an unsettling truth hits far too close to home and cannot be ignored a revelation that may well cost Corie her life.

Praises for Final Decree

Kay Finch keeps readers guessing with a dandy plot and an appealing heroine in her first-rate debut mystery, Final Decree. I predict this will be the first of many adventures for Houston PI Corie McKenna. . . . **Carolyn G. Hart**, Award-Winning Author of *Dare to Die*

Final Decree is a deftly plotted story that pulls the reader along for the ride. The author's lively voice and convincing characters make this debut novel an engrossing read. . . . **Margaret Chittenden,** Author of *Snap Shot*

This is a well-plotted mystery with characters true to life. Corie is an intriguing and stimulating character. We hope we'll be reading more of her adventures in the future. . . . **myshelf.com**